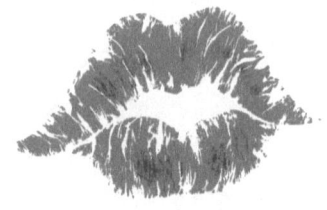

EVERNIGHT PUBLISHING ®

www.evernightpublishing.com

THE CLEANERS

DEDICATION

For Susie, enjoy!

THE CLEANERS

HIS PRIZE

The Cleaners, 1

Doris O'Connor

Copyright © 2016

Chapter One

Incoming bogies in five, Ren.

Ellis Reynolds, known as Ren to his friends and enemies alike, smirked at the crackle in his earpiece, and pushed away from the wall he'd been leaning against. Pulling one long, last drag of smoke into his lungs, he threw the stub on the floor, stamping it out in the process. It wouldn't do to give his position away by the glowing cigarette end. In truth, it was a filthy habit that he needed to break. With a wry grin and a nod into the CCTV camera mounted in the corner of the backyard to indicate he'd heard his boys' warning, he gathered his shoulder length salt-and-pepper hair into a ponytail, and stepped back into the shadows behind the large trash cans.

He heard the fuckers before he saw them. The two goons made enough noise for a herd of elephants. They did have the good sense to stay in the one spot the CCTV couldn't reach, which would only work in his favor. While it would be a matter of seconds to swipe the relevant data, he didn't need evidence of his kill on camera. He was never that careless, which was why he got the big bucks.

The back entrance of the club creaked open, and his target for the night stuck her head out. Myrtle's shiny ebony mass of hair hid her expression as she cautiously looked around, making sure to stay under the camera mounted next to the back door.

The devious little bitch shivered in the cool air, and goosebumps broke out across her dark skin. Clad in only a silk robe, which disguised none of the curves that made her famous at *La Masquerade*, her stunning figure hid an evil, money grabbing soul.

Ren had no problems with working girls. He rather enjoyed them, had lain between this one's thighs a time or two when she first started working for *La Masquerade*'s owner. Owen Huntly was an old friend, and that made this cunt's betrayal personal. No one stole from Owen and got away with it, least of all a woman London's foremost crime lord had made a success.

Ren amused himself by visions of having his big hands wrapped around her throat as he squeezed the life out of her, while Myrtle took out her ever present chewing gum and stuck it over the lens of the camera. So, she thought she was clever, did she?

A low whistle alerted her to the presence of the two goons waiting for her 'round the corner, and a slow, seductive smile spread across her face. Hips sashaying to and fro, she teetered over to them, as though she owned the fucking place.

"It's okay, you can come out."

Thug #2 was pulled back into the shadows by thug #1, who clearly had more brains then the youngster.

"We're good here. You've got the goods?"

Myrtle pouted and dropped her hips, while she

fished a small bag of crack out of her panties, of all places. Ren chuckled to himself and made a mental note to search all of the bitch's orifices when he got rid of her, or maybe while she was still alive. It sure would be fun torturing her a bit. He'd have to cut her tongue off first though, 'cause that bird sure could screech.

"Right here, big boy, and I've got more stashed up there, but I need to see the money first. This wasn't easy to come by."

"Not here for your sob story." Thug #1 gave thug #2 a shove. "Go, check it out, boy."

With a lecherous grin the youngster stumbled forward. Judging by the acne marks on his skin he could only be a teenager—poor bastard.

Ren suppressed a groan when the back door creaked.

"Ah, there you are, Myrtle. The boss wants you on stage and … oh."

Another far too young person he'd be forced to kill now, dammit. He didn't recognize this girl, and he most certainly would, had he seen her before, because she was just his type. Shoulder length red hair framed a heart-shaped pale face, devoid of any make-up. She was too thick to be one of the dancers, so she had to be the new waitress he hadn't had a chance to check out. Owen had mentioned something about her being under his protection. Her blue eyes widened in fear, as it seemed to dawn on her what she'd stumbled into, and Ren readied himself to intervene. His gut twisted at the thought of killing such an innocent, but if she started to scream the place down this whole thing would be fucked, for sure.

"Who the fuck is that?" Thug #1 stepped out of the shadows, and Ren tensed when he drew his Glock on the girl. Of course, the fucker would have a gun. His type always did. There was no fucking skill in killing anyone with one of those, and besides guns could be traced so easily.

Amateurs.

Snapping on his gloves Ren came up silently behind the gun wielding idiot, willing the curvy redhead to stay silent.

"Ah, she's nothing. Kill the stupid girl, for all I care." Myrtle's immediate dismissal of the redhead made Ren's temper spike.

Oh, you'll pay for that, bitch.

Thug #1 laughed.

"Might just take her with. The boss likes the fat ones."

"Hey, I do. More to hold onto when you fuck, and I bet she'll scream nicely." Thug #2 added his foul mouthed assessment, and the girl they were so carelessly discussing blanched. Hands up in the air, she took a step back until Thug #1's barked order stopped her retreat.

"Don't you fucking move, bitch, or I'll blow your head off right now."

A strangled gasp escaped the redhead, and her eyes grew to impossible size when she spotted Ren. Their gazes locked, and Ren held his finger to his lips as he silently came up behind the little group. With Myrtle's attention on the girl and Thug #2 distracted by checking the merchandise, the pathetic trio had no idea he was there. Ren silently willed the terrified girl staring right at him not to scream. Shivers overtook her, but she didn't say a word as he came up behind the thug, who lowered his gun and chuckled.

"I do like a chick who can take orders. You and me wi—"

The sound of his neck breaking put an end to that little speech of his, and the redhead clamped her hand over her mouth as though to stifle a scream.

Good girl.

Ren winked at her, as he let the now lifeless body of Thug #1 slide to the floor. The astonished expression in the other man's dulling eyes made him smirk.

"What the fuck? Argh."

Swinging around he shattered Thug #2's kneecap with one well-placed kick, before the goon even had a chance to pull his gun out. Another kick to his windpipe shut off his screech, and this guy, too, went down, silently twitching his last on the floor.

Ren cut off Myrtle's scream of terror by clamping his large hand around her throat. He indulged himself for a second, holding the lying bitch off the floor. Her hands clasped around his wrists in a desperate effort to get free, and he drank in the sheer terror in her eyes before he brought his free fist up to her temple and knocked the bitch clean out. He flung her on top of the now dead Thug #2 and turned his attention back to the redhead.

She still hadn't screamed, just stood there, both of her hands now held up in a defensive move, which was really rather adorable.

Ren smirked and advanced on her. The fear that literally poured off her curvy frame made him hard as nails, and he made up his mind there and then. This little redhead was his, for the night at least.

****

Oh my God, oh my God, oh my God, he's going to kill me.

Susie couldn't move, couldn't scream, could barely think bar those terrifying few words, which bounced around her brain, as the man she'd just seen kill men twice his bulk with his bare hands slowly walked toward her. He had the long limbed gait of a predator, all sleek lines and deadly intent, and try as she might Susie couldn't tear her gaze away from the intensity of his amber stare. Like a deer trapped in the headlights of a car, she simply stared up the man. Her hands made contact with his hard chest, and a gasp escaped her at the strength of those muscles flexing under her fingers. He didn't stop until he'd stepped right into her personal space, forcing her to step back until the door stopped her. Using his considerable height advantage, he crowded her against the door. The cool metal at her back was a startling contrast against the heat of this stranger's body. He placed his gloved hands either side of her head, while he pushed his body into hers. With her hands trapped against his chest, she had no leverage, and closing her eyes, Susie whimpered.

"Please don't kill me."

Something hard and long twitched against her lower belly, and a shiver of an entirely different kind ran through Susie when she realized what that was. Had he got turned on by killing those guys, or was it her he was responding to? Maybe he got off on the thought of killing her, and what did it matter? She would be dead in seconds anyway.

She felt the low chuckles in his chest before she heard his gravelly laugh in her ear. Puffs of heated air traveled along the sensitive skin on her neck, and Susie pulled in a sharp breath at the sensations that left behind. She was sick in the head, clearly, but being at his mercy like this did something to her. His heat, his strength, the virile scent of aroused man all enveloped her, and had her body react to him against her will. It was insane, that's what this was. This man was a killer, and she ought to be fighting him off, not getting aroused by his harsh breathing in her ear.

He inhaled sharply against her neck, his stubble creating tingles of awareness against the sensitive flesh. She could feel his lips curve into a smile.

"Relax, pumpkin. If I wanted you dead, you'd be toast already."

As if to prove his point, he stepped away to wrap his fist around her throat with just enough force to remind her that he could snap that neck in an instant.

The grin softened the intense lines of his face. Dimples appeared in his cheeks, and laughter lines crinkled the corner of his eyes, deepening the grooves running from his lips to nose. The stranger cocked his head to one side as he studied her. Susie was dimly aware of several men approaching behind him, and her throat went dry when one of them addressed him.

"Usual clean up, boss?" he asked. The burly guy she recognized as one of the bouncers from the club gave her a visual once over that made bile rise in her throat. She was *so* dead. There was no way they would let her live, not after everything she'd seen.

"For the thugs, yes. Take Myrtle to the cellar. The boss will want to ask her a few questions, when the bitch comes around."

Bouncer guy smirked.

"Want me to search her for the rest of the stuff?"

"Oh, no, I'll be doing that, once she's awake and I've broken everyone one of her thieving fingers. That'll get her to talk, I should think."

Susie gasped in horror, and he shifted his attention back to her with a smirk.

"Tell my pumpkin here what else we'll do to bitches who steal and can't keep their mouths shut."

The glint of a knife appeared in Suzie's vision, and she struggled against his hold. The hand on her throat tightened imperceptibly. Not enough to cut off her air supply, but more than enough to get his point across, and she stopped struggling immediately.

"Good girl. I do believe she understands us now,

Ty. Give me five to deal with her, and I'll give you a hand with the mess."

"Sure thing, Ren."

Suzie wanted the ground to swallow her whole when she heard the other man call him that, and Ren's grin deepened as he took in her expression.

"Heard of me then, pumpkin?" he asked. At her silent nod, he laughed, and then, much to her surprise released her. Susie felt strangely bereft without his body heat surrounding her and wrapped her arms around herself in a futile attempt to stop herself from shaking like a leaf. Now that the immediate burst of adrenaline was wearing off, she felt sick to her stomach and utterly disgusted with her reaction to this man. Of course she knew who he was. Ren's reputation preceded him. The best in the business, ruthless, deadly, and fiercely loyal, he was the head of the Cleaners, Huntly's assassination squad. He was also a player, who left a trail of broken hearts behind. No one crossed Ren and lived to tell the tale, and the unfortunate women who snared his attention … rumor was he was into some seriously kinky stuff, not that it should be surprising. The man simply oozed dominance and leashed aggression.

Susie firmly shut down that trail of thought, and squaring her shoulders as best she could, she looked up at him. She had to crane her neck to do so, because he was a good head taller than she was. Amusement danced in his amber eyes, and from somewhere deep inside her, she found the gumption she needed.

"My name is not pumpkin," she said. "It's Susie." When he simply quirked one bushy eyebrow at her, she bit her lip and tried her best to glare at him. Not that it had the slightest effect on him, and besides, her rapid breaths and the heartbeat thudding in her ears gave away her agitation as clearly as though she'd announced the way he affected her.

She was afraid of him, but with that fear came a rush of arousal so intense her knickers were soaked through.

"I'm a waitress, not one of *them*." She spat that word out, and his other eyebrow rose while a slow grin spread over his rugged features. No one knew exactly how old Ren was, but with his weather beaten rough looks, and his shoulder length salt-and-pepper hair, he had to be at least in his late thirties. A good fifteen years her senior, if not more.

"Good to know, *Susie*." The way he dropped his voice when he said her name made her clench her thighs together in helpless need, and he smirked as though he knew exactly what effect he had on her.

"Run along now, pumpkin. Keep your mouth shut, if you know what's good for you, and I'll see you later."

He spun her round by the shoulders, opened the heavy door, and gave her a shove inside. The lock clicked shut behind her with a resounding gong in her head, and Susie just made it to the nearest loo before she was violently sick.

Chapter Two

How long she sat on the grimy floor, puking her guts out, Susie would never know, but eventually her stomach stopped cramping, and she became aware of the fist pounding against the door of her stall.

"Hey, sugar, are you all right in there?"

The concerned voice belonged to none other than Kim, her temporary roommate and the person responsible for having gotten her the job at the club.

"I'm fine." Susie grimaced at the rough quality of her voice, and struggling to her feet, opened the door. Kim stood, hands on hips, clad in the tiny triangles of material which made up her dance costume, and shook her head.

"That asshole hasn't left you knocked up, has he?"

It took a few moments for Suzie's befuddled brain to grasp the meaning behind the words, because Ren's smirking face was still occupying space in her psyche.

"No, of course not. I ... I must have eaten something dodgy, that's all."

Kim didn't look convinced, and to buy herself time, Susie walked over to the sinks, washed her hands and rinsed her mouth out to get rid of the foul taste.

"I'd believe that if I didn't know full well that you've been run off your feet, and you never eat at the club. If that tosser of your ex isn't behind this, then it must be Myrtle. I know you were sent to look for her, so what has the bitch said to you this time? I swear someone needs to staple her foul mouth shut."

Susie couldn't help it. That vision made her laugh. Rather hysterically to be sure, and once she started she couldn't stop, until Kim slapped her hard around the face.

"Jesus, girl, what's wrong with you?"

Susie held her stinging cheek and wiped away the tears that had rolled down her face with an impatient gesture.

"Nothing, I'm just…" Ren's warning ran through her mind and pulling her shoulders back, she straightened her spine, and offered her friend a wobbly smile. "I'm okay now. Go, you're dancing soon, right? And I've got a job to get on with." Not waiting to see if Kim believed her, she all but ran from the toilets, and with a deep breath in, pushed open the door to the club. Loud music assaulted her ears, and plastering a smile on her face, Susie set to collect the empty glasses. If she happened to be glancing a lot toward the empty VIP section then that was for her to know only. Dodging wandering hands as she went about her business, the mind numbing work helped calm her. Besides, she needed this job, and while she was here, she wouldn't have to worry about the loan sharks banging her door down at home. It was, after all, why she'd sought temporary refuge at Kim's place, and had snapped up the chance to waitress at the club.

Say what you would about Owen Huntly, he did look after the girls working for him. While her stomach churned at the thought of spreading her legs for money, she might have to eventually swallow her pride. Owen had made it very clear when he'd hired her, that he would be only too willing to settle her debts for a price.

As though she'd conjured the man up by thinking about him, he entered the VIP area. It wasn't him that made her almost drop the tray of glasses she was carrying however, but the tall, silver haired man by his side. Owen laughed at something that Ren had said, and when both men turned to look in her direction, as though they were talking about her, the proverbial rug was pulled out from under her for the second time this evening.

With his hair now loose from the tie and falling freely down to his shoulders, Ren looked so damn sexy it took her breath away. He'd changed his clothes, and her stomach churned as her imagination went into overdrive. As much as she hadn't liked Myrtle, the thought of what either man might have done to her made bile rise in Susie's throat.

She needed to get out of here. However, Ty had taken up brooding residence by the staff exit, and she would have to cross right in front of the VIP area to leave the club by the front. Neither Owen nor Ren would let her, of that she was sure. Dropping her gaze and doing her best to ignore the feel of Ren's stare on her ass as she turned her back to him, she attempted to pick up the empties on the table in front of her. Unfortunately, the glass in her hand slipped, and she watched in growing horror as it crashed down onto to the table, knocking over the half empty beer bottles. The pale liquid fizzed over the surface and soaked the customer, who'd been staring down her exposed cleavage.

"Fuck, you bitch did that on purpose."

Susie cried out in shock as the guy's fingers clamped painfully around her wrist. He staggered to his feet, and his alcohol laced breath blasted her straight in the face as he yanked her closer to him. The heavy tray clattered to the floor, glass broke, and liquid splashed up her bare legs. Before she could even formulate a reply Ty appeared behind the swaying customer. He glanced behind her as though looking for permission, and in the temporary lull of the music, she heard glass crunch under heavy footsteps, seconds before a familiar scent engulfed her.

"Take your hands off what's mine, mister."

Ren's gravelly drawl held a dangerous edge, which made her stomach do flip-flops, especially when Ren put his solid arm around her waist and clamped his large hand over the other man's wrist.

Sweat broke out on the inebriated man's forehead, but he was either too stupid or too drunk to grasp the danger he was in, because instead of letting go, his beefy fingers dug into her wrist even more. Tears sprang into Susie's eyes, and she couldn't suppress a whimper.

Ty exchanged a glance with Ren, and in the next instant brought his hands down either side of inebriated guy's neck in a karate move that meant the overweight guy slumped immediately. Ty held him up by the scruff of the neck, while Ren uncurled the man's fingers from around her wrists, and in the next instant the world tilted and she was tucked up in his arms cradled high against his chest, as he strode away with her in his arms.

"Take out the trash, Ty."

"Sure thing, boss."

Susie risked a quick glance up the man who was carrying her as though she weighed no more than a feather, and his dark gaze briefly connected with hers as they left the busy club behind. Her heart beat faster at the quiet determination she saw in his eyes, only to turn into a jackhammer when they entered Owen Huntly's office. She'd only been in here once, the day he'd hired her, and the place had seemed ominous then. With its dark mahogany furnishings, the massive desk, and the floor to ceiling window—one way glass she knew—that afforded an unrivalled view over the club below, it screamed extreme wealth and power, and made her so nervous she could barely breathe. Why on earth had Ren brought her here? A door banged shut behind them, and in the next instant, Ren had set her on top of the club owner's desk.

Susie didn't know where to look when Owen Huntly himself stepped up to her, grasped her hand and clucked his tongue.

"Best ice that, Ren. Seems your prize is somewhat fragile?"

His prize?

Before she could question that odd choice of words, Ren was back, and she jumped when he wrapped a cold icepack around her hurting wrist.

"It's okay, pumpkin. It will help, trust me."

His large hand held the pack in place, while he grasped her chin with his free hand and nudged her head up until she had no choice but to look at him.

The quiet fury that emanated from his frame made the fine hair on her neck rise to attention. It seemed so out of proportion to what had happened, and surely he wouldn't be that furious because she got hurt? A muscle ticked in his jaw, and she forgot to breathe altogether when he rubbed his thumb over her bottom lip, in an almost absent minded gesture, while he addressed Owen.

"That was unacceptable, Huntly."

The other man chuckled.

"Not like you to be this possessive, Ren." The far too arousing moves of his digit across her lips stopped, and he flashed her a brief smile. Releasing her, he stepped away, and Susie made a quick grab for the icepack. It did soothe her sore wrist, after all.

"I'm not, just don't like my property being damaged, that's all."

****

Susie gasped and dropped the ice pack when he said that, while Owen shook his head and smirked. If the man wasn't one of his oldest friends, he'd deck him for sure. Instead he bent down to pick up the ice pack and handed it back to her.

"Keep that on. It'll help keep the bruising down."

Already ugly fingerprints marred her delicate skin, and it took every ounce of self-control he possessed to not storm out of the club, hunt that fucker down and beat him to a pulp, for hurting his pumpkin. The possessive nature of his feelings made him angrier. Why her, and why now, he had no idea, but no other man was ever going to put his hands on her again. He scowled at her, disgusted with his thought processes, and a faint blush appeared on her cheekbones as she dropped her gaze again and dutifully wrapped the pack around her wrist.

"If you say so, Ren." Owen laughed, and then sobering, turned his attention to Susie.

"You will recall I gave you a choice when you started working for me, Susie?"

"Yes, sir?" Susie raised her head to look at Owen, and the slight tremble in her voice as she addressed Owen made Ren hard as freaking nails. He needed to get them out of there, so that he could fuck her senseless. That would surely stop these conflicting emotions that made him act so out of character.

"You also said I could work here as a waitress. I'm not ready for anything else, and with all due respect, sir, you can't make me."

"He isn't. I am. I'm claiming you as payment for services rendered, and besides, this way I can ensure you can't squeal about what you saw out there."

It was immensely satisfying to see her head whip round to look at him. Mouth slightly open, her breathing sped up, and Ren watched her reaction.

"I won't sleep with you. I'm not a whore."

Owen chuckled as though watching this interchange was the most amusing thing ever. Ren flipped him the finger, without breaking eye contact with the curvy redhead in front of him.

"I never said you were, and I agree you will not be sleeping with me."

Her eyes widened, and the flare of hope in their blue depths pissed him off.

"More like pass out after I've fucked you raw. You're mine now, to do with as I please, and you best remember that."

Her reaction would have been comical in any other circumstances and with any other woman, but the way she wrapped her arms around herself, while biting down on her lip so hard she was drawing blood, made his already dark mood worse.

Especially when she wrenched her tear-stained gaze to his, seemingly determined to have the last word.

"So, murder isn't enough for you now? You're gonna add rape to your repertoire, because that's the only way you'll get anywhere near me."

The words were brave, but she flinched when he stepped up to her, wrapped his hands in her hair and yanked her off the desk. Another swift move had her face down on the piece of furniture, and she gasped when he kicked her legs apart and cupped her pussy through her underwear.

Owen smirked at him over the prone girl's body. Lifting Susie's head to make her look at him, Ren traced one finger along her slit, satisfied to feel the dampness under his fingertips. Oh yes, his little pumpkin could protest all she wanted, but she wasn't immune to him. To prove his point, he nudged the elastic of her underwear away, and sank two fingers into her hole, while circling her clit with his thumb. The girl bucked underneath him, and her internal muscles squeezed the shit out of his fingers when he found the spot he was looking for. Her whole body tensed underneath him, and having proven his point he withdrew his fingers and smacked her ass twice. The flesh wobbled and pinked up nicely. Pulling her back up by her hair, he made a point of licking his fingers clean, before he grasped her chin with that hand, and smiled at her.

"It's not rape if you're enjoying it, pumpkin, and trust me, by the time I'm done with you, you'll be begging me for my cock."

"Never." The word was barely above a whisper, but Ren heard it anyway, as did Owen, because he laughed again.

"As entertaining as this is, I've got things to do, so take your toy home with you, Ren." Owen smirked at Susie when she shook her head, as best she could with Ren's fist still buried in her hair. He loosened his hold on her and dropped his hand to her nape. Whether to reassure her or to make sure she wouldn't run, he wasn't entirely sure himself, but she'd gone so pale, the enticing line of freckles dusted over her nose stood out in dark contrast. Definitely a natural redhead, if he had to guess.

"You can't just pass me off to him. It's not right. It's—"

She stopped speaking and reared back when Owen shot to his feet with so much force that his chair went flying and crashed into the glass wall behind him. Ren tightened his hold on the girl's neck, but he needn't have worried, because she pushed back against him as though she was seeking his protection.

"*Enough,* girl! My mind is made up, and I'm not in the habit of repeating myself. You accepted my protection when you sought out employment here, which makes you my property. I made my terms perfectly clear, so either shut up or instead of letting him fuck you, I'll put you to work on the floor. Ren wants you, so you're his, for as long he deems you useful. So, I suggest you keep your ungrateful little trap shut, and keep my man happy. Are we clear here?"

Susie's shoulders slumped. She started trembling, but she did nod.

"Excellent. Enjoy your prize, Ren. You've certainly earned it today." Owen regarded the trembling woman through dispassionate eyes. "It would be far easier to simply kill this one, too. I know you like a challenge…"

"Please, I'll be good. I don't want to die."

Owen waved a hand in dismissal, and Ren threw his newly acquired bundle of curves over his shoulder. She struggled, so he swatted her ass several more times in quick succession, until she went limp against him. Her sweet feminine musk hit Ren's nostrils, and he winked at Owen while adjusting himself with his free hand.

"Like I told you earlier, pumpkin, if I wanted you dead, you'd be floating in the canal already. Now be a good girl, and thank Mr. Huntly for taking care of you."

Something sounding suspiciously like a muffled *Fuck You!* came from the girl flung over his back, and Ren pinched the ample thigh under his restraining arm.

"I'm waiting, pumpkin," he said.

"Thanks for nothing." The sassy reply made Ren grin, and his boss shook his head with a wry grin in his direction.

"Have fun taming that one, Ren," Owen said.

"Oh, I intend to."

Chapter Three

Being carted out of the club, flung over Ren's shoulder as though she was nothing more than a sack of spuds, shouldn't be a turn-on, especially after the way both Ren and Huntly had talked about her as though she was nothing more than an object of payment. Damn the sorry lot of them, and damn her hormones. Maybe it was just the threat to her life that made her act so out of character. They said that, didn't they? Sex was life affirming, after all, and with all your senses heightened it made some sort of convoluted sense that she was turned on … maybe?

Susie gave up trying to make sense of it as she bounced over Ren's shoulder. She couldn't see much with her hair obscuring her vision, which was probably just as well. She didn't want to see other people's smirks at her humiliation, especially as she found the rhythmic clenching of Ren's ass cheeks a far too arousing view. Her work uniform consisted of nothing more than a tiny skirt and low cut blouse, and with his hand clamped firmly under her ass, he would know how embarrassingly wet she was getting at this blatant caveman act. It spoke to the deeply buried submissive part of her, the one that was always attracted to the bad boys. The one awakened by her ex. The one that had meant he'd taken full advantage of her need to please him. Little had she known it had all been an act to groom her to bend to his will, and when that hadn't worked, he'd run up debts in her name she would never be able to pay off in her lifetime, unless she did what he wanted her to. As she wasn't prepared to do that, the circling loan sharks had forced her out of her home and into seeking refuge here at this club and with Huntly. Talk about jumping from the frying pan and into the fire.

She'd known Brian was bad news, hadn't she? Just like she knew Ren was even worse news, yet that thought just turned her on even more. She was turning into a fucking cliché, and there wasn't a thing she could do about it, even if she wanted to.

Her life was spiraling out of control and down the proverbial drain at a speed that left her breathless. Cold air hit her exposed flesh when they left the club behind. A car alarm beeped, and in the next instant she was on her feet. Ren's hand dug into her elbow, as he wrenched open the door to an old, silver E-type Jaguar. Susie didn't know much about cars, but she knew this one had to be worth a fortune. From the brief glimpse she got, before he pushed her inside the plush interior, it was in pristine condition. Her heart turned into a jackhammer when he reached across her to strap her into the seatbelt.

"Don't even think of trying to make a run for it, pumpkin. While it would be fun to chase you, it wouldn't end well … for *you.*"

He smirked at her sharp intake of breath and tightened the seatbelt over her breasts. She screwed her eyes shut when he ran his fingers over her nipples. His hot breaths ghosted across her face, bringing with it the faint scent of tobacco, mint, and a whiff of whatever cologne he used. Something dark and spicy, dangerous like the man himself. Susie couldn't stop her whimper of need when he pinched each of her nipples. Even through the fabric of her blouse and the thin lace of her bra those traitorous points responded and sent darts of need down to her clit. That little bundle of nerves contracted, and her pussy muscles clenched, further soaking the gusset of her knickers with her arousal. Heat stained her cheeks, and she shook her head in denial at his breathy words.

"So responsive, pumpkin. I'm going to have fun torturing these, until you beg me to fuck you."

"Never." Even to her own ears that reply was far too breathy, and sure enough his dark laughter washed over her. She breathed a sigh of relief when the air displaced with his retreat. Her car door slammed shut, his opened, and the car dipped as he slid into his seat. Seconds later the powerful engine throbbed into life. Country music filled the space, and Susie cautiously opened her eyes. A grim smile played around his lips as he pulled away, and she knew her mouth fell open when he startled to whistle along to the tune of an old Dolly Parton song. He glanced over to her and reaching across snapped her mouth shut for her. The devilish wink which accompanied those actions made her insides clench. Whether in fear or arousal she wasn't entirely sure, but in the close confines of the car, his sheer masculine presence was overwhelming. It made breathing difficult, especially when he slid his large hand down to her thigh.

"Open up, girl."

She didn't even think to disobey that clipped command, and goosebumps broke out over her skin when he murmured his approval at her compliance.

"Good girl."

He slowly slid the calloused pads of his digits up her thighs, until he reached the sodden crotch of her underwear, and his smirk deepened.

"Such a naughty girl, too." Susie bit the inside of her mouth to stop herself from moaning as he traced the seam of her slit through the cloth with maddeningly slow strokes, designed to drive her insane. "Take them off for me, pull your skirt up, and let me see what's mine."

"Wh-at?" Her squeak of an answer seemed to amuse him, and in the next instant, she screeched when he slapped her hard across her pussy.

"Let's get one thing straight, girl. When I tell you to do something you do it, and the correct address is Sir.

Are we clear?"

The ache in her cunt turned to a soothing caress when he rubbed his palm up and down her slit, before he released her with a sharp pinch to her inside thigh.

"I'm waiting, girl. You've already earned yourself a punishment, so don't make this worse for you."

"Yes, Sir." Susie ground the words out through gritted teeth, and his low laughter washed over her as she shimmied out of her embarrassingly wet knickers. Heat stained her cheeks when she handed them over and saw him lift them to his nose.

"See, that wasn't so hard now, was it? We'll get along just fine, as long as you do as you're told."

Suzie thought it wisest not to comment on that. She crossed her arms instead, and stared straight ahead, determined to ignore him. It was only when they pulled up in her street, that she broke her silence with a groan. Her front door was open, the living room window was broken, and some of her clothes were strewn all over the garden path. By far more frightening, however, were the painted words across the door.

Time to pay, Bitch.

She felt rather than saw Ren's whole demeanor change. One of his large hands clamped down on her shoulder, and she didn't need his harsh command to stay rooted in her seat to comply. There was no way she was going anywhere until she knew whoever had done that to her house wasn't still there.

The locks clicked on the car, and in the next instant, Ren had disappeared inside her grandmother's house like a hulking shadow of doom. When he reappeared moments later, he looked even more furious, if that was possible. She cried out in pain when he wrenched her out of his car by her arm and propelled her into the wrecked interior of her house. Tears filled her eyes at the devastation she saw. Everything had been turned upside down, anything valuable stolen, and on the inside of the living room wall was another message.

Pay up or die.

"What sort of shit are you involved in, girl?"

Ren's voice had dropped to a deep growl, and the fingers still clamped around her forearm tightened painfully. She would have bruises there tomorrow, for sure, yet she felt oddly safe with him.

"Answer me, dammit."

Ren gave her a shake, and when she looked up it was the concern she saw in his amber gaze that made her answer. Besides, what else could she do? He would find out sooner or later, anyway, and she was as good as dead anyway.

"I'm not, it's Brian Monk. He's my ex, works for..." She flinched when Ren ran a hand through his hair, and shook his head.

"The Priestly brothers, right?"

Ren swore softly when she simply nodded. Susie stumbled as he gave her a shove away, as though he couldn't bear to touch her right now.

He kicked what had been her grandma's favorite armchair with so much force the stuffing flew in the air, and clasping her arms around her midriff, Susie screwed her eyes shut. The only consolation was that her beloved grandma was not here to see how far she'd fallen into the criminal underbelly that ruled these streets. There was some comfort in the fact that her grandmother's mental decline had meant she had been blissfully unaware of the estate's fall from grace, as so aptly witnessed by the state of the place. No doubt the neighbors had been through the place, too. Certainly none of them would have come to Susie's aid, had she been here when the loan sharks had turned up. The fact that she was truly alone hit her hard, as did Ren's next words.

"So much for your protestations of not being a whore." There was an odd undertone to Ren's voice, almost as though he was disappointed, and it made her feel even more wretched inside.

"I'm *not* a whore." She risked a peek up at him, only to find him not paying attention to her. In a fit of madness she picked up one of the cushions and threw it at his back. Ren swung 'round so fast that she took several steps back until the wall stopped her. Like an avenging angel he stalked her every move, and her stomach hollowed out when he grasped her arms and pinned them high above her head, while he got right in her face.

"Wouldn't matter to me if you were, but I cannot abide liars, let alone someone working for the competition. Give me one good reason why I shouldn't march you right back to Huntly now and hand you over. You can work off your debt for him, if he lets you live that is."

The smirk which accompanied those words was utterly terrifying, and Susie shook her head in an attempt to make him see sense.

"No?" Ren laughed, and transferring both her wrists into one of his large hands, grasped her chin. His fingers dug into her cheeks, and she lost herself in the intensity of his gaze. "I suppose, I could keep you and pass you 'round my boys instead."

"No, please, Sir. I'm not—"

"A whore, yeah, so you keep saying, girl. Trouble is, I don't believe a fucking word coming out of your mouth right now."

He stepped away, leaving her curiously bereft, and Susie did the only thing she knew that might get through to him. Sinking to her knees in front of him, she grasped hold of his ankles, and kissed his boots.

"Please, Sir, let me explain."

****

Seeing her submit like this should have been a huge turn-on, but this all felt wrong. He was missing something here, and Ren didn't like that feeling one little bit. Neither did he like the gnawing ache of disappointment in his guts.

Schooling his features into a mask of indifference, he crossed his arms over his chest, and shook the girl's trembling fingers off his legs. Her face dropped at his actions, and parking his butt on the edge of the chair, he put distance between them.

"Go, on, explain, and you better tell me the truth, girl, or so help me, I'll leave you here for them to find you and finish off the job."

Her expressive eyes widened in horror, and she swallowed convulsively as though to hold back tears. A grudging respect rose in his chest for her. She was clearly terrified and in a shitload of trouble, yet she held it together, just like she had when she'd stumbled into the mess with Myrtle. Ren realized with a start that he wanted her to be innocent in all this, and that made his mood darken further. She was just a series of warm holes for him to fill, after all. He would have his fun, and then pass her on, so her past shouldn't matter to him one iota.

"Please, Sir, I *am* telling the truth. I'm not a whore."

At his disgusted snort, her mouth firmed into a thin line. She threw her shoulders back, which gave him an even better view down her blouse. Several buttons had come undone in his manhandling of her, and the heavy orbs quivered and strained with the force of her breathing. His fingers itched to test their weight, and to have this woman squirming underneath him, but he wanted … needed answers first.

"If you're not one of Brian's girls, then what are you? His *girlfriend*?" He smirked as he said that, but her reaction left him speechless. Red spots appeared on her cheeks, and she dropped her gaze to the floor, her voice so quiet that he had to strain to hear her.

"I was, or at least I thought I was. I met him just after my Gran died, and he was…" She looked up at him, and the moisture lurking in her gaze hit him in the gut with the force of a runaway train. He could read nothing but absolute honesty in her blue eyes right now, filled with painful memories that made him feel like an ass for having doubted her in the first place.

"Let me guess. This was your grandmother's house." He made a sweeping gesture around the wrecked room. The torn doilies on the back of the settee and the smashed knickknacks in the dresser took on a new meaning when she nodded.

"Yes, I grew up here, and she'd turn in her grave if she saw what those bastards had done to it. I could kill him, I really could."

She flinched at Ren's short laugh in response, and when he held his hand out to her, struggled to her feet.

"You are many things, pumpkin, but a killer you're not."

She gave him a half smile, and he rubbed his thumb over the back of her hand in a silent bid for her to carry on talking, while he steered her onto the tattered couch. She swiped a tear off her face, while she attempted to push some of the stuffing back into the seat, and eventually gave up.

"I wouldn't be too sure on that. If he was here now…"

"I'd be forced to take him out, but that's neither here nor there, pumpkin." He nudged her chin up to see her expression and grinned at the silent determination on her face.

"Not if I get to him first," she said. "The bastard did nothing but lie to me, from the moment I met him, and like a stupid fool I believed him. I was so lonely after Gran died, and he…" She bit her lip, and Ren took pity on her.

"Wined and dined you, promised you the earth, told you he loved you?"

Susie swiped away the silent tear that had escaped her eyes, and nodded.

"Like I said, I was a fool. By the time I realized who he was and what he was involved in, it was too late. Had he not gone down for that bank job, lord only knows where I'd have ended up. Anyway, I thought I was rid of him, only to find out that he owed folks a shit ton of money, debts he'd run up in my name, and with him behind bars they came looking for me. I ran away to the only person I thought might be able to help me." She glanced up at him nervously, and at his nod continued. "I didn't really want to work for Huntly either. Kind of like jumping out of the frying pan into the fire, but he has a better reputation than the Priestlys, and Kim put in a good word for me, when she heard of my troubles."

Ren smirked at that, and Susie frowned.

"You know Kim?" she asked. "She's a college friend of mine, see, and—"

"Intimately, pumpkin, though it amuses me to hear that she ever went to college. Her talents definitely lie elsewhere and not in academia." His amusement deepened when the meaning of his words seemed to sink in, and she tried her best not to react, yet failed miserably. Her blue eyes sparked fire at him, and his cock twitched against his zipper. It would be fun leashing all that passion, for sure.

"She was very good, in fact. I don't know why she chose to ... well, you know."

"Do spit it out, pumpkin, and I know Kim is a clever little cunt." Susie's sharp intake of breath lightened his dark mood, and he flicked her nose with his index finger. "She wouldn't have gotten as far as she has if she wasn't. Besides, I happen to be very fond of the girls at the club, as you'll find out soon enough."

The girl gasped when he sprang to his feet and pulled her up, too.

"You've got five minutes to grab what you need. You won't be coming back here."

"But—"

He silenced her protest by clamping his large hands over her mouth. Her eyes widened and her nostrils flared with the effort to draw air into her lungs. Her fear was an almost palpable presence that Ren drank in.

"You heard me. Five minutes. What you can't get in that time, you'll leave. I have some phone calls to make to clear up this mess once and for all. You, girl." He took his hand off of her mouth and winked at her. "I own you after this, and you *will* do as you're told, or else…"

It was almost comical to witness the speed with which she complied, especially after he swiped his phone and started talking to Huntly.

"Owen, we have a new problem. Seems the Priestly brothers think they can throw their weight around in our territory…Yeah, thought you'd say that… I'm on it, boss."

He raised his eyebrows at Susie when she stopped at the bottom of the stairs, seemingly trying to listen in on the conversation. She thundered up the staircase as he filled Huntly in on what he'd gathered here. It took exactly four minutes and forty-five seconds before a breathless Susie reappeared at the top of the stairs, carrying two old fashioned suitcases, just as he finished his call.

"Yeah, she's involved, but don'tcha worry. She won't be a problem, Owen. I'll make sure of that."

Chapter Four

Those ominous words she heard him end the phone call with bounced around in her brain over and over, yet she couldn't bring herself to ask him about their meaning. Ren looked utterly unapproachable on the drive to his place, and the silence in the car was only relieved by the frequent phone calls he took. The fact that he didn't hide his plans to take out as many of the Priestly gang as he could terrified Susie even more.

Everyone knew that Huntly and the Priestly brothers barely tolerated each other, but this was all escalating far too fast, not least because it seemed that Myrtle had been selling off Huntly's drugs to Priestly goons.

By the time they pulled up outside a multi-story town house in a rather affluent part of London, Susie's nerves were shot to pieces. Three large people carriers were parked on the drive, and she jumped when the door flung open and a small army of dark clothed bad boys spilled onto the drive. Ty appeared to be the leader of this motley crew, and he nodded at Ren once, smirked at Susie, and then barked a series of orders at the assembled men.

Ren's earlier words of sharing her around his men came back to haunt her as Ty opened her car door and pulled her out and on her feet.

"What do you want me to do with this one, Ren?"

The men laughed, and Susie dropped her gaze. There was no point in antagonizing these guys, after all. That would just get her killed faster. She didn't even want to contemplate what they might do to her, before they killed her.

"Put her in the cellar for now. I'll deal with her personally once we're done. After that, we'll see."

"Wouldn't mind having a piece of that ass, boss."

"Me neither. Been a while since we had fresh cunt in here, after all."

Suzie swallowed her gasp at the rude comments and suggestions thrown her way, as Ty steered her through the men. Their lecherous laughter made bile rise in her throat, and she stumbled along, not daring to look up. The steep stairs leading down to the cellar almost made her hyperventilate, especially when they reached the bottom and the harsh fluorescent lighting illuminated a fully equipped BDSM dungeon that wouldn't have looked out of place in one of the clubs Brian had taken her to in an effort to get her trained. Back then, it had seemed a fun thing to do. In fact, Susie had quickly learned that with the right Dom she could fly. That hadn't been Brian, however, which was another reason why she'd run the first chance she could. Unbidden her thoughts strayed to the enigmatic Ren, and the way he could hold her in place with just a look. She could see herself submitting to him, but the rest of his men... A shudder went through her, and she spun 'round to face Ty, who was watching her reaction to what she saw. No doubt he would report right back to Ren.

Ty threw her suitcases on the huge bed dominating one corner of the room and flashed her a quick smile, when she risked a peek up at him.

"Make yourself at home. Bathroom is through there, if you need it."

With that, he stomped up the stairs, and the heavy door at the top slammed shut. The click of the lock sounded too loud in the stillness of the room, and Susie realized that it must be soundproof. She couldn't hear a thing through the thick walls, and renewed horror coursed through her veins. She could die down here, and no one would be any the wiser.

Don't be such a ninny. If he wanted you dead, he'd have killed you already.

The mental pep talk did little to calm her nerves, and before panic could completely take hold of her, Suzie explored her luxurious prison. She had to give it to Ren. All the equipment was clean, and the smell of polished leather and wax was somehow soothing. It reminded her of long gone days of her childhood when Gran had been alive, and she'd helped her polish every surface in her house until it gleamed.

With thoughts of her beloved Grammy came tears, and once she started she couldn't stop. Really, what on earth was she going to do? Seeing her bedraggled reflection stare back at herself from the full length mirror opposite the St. Andrew's Cross proved the last straw. With jerky, uncoordinated moves, Susie stripped off her club uniform and sought refuge in the shower. The power shower drowned out her sobs, and she only came out of it when she'd scrubbed her skin almost raw. She still felt dirty, probably always would, and her stomach churned anew at the thought of what she had gotten into. Exhaustion claimed her, and having managed to brush her teeth with the brand new toothbrush left on the sink, Susie wrapped herself up in one of the fluffy towels, and threw herself face down onto the surprisingly comfortable bed.

If she was going to be held prisoner to do God only knew what things in this room, she might as well enjoy the creature comforts.

Susie woke up hours later, not sure what had awoken her, but the fine hair on her arms rose. The previously bright room was bathed in the soft lighting coming from a series of uplighters attached to the corners of this vast room, and she could sense Ren's stare on her. How she knew it was him she couldn't say, but his presence made breathing difficult. She screeched and kicked out when his large hand grasped her ankle, but she should have known that would prove useless. Her shoulders protested as she fought to bring her arms up in a defensive move, and realized she was restrained. Thick, padded leather cuffs secured her wrists to a length of chain attached to the bed frame. The metal clanked as she yanked on her restraints, and in the next instant another heavy cuff wrapped itself around her free ankle. More clanking later and her legs were pulled apart at an obscene angle. Cool air skittered over her exposed pussy, and to her instant shame Susie realized she was getting wet. Ren laughed.

"Isn't that a pretty sight to come home to, Ty? You can go now. I'll take it from here."

Ty's grunt in answer from somewhere up by her head made Susie screw her eyes shut as more heat washed into her cheeks. The bed dipped, and Ren's spicy scent enveloped her as a blindfold was slipped over her eyes. Plunged into darkness and unable to move, her heartbeat went into overdrive as she strained to listen to his movements around the room.

There was the thunk of something heavy hitting the floor—his boots perhaps—then the rustle of clothing, and Suzie whimpered as the bed dipped anew.

"Easy there, pumpkin. Nice deep breaths for me now. I don't want you to pass out *yet*. I'm going to claim my reward first for solving one of your problems." Pressure on her bottom lip made her open her mouth. Her nostrils flared when he pushed several fingers past her lips and pushed down on her tongue.

"That's my girl, breathe nice and slow now, because I'm going to fuck your mouth." Another whimper escaped her as he withdrew his digits, and she felt his thick cock head slip past her lips. His spicy musk enveloped her, and she swallowed convulsively as he pushed in deep, flattening her tongue until his tip hit the back of her throat. Susie gagged around the invasion, before he withdrew slightly with a grunt. She clenched her jaw, and his fingers dug painfully into her cheeks, forcing her mouth wide open.

"None of that, girl. You best not think about biting down, or I'll keep this luscious mouth open with a spider gag, leaving you with no choice but to take what I'll give you. Are we clear?"

He withdrew, and she drew a hasty breath into her lungs.

"Yes, Sir?"

The bruising hold on her face gentled, and in the next instant his warm lips covered hers. It was a mere brush of a touch, as light as a butterfly's wings, yet it made this whole encounter less impersonal.

"Good girl."

The warmth of his approval in those two words alone meant she opened wide, when she sensed him draw closer again. Susie had always enjoyed giving head, and robbed of her senses and with her choices taken away, this experience proved a sensory overload, which left her growing embarrassingly wet. She ought to be fighting him off, yet that thought didn't even enter her head as he took possession of her mouth as though it was his God-given right, as though he owned her.

Which, in a sense he did right now. With that knowledge came peace, as his breathing sped up, and hands fisting in her hair he thrust in deep on every down stroke. Susie wrapped her tongue around the flared mushroom tip of his shaft, ran it around his corona and licked up the thick vein, before she relaxed her throat and simply let him set the pace. Tiny spurts of his salty essence were her reward, and she eagerly swallowed them down, as his guttural praise of her actions spurred her on. He grew bigger, longer in her mouth, and the pulsing along his vein gave her a moment's warning, before Ren pushed in all the way, and emptied himself down the back of her throat with a hoarse shout. Susie tried her best to swallow it all. Like everything else about this man, his manhandling of her turned her on, and she moaned her denial when he pulled out of her mouth. Ren splashed the rest of his essence over her tits instead. Hot and sticky, his cum branded her, grounded her in a way, as the reality of her situation finally sank in. Shame at her actions followed suit. What was it about him that made her forget everything else and simply made her his puppet, eager to please?

In the heat of the moment she'd almost forgotten that she wasn't a willing participant in this game, and she made a futile attempt at pulling on her restraints.

His dark laughter washed over her.

"I thought you were being far too compliant, there, my little pumpkin. Stop that now, or you'll hurt yourself, and I shan't tell you the good news."

"Good news, Sir?" She echoed the words, and the bed dipped again. In the next instant her blindfold came off and Susie blinked in the sudden light. Her throat went dry when she took in the sight of a naked Ren. Despite his earlier release his cock still stood at half mast and bopped with his chuckles of amusement.

"Eyes up here, girl."

With heat staining her cheeks, Susie tore her gaze away from the sight of his magnificent dick. He'd felt huge, but seeing him up close, and already hardening again, as Ren reached forward and lifted one of her breasts as though he was weighing it in his hands—that reality meant her mouth went dry and her pussy muscles contracted in helpless need.

Susie liked sex as much as the next girl, but this … this unreasonable lust she felt was something else. She couldn't even begin to explain to it herself.

Amusement danced in Ren's dark eyes when she finally brought her gaze up to meet his.

"Aren't you going to ask me which one of your problems I solved?"

****

She really had the most expressive face, and seeing her all flushed with his cum drying all over her large tits… Yeah, that was such a fucking turn-on, Ren's cock rose to the occasion again. Killing always gave him an appetite for sex, and when he'd found her fast asleep on the bed, curled into a little ball, a plan had formed in his mind. Seeing Ty's reaction to her had only cemented that initial gut reaction he'd had. Susie was his, and he had no intention of sharing her with anyone. While Ty's help made restraining her before she woke up fully much easier, he hated seeing the other man's hand wrapped around her creamy flesh. Something Ty clearly knew, because he didn't linger and scarpered back up those stairs with a smirk on his face.

Ren could expect some ribbing from his men, after his blatant claim of ownership of the newest fuck toy to enter the house, but so be it.

"Problem, Sir?" she asked and did her best to glare at him. "You mean apart from being kept a prisoner by you?"

Her frown deepened when Ren swung his head back and laughed.

"Yes, apart from that small detail. And watch the sass. You're not in a position to exhibit any. I still owe you a punishment as it stands. I'm referring to the loan sharks, for starters."

He paused to assess her reaction, and when she

simply stared at him, seemingly lost for words, he smirked.

"They won't bother you again, as I've pointed out the error of their ways of collecting on our territory. Once they realized you were a Huntly girl, they couldn't have been more cooperative. Shame, really, I'd have enjoyed killing them…"

A strangled groan escaped her at his words, and he drank in her sudden fear.

"Which leaves *your* punishment."

Her eyes widened when he walked over to the rack where he kept his assortment of impact play toys. Running his fingers slowly along them he kept an eye on her expression. The whip made her tense, whereas the flogger made her breathing speed up in seeming anticipation. The cane elicited a similar reaction to the whip, whereas the paddles didn't seem to faze her at all. In the end he settled for one of his personal favorites. He knew he made the right decision when she didn't seem capable of tearing her eyes away from the riding crop. She jumped when he slapped it into his open hand, and shivers raced over her skin as he traced the end around her nipples. The little pink nubs firmed under the gentle pressure he used, and Susie gasped when he slapped the underside of each breasts with the end of the crop. Not hard enough to truly hurt her, just enough to leave a very satisfactory red mark behind. Her sweet musk increased, and a quick glance between her open legs confirmed what Ren already knew. She was getting off on this.

Her ex had been most informative in the end. Then again, being strung up by one's balls tended to make a man sing like a fucking canary. Ren knew all he needed to about this delightful young woman. A natural submissive, she'd thrived under the experienced Doms in the club, Ren, too, occasionally attended. She had been less responsive to Brian's brand of sadism. Then again that wanker wouldn't know what to do with true submission if it hit him in the ass and bit him. He'd only been interested in getting Suzie trained up, so that he could sell her on. When the redhead had realized his plans, she'd run. Straight to Huntly and ultimately Ren, which meant her delectable curves were now his for the taking.

He ran the tip of the crop lower, over the quivering flesh of her rounded belly, until he hit the juncture of her thighs. A groan escaped his girl when he teased the crop up and down either side of her slit, and her puffy lips swelled further as more blood rushed to the area. Her clit stood even more erect, and Suzie's whole body stiffened when he ran lazy circles around that bundle of nerves. The chains clanked, her toes curled under, and her breaths came in short, staccato bursts. More of her sweet musk escaped her clenching hole and dribbled down into the cleft of her ass, as her body climbed toward release.

"I haven't given you permission to come, pumpkin, remember that."

Another one of those cock hardening groans was her response, and chuckling, Ren increased the pressure he used, while Suzie bit her lips so hard she drew blood in her seeming effort to control her body. The fact that she did wasn't lost on him. The girl's submissive streak ran deep, and she had been well trained indeed to respond to his command so instinctively.

"Good girl, how close are you right now?"

Ren withdrew the crop after one long last swipe through her sodden slit, which left the leather soaked in her juices. *Such a fucking turn-on.*

When she didn't answer him, he brought the crop down hard on her quivering clit.

Susie screamed and bucked against her restraints, and the fire in her passion glazed eyes when she glared at him made his balls ache anew. There she was, his little hell cat.

"I asked you a question, and I expect an answer, girl, otherwise, I shall leave you strapped up liked this all night, and in a chastity belt to boot, with both your holes plugged and no chance of any relief soon."

Ren smirked at the way she frantically shook her head.

"Sir, please. I … don't I get a safeword?"

Tears streamed down Susie's face, and Ren shook his head in wry amusement.

"How cute that you think this is an option here. Let's get one thing straight, girl. You're mine, and I'm going to do to you what I damn well please, and there isn't a thing you can do to stop me."

Susie sniffed and gave a reluctant nod.

"Fine, but I hate you."

The words were brave, but there was no conviction behind them, and when Ren resumed the slow torture of her clit with the end of the crop, Suzie's feminine mewls of need told him an entirely different story.

"So you say, but your body wants me anyway. Here, taste how wet you are for the man you profess to hate."

Ren slowly brought the crop up her curves, leaving a wet trail of her arousal behind on her flawless skin, and it was a matter of moments to shove the crop past her lips.

A gasp was his reward, and Ren smiled.

"Lick it clean, and then tell me again how much you hate what I'm doing to you."

Chapter Five

Oh, the man was infuriating and relentless, as he gave her no choice but to follow his demands. His voice alone, that deep, gravelly drawl ensured her submission. Susie wanted to rally and scream, but there was no denying that he played her body like a fine instrument. Tasting her own musk on her tongue simply confirmed he was right, and then there was the burning need building between her thighs.

Never in all of her life had Susie been this turned on, so desperate for release that she would do anything, and yet utterly unable to let go and tumble into the sweet abyss that hovered just outside her reach. Damn the man for tapping so effortlessly into her psyche that she only wanted to please him. This shouldn't be happening, not now, not here, not with him, yet Susie was unable to stop her response. Ren demanded her complete surrender, and unlike before, where she'd known there was an out, where submission had come on her terms, with him, she couldn't hold onto that tiny portion of herself. As mini contractions rocked her body, a prelude to what was to come, if only he'd give her permission to truly fly, she couldn't recall why holding onto that part of herself had always seemed so important.

"I don't ... I can't ... oh fuck."

Ren's laughter pitched her deeper into that chasm, and she screwed her eyes shut when he took the crop away. The bed dipped and then his mouth was on hers, devouring her with a heat and intensity that left no room for doubt. He grunted into the kiss, when she kissed him back, and Susie lifted her head to prolong the contact when he withdrew.

His amber eyes held her spellbound with their heated lust.

"Give me what I want, baby, and I'll make this so damn good for you."

Not trusting her voice to work, Susie shook her head, and her insides twisted in fevered anticipation, as Ren's jaw clenched.

"Wrong answer, pumpkin." Ren dipped his head, and delivering tiny bites of pain along her neck, he worked his way south with exquisite slowness that made her want to scream, beg, do whatever he wanted of her, and still she clung on to her refusal.

Every graze of his teeth, soothed by the lap of his tongue, every sharp bite, followed by the scrape of his stubble across her overheated flesh, marked her further as his, whether she wanted to admit it or not. Susie arched her spine when he closed his lips round one of her nipples while he pinched the other between his fingers and pulled hard, while biting down on the one in his mouth. Suzie screamed, not in pain, but pure need, as the burn between her legs reached unbearable levels.

"Please, Sir, I can't…"

Ren's dark gaze pulled her into him, as he raised his head, both his hands now busy keeping up the sweet torture to her nipples.

"You beg so nicely, my sweet. What is it you need? You only have to ask me for it."

Susie slammed her mouth shut and shook her head, and his grin turned sinful.

"I was hoping you'd resist. It gives me a chance to use these."

He released her breasts, and Suzie whimpered as the blood rushed back into her abused flesh. She didn't want to know what he was getting, but she couldn't *not* look either, and when he turned back round with a set of nipple clamps in his hands, she let out a shaky breath.

Much to her surprise he kissed her again, leaving

her a panting, needy mess, before the intense pain flooding her system made her scream. It spiraled out from her nipples, when he attached both clamps at the same time and cruelly tightened them.

"Shush, girl, take this for me. Breathe through the pain. Let it all go and see what happens. That's my girl … beautiful. That's it."

Listening to the deep, gravelly cadence of his smoky voice did indeed ground her, and the pain slowed to a dull ebb. Then to a pleasant reminder of being his, as he continued to bite a path of pleasuring pain down toward her mound. By the time he reached her pussy and blew a stream of hot air across her slit, Susie was floating in that marvelous space she'd only experienced a few times before. Where nothing mattered but Sir's voice praising her, the knowledge that she was his to do with as he pleased. Freedom, and peace, at last.

Two fingers slid into her tight channel, while hot wet heat engulfed her clit, and her hips bucked off the bed as pleasure so intense she saw stars threatened to consume her. Susie didn't know what she was saying as Ren's oh so talented fingers and tongue took her right up to the crest of an orgasm so intense, she wasn't sure if she was to survive it. Whatever she had been mumbling must have been what he had been waiting for, because he finally said those magic words.

"Good girl. Let go and come for me now. I want to hear you scream, when you do."

Susie had no problems whatsoever to follow that command. She screamed until her voice was hoarse, right through the seemingly never ending set of multiple orgasms he wrung out of her with breathtaking determination. It left Susie a crying, spent mass of over sensitized nerve endings, and when he finally stopped and released the nipple clamps, even that shock registered simply as exquisite agony which had her miraculously hovering on the edge of another orgasm.

Pain, pleasure, she couldn't distinguish between them anymore, every cell in her body only existing to bend to his will. When something cold touched her lips, she obediently followed his growled demand to drink. The cool water slid down her throat and lubricated her vocal cords enough for her to croak a reply.

"Thank you, Sir."

Another kiss was her seeming reward. This one was warm and tender, yet no less possessive than his previous ones. She sighed when he withdrew, and his low laughter skittered over the sensitive skin under her ear, as he nuzzled into her neck.

"Look at me, pumpkin."

From somewhere she found the strength to pry open her heavy eyelids, and the heated intensity in his dark gaze pinned her in place.

"You're welcome, sweetheart, but I'm still waiting."

The unexpected endearment made her blink, and she didn't even question what he meant. Not when she could feel his cock dig into her thigh as he settled himself between her splayed legs. With his hands flat on the mattress either side of her face, his biceps bunched with the effort required to keep his weight off of her. Beads of perspiration marred his harsh features, and with his hair falling between them it created an illusion of intimacy, as though they were the only two people in the entire universe. Susie couldn't have looked away if her life had depended on it. Almost without conscious effort on her part, the words spilled from her mouth.

"Please, Sir, I want you to fuck me."

A brilliant smile lit up Ren's features, and with a wink and a flick of his hips, he slid home.

"Your wish is my command, pumpkin. See, I told you, we'd get along just fine."

Susie gasped at his entry. As aroused as she was her tissues struggled to accept him, as he slowly and inexorably pushed into her tight channel, until he at long last bottomed out. Ren caught her whimper of distress in his mouth. He nibbled and licked along the seam of her lips, flicking his tongue against hers, in a bold imitation of what she wanted, needed him to do between her legs. The initial burn gave way to pleasure as he slowly pulled out and rocked back into her body, grinding against her clit as he did so.

When she moaned, he did it again with a wicked smirk that made her heart miss a beat.

"You feel so damn good, and tight, pumpkin. I'm going to fuck that sweet pussy now, until you scream for me again."

True to his word, Ren increased both the force and speed of his possession of her. The bed rocked, and Susie found herself lifting into every one of his possessive strokes into her. Her internal muscles gripped tight around his shaft, making him grunt in pleasure. Ren got to his knees, and grasping her ass cheeks slammed into her in increasingly uncoordinated moves. Susie's eyes drifted shut again as the pressure built in tightening circles. She yanked on her restraints, desperate to touch him, to explore the sweat slicked planes of his torso, but it was useless. Pinned by him and the cuffs keeping her open to him, she could only throw her head back, as the contractions gripped her again. Susie knew she was saying something, pleading with him no doubt, but she couldn't hear the words over the rushing in her ears, as she was sucked into the maelstrom of sensations, and took Ren right with her. The air whooshed out of her lungs, as he collapsed on top of her, his harsh breathing in her neck, confirming his own release, as his cock pulsed inside her, triggering another, smaller set of mini orgasms which made him groan.

"Fuck, that was intense. And your greedy little cunt is still rippling along my dick."

Something indecipherable in the tone of his voice made warmth spread through her veins. It was almost as though he cared, as though this had been as mind blowing for him as it had been for her. Not that Susie had a lot of men to compare him with. Teenage fumbles notwithstanding, Brian had been her first, and the few Doms she had been with at Brian's insistence had not touched her in a sexual way. Maybe that was the hold this man had over her.

Great sex was addictive, is that not what they said? Yes, that had to be it, because the alternative, the fact that she might actually be developing feelings for this man, this killer, was too horrific to contemplate.

She felt his lips curl up into a smile against her neck, and another shiver of pure need raced through her when he nibbled her earlobe, and shifting slightly buried his hands in her hair, and gave a sharp tug.

"Talk to me, pumpkin. Or have I worn you out?"

He laughed when she moaned and reluctantly opened her eyes again to find him studying her.

"Hello there, sweetheart."

Oh, the way he rolled that simple endearment around his tongue, it did something to her, and against her better judgment she smiled at him.

"Hi." She wriggled, and taking the hint at last Ren reached between them and slowly withdrew. Her internal muscles protested the move, and Susie winced at the soreness left behind. Much to her surprise, Ren reached up and released her wrists from the cuffs. Not that she could bring her arms down, and seemingly realizing her predicament, Ren swore softly under his breath.

"Stay right there. I'll take care of you. Let me just get rid of this thing."

Belatedly she realized he was wearing a condom, and she breathed a sigh of relief at his foresight. She had been in no position to demand he did so, that's if she'd even remembered to make sure he protected her, which she hadn't of course.

Susie winced as she tried to shift her arms and couldn't. They didn't seem to belong to her anymore, and she grunted her frustration when she could manage the barest twitch of her fingers. Her legs, at least fared better, as she managed to turn her ankles.

"That's it, keep wriggling those pinkies for me. Get that circulation going again. I'm sorry, pumpkin, but this will hurt."

The concern in Ren's deep drawl meant her heart gave several more suspicious bumps against her chest bone, before she cried out in pain, when he brought first one and then the other arm down. She couldn't see his expression, hidden as it was by his hair, as he concentrated on the task of massaging each one of her limbs until the feeling returned to them, but he kept up a soothing monologue of praise, which meant she would have taken anything for him right now.

When he at long last seemed satisfied that she was back to normal, and having freed her out of all restraints, he surprised her again, by fetching a warm wash cloth from the bathroom. By the time he'd tenderly washed her down, Susie could barely keep her eyes open.

Ren laughed when she yawned out loud, and climbing back into bed with her, spooned his big body around her in a lover's embrace that seemed utterly out of sorts to the odd relationship they seemed to be having.

Could you call this a relationship at all?

"Stop overthinking things, and go to sleep, pumpkin." Ren's gentle admonishment freed her of the thoughts swirling in her brain, and sighing she relaxed into the cuddle he offered. "That's my girl. We'll talk in the morning. It's been one hell of a day, and I need my sleep."

His even breathing told her that he must have fallen asleep almost immediately, and soothed by his presence Susie, too, eventually drifted back off again. Nightmares plagued her sleep however. Cruel, twisted images of Ren covered in blood, and doing unspeakable acts to God only knew who. Brian's sneering face also loomed large. In her dreams he had come for her, and Ren handed her over to him with a smirk. Gasping for breath she woke up, only to find Ren awake and watching her.

"Let it go, pumpkin. I told you I took care of your problems, didn't I?" His firm lips kicked up into a grim smile, when she whispered Brian's name.

"Yeah, he's fish food, baby, as are most of his goons. It was rather satisfying to clean house, and I'll have to thank that judge for putting him out on bail. Made getting to the fucker that much easier, especially as I prefer to work with my hands. He squealed like a fucking girl in the end. I should have filmed it to show you really."

Susie shook her head and swallowed convulsively to stop herself from being sick, especially as there was no mistaking the hard rod prodding against her thigh. Violence seemed to turn Ren on, and that should terrify her. However her mind might scream at the wrongness of it all, her body wasn't listening. Not when Ren looked at her with that hooded, lustful expression, and rubbed his thumb over her rapidly hardening nipples. Still sore from his earlier attention to them, the slight abrasion of his calloused pad sent shivers of need across her body, and her breathing sped up. Ren pushed one of his thighs between hers, and everything inside of her tensed, when the action meant the thick head of his cock slid through her pussy lips.

"Always so fucking wet for me, girl."

With that he slid into her body, and Susie moaned at the feel of his large shaft stretching her. Slowly and with surprising tenderness, Ren took ownership of her body again, while he claimed her mouth in a kiss.

"Relax, baby, let me in."

The soothing command was all she needed to let go, and Susie's breathing sped up in tune to his thrusts in and out of her. Unlike his earlier claim, this was a slow, tender coupling that only served to further scramble her brains. Every thrust and retreat made her sink further into his ownership, and when he reached around and flicked her clit with his thumb, Susie shuddered her release. Only then did Ren flip her over. Pinned under his body weight, he brought her arms up, and clasping their fingers together, he surged back into her.

Driving deep on every down stroke he pounded her into the mattress, while holding her gaze, and he murmured his approval, when she brought her legs up. Pushing down on his calves she lifted her hips up to meet him halfway, and the tingles of need started again. Ren smirked at her needy moan, and shifted slightly until he hit her sweet spot with every thrust.

"Let go for me, pumpkin. One more time. Show me how much my sweet little cunt wants my cock. That's it. So fucking good."

The dirty words, panted as they were, as he lost control proved the ultimate catalyst, and throwing her head back, Susie gave herself over to the carnal pleasures

Ren wrung from her. He joined her moments later, stiffening above her, before he came with a shout. Head buried in her breasts, he pumped into her a few more times, before he stilled, and they lay there panting for breath. Eventually, he moved off her, and stalked back to bathroom pulling the protection off as he walked. Susie indulged herself by admiring his ass. In the dim light, she could see the myriad of scars marring his body, and she shivered. Whether it was due to the cool air skittering over her sweaty skin, or the realization why he had those scars, she couldn't be sure.

The toilet flushed, and moments later Susie was treated to a full frontal view of Ren. His torso held even more scars. Several holes, which must have been bullets, old knife scars, a nasty burn mark on his shoulder, and a fresh and angry looking bruise across his right pectoral.

Susie scooted into a sitting position when Ren joined her on the bed, and his jaw tensed when she traced the purple mark with her fingertips.

"What happened?" she asked. Ren stopped her frantic exploration of his scars by grasping her hand and lifting it up to his mouth. Her mouth went dry when he turned her hand over and pressed a lingering kiss to her palm.

"Occupational hazard, pumpkin, that's all. It's nothing."

He held onto her hand when she would have pulled away. Ren wrapped his free hand in her hair and tilted her head so that she had no choice but to look at him. A whimper escaped her when he tightened his hold on her. Not so much that it hurt, just enough to ground her, to let her know he was still very much in charge here, and the submissive inside her sighed in relief. This was what she needed after all, to stop the thoughts swirling in her head, and she offered him a tentative smile.

"Can I ask you something, Sir?"

Heat flared in his eyes at the use of the title, and his smile of approval further grounded her in this moment. To hell with thoughts of right and wrong. When he looked at her like that, all she wanted to do was sink to her knees, curl around his legs and let him take care of everything else.

"Of course, sweetheart, though you might not like the answer." His accompanying wink took away some of the underlying threat his words appeared to imply, and Susie rushed on before she lost her nerve.

"Why did you kill Brian?" The hand in her hair tightened imperceptibly, and his jaw clenched. The subtle reaction to her question made her heart beat faster, especially when he didn't meet her gaze.

"He had it coming, that's all."

"Why now though?" A tick appeared in his jaw, and he still wouldn't look at her, but at a spot above her shoulder. It gave her the courage to press on with her questioning. "I mean, he's been working for the Priestly brothers like forever, and now you chose to take him out. Start a whole turf war from the sounds of it. I..."

She stopped talking when he released her, ran a hand over his face, and then climbed into bed next to her. Without saying a word he stretched out, pulled the covers up, and folded his hands behind his head. He looked the picture of nonchalance if you ignored that tell-tale tic in his jaw.

"Like I said he had it coming. Huntly doesn't look kindly on scum that is involved in human trafficking. Let alone when it happens on his turf. Like it or not your grandmother's house is in our territory, and an attack like that, especially to one of our girls, is unacceptable." He paused, flicked her a glance, and

Susie's mouth went dry. "And he hurt *you*."

Ren gave a sharp nod when she gasped in answer.

"I told you. You're mine, and I look after what's mine. Those fuckers would have come looking for you again, so the boys and I took care of them. Brian, I dealt with on my own. When they find his body it will set a nice example as to what happens to people who cross me."

Susie couldn't help her shiver, and Ren frowned when she drew her knees up to her chest in a futile effort to make herself as small as possible. He reached across to her, and his expression grew murderous when she flinched away from him. Susie regretted that move immediately, because Ren turned his back on her. He picked up a remote from the night stand, and the room descended into complete darkness.

"Go to sleep, girl, and don't even think of escaping. I'll only hunt you down and make you pay for crossing me."

With those ominous words, he went back to sleep, if his even breathing was anything to go by. Susie tried her best to do the same, but it proved useless. Her mind just wouldn't shut up, and when she couldn't ignore the urgent demands of her bladder anymore, she kicked off the cover, and gingerly made her way round the bed. She breathed a sigh of relief when her fingertips found the remote she had seen him use, and eventually she got the lights to work enough so that she could see, without fearing she was going to break her neck. Ren's harsh features had relaxed in his sleep. It meant he looked less menacing, yet still sexy as hell.

How long she stood there watching him sleep, she couldn't say, but eventually she had to move. Having relieved herself, she rummaged through her suitcases for something to wear, and breathed a sigh of relief when she found the sport bra and shorts right at the top. Leggings and an oversized t-shirt later, she felt far less exposed, and also very aware of how long it had been since she'd last eaten.

There was no food down here, as far as she could tell, but there had to be a fully stocked larder somewhere in this house. Ren seemed to share this place with his men, and they would need food to keep going. Susie approached the bottom of the stairs and froze when Ren mumbled something. Was he awake? Was she about to get another punishment for having moved and gotten dressed without his permission? Then again, he wouldn't have gone through the trouble of letting her pack something, if he intended to keep her locked up and naked forever more, would he? Her head started to throb in protest at her convoluted thought processes. A quick glance over to the bed showed Ren to be still fast asleep, one arm flung over his head, the other one curled into the pillow Susie had been using moments before. The sheet slipped, exposing more of his toned body, and her gaze was drawn to the impressive bulge between his legs. Even in his sleep, he stole her breath, and made her pussy tingle in need. Would she still feel this way, had they met in other circumstances? The sad truth was, she would never know. She was his now to do with as he pleased, and she wouldn't risk setting him off. From the sounds of it he'd come straight to her after killing Brian, and God only knew how many more people last night. They were criminals for sure, but they were still human beings, and she couldn't reconcile the rare tender moments he had shown her with the certain knowledge that this man was a killer. He could rip her apart with his bare hands if he so chose, and no one would come to her aid.

It was a sobering thought indeed, and with her heartbeat pounding in her ears, Susie ascended the stairs.

Much to her surprise the handle turned and the heavy door swung open easily enough. It opened into a long hallway, and taking a deep breath in, Susie stepped onto the long oriental runner that sat on top the polished oak flooring. The door whooshed shut behind her, and a clock chimed the hour somewhere in the house.

Eight gongs later, Susie had her answer. It was breakfast time, and her tummy rumbled its approval at that thought. Male laughter traveled down the hall, as a door opened and brought with it the enticing smell of coffee. Nose in the air, Susie followed that scent, straight past the front door. After all, there was no point in running, if she wanted to live.

Chapter Six

Ren reached across the bed, expecting to find a soft female body and frowned when his fingers encountered nothing but a cushion.

"What the fuck?"

The light was on, dimmed so as not to wake him, and he swore under his breath when he saw her open suitcase. Disappointment sat heavy in his gut. She wouldn't get very far if she'd run, but, dammit, he'd hoped she wouldn't. He'd have to kill her, and that thought made his gut twist in horror.

Fuck.

He deliberately hadn't locked the door, testing her, safe in the knowledge that he'd wake up the minute she stirred and thus would be able to stop her. The fact that he hadn't, and judging by the stone cold sheet on her side, she had been gone a while didn't sit well with him. He never slept that soundly, so what the fuck was that all about?

Pulling on some joggers, he took the stairs three at a time, and stopped dead when he yanked open the fire door at the top.

Someone was cooking breakfast, and there was bacon involved, unless he was very much mistaken. The delicious smell made his stomach growl in need, reminding him that it had been hours since he'd last eaten, and he'd used up a fair amount of calories since then. Unbidden an image of Susie, bound, naked and at his mercy popped in his head, and predictably his cock stiffened in answer. She'd been so beautifully responsive to him it made her apparent betrayal even harder to swallow. A glance at the front door showed it to be unlocked, and Ren swore under his breath. Someone would pay for this, all right.

Feminine laughter, which could only belong to his little pumpkin, joined the gruff rumble of his men, and breathing a sigh of relief that she was still here, Ren crossed the distance to the kitchen in record time. His mood darkened further, however, when he entered the kitchen to find a positive picture postcard scene of domestic bliss.

Four of his men sat round the kitchen table, munching themselves through what looked like their body weight in pancakes. His unruly prize was laughing at something Ty said to her, as he put his empty plate in the kitchen sink, where she seemed to be stirring more pancake mixture.

Ren barely swallowed his growl of annoyance when his right hand man leaned in to swipe a speck of flour off her cheek.

"Well, isn't this fucking cozy? What the hell is going on here?"

Chairs scraped back as his men shot to their feet. Susie jumped and dropped the bowl. Pancake mixture splattered across the floor, the kitchen units and up Ty's trouser legs in result. The other man took a step away and over the worst of the mess, while shaking his head at Ren.

"Jeez, boss, relax. Now, look what you made her do."

"I didn't make her do anything. Seems to me she's taken this all on by herself rather than waiting for my instructions. Did I give you permission to leave the cellar, girl?"

Susie swallowed hard, clearly worried at his reaction, which she damn well ought to be. Right now he wanted to pummel her ass for her insolence and then fuck her silly, because she was here.

She didn't run away.

The relief that flooded him at finding her here in his kitchen, safe and sound made his heart beat faster and his chest tighten in emotion, which only served to make him angrier. He didn't want to fucking care about her.

Her gaze flitted from Ty to Ren's, which only served to piss him off more. Especially as Ty put his hands on her shoulders and flashed her a grin, guaranteed to melt any women's panties. Heat blossomed in Susie's cheeks, and Ren mentally rearranged Ty's face with his fists.

"Get your fucking hands off my property, Ty."

Ty blew out a breath, and turned around to face him.

"Ren, seriously. She just made us breakfast. It's damn good. You should try some." Ty's attempt at a smile changed to a frown when Ren's mood seemed to dawn on him, and with a sigh he lifted his hands off the girl at last.

Ren gave him a sharp nod, and taking the hint, Ty stepped away and joined the other men. The tension in the room went up tenfold, a far cry from the happy scene he'd interrupted.

"I asked you a question, girl, I expect an answer."

Susie flinched at his growled question, and sank to her knees right in the mess on the floor, when he pointed downward.

"No, Sir, you didn't."

Her voice sounded very lost and quiet.

"Then what the fuck are you doing here?" She flinched anew, and a rumble of discontent went up between his men. Ty looked ready to murder him, and the other four all looked as though they wanted to be anywhere but here, which would have been amusing under any other circumstances. Right now, Ren's sense of humor would appear to have deserted him, however, especially when she mumbled something he couldn't quite catch.

"What was that, girl? Speak up when you're fucking talking to me, and crawl over here to greet your owner properly." A shiver went through her frame, but she dutifully started to crawl, right through the sticky mess on the floor, until her fingertips touched his bare feet.

"Don't touch me with your filthy hands, just use your mouth."

Ty swore again, and Ren flipped him the finger, daring him to disagree with his treatment of the girl. His cock jumped further to attention when she nuzzled into his groin, and Ren fisted his hands into tight balls.

"I'm sorry, Sir, but I did make you breakfast, too, and the men were hungry. I didn't think you'd mind if I cooked them something." She glanced up at him, looking for reassurance he was in no mood to give right now, and something hot and angry flashed in her eyes.

"The next batch was going to be yours, and I was going to take them down to you. I can't do that now, of course, because they're all over the floor and ow…" Her voice trailed off, and the defiance left her eyes, when he yanked her head up by her hair.

"Enough, girl. I'm in no mood to hear your excuses. You're mine, and your responsibility is to me not my men. Of course, if you like them so much, you won't mind me ordering you to suck them off, after you've dealt with this." Her pupils widened, and her breathing sped up, and it was sorely tempting to pull his rock hard dick out, and make her give him the relief he so sorely needed right now. Susie tried to shake her head.

"What? Don't want to go down on my men?"

"No, Sir, please … I…"

Ren growled his annoyance, and she stopped

speaking when he pushed her back down on the floor, and glared at her. "You're here for me to fuck your holes. That's what I want from you, not fucking breakfast."

Seeing her subjugated on the mess on the floor soothed the savage inside him that had risen the moment he'd seen her giving her attention to someone other than him.

Susie didn't say anything, made no attempt to defend her actions further, and guilt at his treatment of her followed hard on the heels of his outburst, not helped by Ty shaking his head, and the other four piling out of the kitchen. None of his men met his gaze, in fact, and as for his little pumpkin, the dejected fall of her shoulders made him feel ten times worse.

"Go clean yourself up, and then come back here, and clean that mess you made." His words came out much harsher than he intended them to, but, *fuck it*, he didn't know what else to do with this strange tightness in his chest. It made him stop her when she would have risen to her feet.

"*No*. Crawl, until I can't see you anymore. Then you may walk, and hurry up about it."

"Yes, Sir."

He almost didn't hear her murmured response, and watched her retreat out of the kitchen with mixed emotions. He wasn't entirely surprised when Ty punched him hard on the shoulder.

"Fuck, boss, why are you being such an ass? The girl did nothing wrong here."

Ren spun round to face the other man and blocked the uppercut aimed at his chin.

Giving Ty a hard shove out of the way, he walked over to the sink, and poured himself a much needed glass of water.

"Since when are you concerned about the way I

treat the girls we bring here?" He countered Ty's question with one of his own, and having downed the glass in one go, slammed it down on the sink.

"Since you made it pretty clear that she is not to be shared. Fuck, Ren, you treat the working girls better than this, and we pay them well. She's not one of them. You know that. She was terrified when she came into the kitchen and saw us all here. I'm pretty sure she expected us all to jump her or something, and had it not been for your earlier order we sure as fuck would have done. Your girl is fucking hot, after all." Ty nodded when Ren smiled grimly at that.

"Anyway, Josh was moaning about being hungry and the next thing we know, she's asking us if you like pancakes, and if you'd mind if she made some."

Ren didn't like where this was going, and the fine hair on his neck rose when Ty gave a short laugh.

"You can imagine what Josh's response to that was. The man only ever thinks with two things, his Johnson and his stomach. Needless to say his stomach won out, and he all but ordered her to make them. She still hesitated, wanting to know if you'd mind."

Ren swore softly, and Ty rolled his eyes.

"Yeah, you get the picture now, I take it. Anyway, she got to cooking, they tucked in, and fuck, I tell you, that girl makes a mean pancake. They're some still in the oven to keep them warm, so go eat them, and then you'll see. We were all having fun, until you turned up with a giant stick up your ass and go all caveman on the girl."

Ty fell silent, seemingly letting his words sink in, and when Ren sighed and opened the oven door, he continued.

"She wanted to make you fresh ones. Otherwise, she'd have been down there already with those ones."

Picking up the oven gloves Ren took the little

plate piled high with pancakes out of the oven, and his stomach rumbled loudly when the delicious smell hit his nostrils.

"They sure smell good." He murmured the words under his breath, and then closed his eyes, as he took his first bite.

"Told you, they're fucking good, right?" Ty's gruff voice softened slightly with hidden laughter, and sure enough, when Ren opened his eyes it was to see his second in command openly smirk at him.

Ren flipped him the finger again and carried on eating. The flavor and fluffy texture exploded on his taste buds. He savored every mouthful, until his gaze fell to the mess on the floor, and his appetite left him.

Arms crossed over his wide chest, Ty stood right in the middle of it all, and Ren pushed the plate away with a sigh.

"All right, I admit it, I fucked up. But the girl is my property. She's not here on freaking vacation and we don't pay her to cook us breakfast, so…"

His words trailed off, as Ty's expression grew murderous.

"That's bullshit, and you know it, Ren. I've never seen you act like that around a bit of pussy." He smirked when Ren shot out of his chair.

"Don't you fucking call her that!"

"Why not? That's exactly how you treated her after all, which would be all fine and dandy, if I hadn't been there when you took out that Brian fucker. This was personal from the start, and as a result, we're gonna have weeks of clean up in front of us, not to mention a fucking turf war. The Priestly asses had it coming, but you can't tell me you'd have been this bothered about a turf violation, had it been any other chick involved." He laughed when Ren kept quiet and glared at him. "Yeah, thought so. You've got it bad, boss, and that's why you're taking your shit out on her ass."

Ren continued to glare at Ty, and it was on the top of his tongue to refute the other man's ridiculous accusations, but Ty knew him better than anyone. They'd been through too much fucked up shit, had shared too many women, killed too many assholes together for Ren to even entertain the notion of lying to him.

"Fuck! I don't need this shit right now."

Ty laughed in answer, strolled across to the utility room, and pulled out the bucket and mop.

"From what I can gather, one never has time in one's life for that. At least that's what my old man always said. You just know when it hits you, and it's up to you to figure out what to do about it. The way I see it, Susie ain't going nowhere in a hurry, though I dare say after that earlier scene she'll wanna run far away from you."

Ren made a disgusted sound at the back of his throat, and chuckling to himself, Ty dumped the bucket under the tap to fill it up.

"Go, make your peace with her, or, if you don't want her around, let her go. I know what outcome my money will be on, and for what it's worth, you couldn't have picked better. The girl is fucking hot, she can cook, and she's yours by proxy. Win-win, if you ask me." He heaved the bucket out of the sink, and swirled the mop around in it with great flourish. It reminded Ren of their time in the army, when they'd been mere rookies, and had had to clean out their quarters.

"Go, I'll clean this mess up. You'll either be fucking her brains out, or escorting her out of here. Whichever it is, she won't be cleaning this up herself."

"Smart fucking ass."

"Always." Ty countered. "Compared to you, Ren, I'm a fucking genius, after all."

Ren punched him in the shoulder, and Ty's mocking laughter followed him all the way down the corridor. He scowled when he came across Josh lurking outside the door, leading to the cellar. The younger man stared him down, and Ren inwardly sighed. It seemed Susie had made another ally in the former MMA fighter, because face set in a stern mask, he pushed away from the wall and got right into Ren's face.

"If you've got something to say to me, spit it out already, Josh, otherwise, move out my fucking way, so that I can get to my girl."

A muscle ticked in Josh's jaw, and seconds passed by, during which Ren readied himself to take the guy down a notch. Not that he was looking forward to that. Josh threw a mean punch, and that was when he wasn't personally invested, which he clearly was right now.

"So you remembered she's your girl, at last then? Funny that. After the shit you pulled in that kitchen, we all thought your orders last night were chicken shit. You don't treat her like that, boss, ever, do you hear me?"

"Or?"

Josh stepped back and cracked his knuckles.

"Or I'll have something to say about it, that's what. The girl is an innocent, you fuckin' know that after last night, and we don't mess with those. Least of all when she's under Huntly's protection, and knows enough to blow the whistle on all of us. I don't wanna fucking kill her, but if she tries to run, because her *owner,*" he mimed quotation marks around the word, "is treating her like shit, then us cleaners will have to hunt her down. None of us fucking want that. So, you sort it, boss."

With that Josh stalked away. The front door slammed shut behind him with enough force to rattle the window frames, and Ren smirked.

What was it about his little pumpkin that garnered

such loyalty in his men?

Chapter Seven

Susie stood under the hot spray and let the water wash away the hateful words that seemed to have lodged in her skin. It also hid the tears she couldn't hold back anymore. Tears which made her angry at herself. Why couldn't she simply stand up to him, and tell him to take a fucking hike? That's certainly what she would have done before, if any other man had tried to pull that stunt on her. The urge to disobey him, to call him out on his crap had been overwhelmingly strong for all of one second, before he'd grasped her hair, exerting his dominance, and his disapproval at her action had robbed her of any suitable comeback.

She still felt the injustice of it all. It festered in her side like a poisoned dart and warred with the need to please him. She still couldn't understand what she'd done so wrong. His men had to eat, after all. It's not as though she'd tried to run away. The thought of freedom made her cry harder with the knowledge that that thought hadn't even occurred to her. No, like the lamb to the slaughter she had trotted right past the front door, and entered the kitchen. Her stomach cramped, reliving that moment she'd pushed open the slightly ajar door, and had found herself at the receiving end of five pairs of assessing male eyes.

Each one of Ren's men was a drool-worthy specimen male in its prime, and that's without the underlying air of danger, leashed aggression, and pure male dominance that was an almost palpable force in the room, as their attention as one shifted to her. Susie didn't have the visceral reaction to Ren's men like she had to him, but she was certainly not immune to them either.

No woman would be with that much testosterone filling the space. Josh, the biggest and meanest looking of them all, had tipped his chair back on its legs and given her a sinful smile that had promised all sorts of wicked delights. Like the majority of them, he'd been shirtless, wearing just loose fitting pajama bottoms, and Susie hadn't managed to look away from the myriad of tattoos gracing his impressive chest. He looked the sort to hit first and ask questions later, and she would have backed away, had the "sin brothers", as these two members of Ren's team were known among the dancers, had not come up behind her, and barred her escape from the room. Six foot three of lean muscle they had surrounded her, one large hand on each of her shoulders. Not restraining her exactly, but letting her know she wasn't going anywhere either. She'd flicked a nervous glance at each one of them, and Alex and James Synn had both grinned at her. Alex, the older one, had more muscle mass than his slightly leaner brother James, but they'd both still towered over her, making her feel small, feminine, and like the prey they were about to devour. Maybe it hadn't been such a good idea to leave Ren's protection.

Two sets of identical amber eyes had crinkled up at the corners in seeming amusement at her clearly far too obvious thought processes.

"Relax, little lady. If we wanted to eat you, you'd be strapped to this table already," James said, and Alex laughed and ran his thumb up her neck, over her rapidly beating pulse point.

"You'd enjoy it too, wouldn't she, bro?"

James winked at his brother's statement, and Susie had swallowed hard.

"The boss would have your hide, so leave her alone."

Ty Mason, Ren's brooding, dark haired second in command, and the one man apart from Ren, who Susie knew best, intervened, and she flashed him a grateful smile. Chuckling, the sin brothers stepped away from her. They'd still barred her exit route, however, and when Josh rose to his feet, gathered his shoulder length brown hair and tied it back behind his nape, she took an involuntary step back.

He'd smirked and addressed Ty, his deep gravelly voice sending shivers of unease through her.

"So, if we can't eat her, what's for breakfast, Ty? I'm fucking starving."

Ty had shaken his head, but before he could say anything the last remaining member of Ren's team, had spoken up. The enigmatic Ace Jackson had made her more nervous than the other four put together.

"She looks as though she knows her way around a kitchen." His dark eyes had taken a leisurely tour around her body, making Susie feel as though he could look right through her protective layers. He'd licked his lips lingering on her breasts, and his cruel looking lips had curved into the semblance of a smile, which had only served to send yet more adrenaline through her body. Ace so rarely smiled. It didn't bode well when he did. Susie had never wanted to run more, yet she also knew she wouldn't get anywhere. So, instead she'd crossed her arms over her chest and dropped her gaze to the floorboards.

"After all, you don't get those curves unless you like your food." The inherent insult had brought her head up, and she'd done her best to glare at him. Not that it had any effect on the man. He'd simply stared her down, raised an eyebrow, and smirked some more.

"What are you doing here, girl?" Ty's gentle voice had broken the tense moment, and she breathed a sigh of relief. Not thinking of the consequences she'd blurted out the first thing on her mind.

"Well, Ren is still asleep, and I figured he would want some breakfast."

A collective murmur had gone through the men. Cocking his head to one side Ty had studied her with the most curious expression on his face.

"You're telling me the boss is still sleeping, and doesn't know you're here?" he'd asked.

She'd only managed a nod in response, as the tension in the room seemed to hit boiling point again, and she jumped at Josh's response.

"Well, I'll be fuckin' damned. You best get on with making that breakfast then, girl. What'cha thinking of doing?"

"Pancakes?" She'd hated the way her voice had wobbled, but Josh's grim face had broken into a wide grin, and he'd slapped his rock hard abs.

"With bacon and stuff?" he'd asked. "Not the flimsy kind you chicks like, right?"

"If you like...."

Josh had sat down and hitched his thumb over his massive shoulder.

"Get on with it then, girl. I'm hungry."

That had set the mood for the rest of the hour, and the men had become rapidly more relaxed, once she'd started cooking. In truth it had felt good to see them all enjoying her cooking for them so heartily. They'd cracked jokes, and for a few precious minutes Susie had forgotten why she was there. It had felt as though she'd belonged in this kitchen, safely surrounded by men who meant her no harm it seemed, even though they all looked as though they could break her neck without even breaking into a sweat. That was until Ren had walked in, all furious and cold.

She should hate him, but the opposite was true, and she knew full well that, should he turn up now, she'd be putty in his hands again. It was freaking insane, that's what this was. How had she managed to successfully run from Brian, only to be ensnared by someone far more dangerous than that man had ever been?

Ren's dark words came back to haunt her.

He's fish food, baby... he hurt you.

That had made it sound as though he cared about her, as though she meant more to him than just a convenient fuck, but after the impersonal way he'd treated her in the kitchen, and in front of his men...

Susie angrily blinked away her tears. He had no right, and she would tell him so. Consequences be fucked. As though she'd conjured him up with her thoughts the sound of the door guarding the wet room opening and shutting made her flinch. His scent enveloped her seconds before his heavy hands landed on her shoulder and pulled her back against his naked frame. Against her will her breathing hitched, as she felt him hardening against her ass. He kicked her legs apart, and she put her hands up against the tiled wall for support, as he slid his hair roughened thigh between her open legs. Ren brought his hands slowly round to her front, cupping her heavy breasts as though to test their weight, and her traitorous body responded to him like a puppet on a string. She ought to be screaming at him, not pushing against him, melting under his touch as he flicked his thumb over her nipples, and nuzzled into her neck.

"Forgive me, pumpkin. I was an ass back then."

Susie bit back her groan in answer, as he slid his thigh through her pussy lips, while rubbing his morning stubble along the sensitive skin of her neck. Ren nibbled on her earlobe, his heavy breathing audible even over the stream of water cascading on them both.

"Please, don't."

He stopped the movement of his thigh along her

slit, and Susie gasped, as he swung her up and around without much effort at all, as though she weighed no more than a feather. The marble countertop he perched her on felt cool under her bare ass, and she hastily braced her hands behind her back, as he yanked her thighs apart and lifted them up. There was no mistaking his intention as he stared at her exposed cunt, and to her shame Susie grew wet for him. Even more so when he dropped to his knees, so that he was eyelevel with her most intimate parts. His hot breath ghosted across moist flesh rapidly swelling in readiness for him, and screwing her eyes shut she whispered her denial.

"I hate you."

Ren's laughter washed over her, seconds before he flung her legs over his shoulders, parted her labia with his thumbs, exposing her clit, and flicked his tongue over that needy bundle of nerves. Susie tensed and bit her tongue to stop herself from groaning out loud, as Ren set to work. *Oh, God*, he could eat pussy, and her body didn't care one iota about her misgivings. Her mind might scream at her, but the rational part of her wasn't in charge right now. In truth, it never was where Ren was concerned. He drew her like a moth to the flame, knowing she would get burned, yet she still flew anyway.

Ren shifted his hands under her ass cheeks, and lifting her higher he switched his attention from her clit to her pussy hole. The appreciative murmurs as he tunneled his tongue inside her and lapped up her arousal only served to make her wetter. Her hips took on a life of their own, grinding against him, as he alternated tongue fucking her hole with sucking her clit into his mouth until she miraculously hovered on the brink of orgasm. Ren withdrew, and when she moaned her denial he laughed. Trailing kisses up over her mound, he licked the shower induced moisture off her skin. His open mouthed adoration of her body left tingles of awareness in its wake. She jerked when he reached her breasts, tonguing each nipple, before drawing the needy points into his mouth and suckling on each point hard in turn. The action left her a panting mess, desperate to come. His hard cock probed her thigh, and fisting one of his hands in her hair, Ren kissed her at the same time, as he impaled himself inside her body with one long hard thrust that lifted her off the counter. Susie screamed into the kiss and braced her feet on the wall opposite for leverage as her long denied orgasm raced through her.

Triumph flared in Ren's dark gaze as he pulled away, and flexing his hips, pistoned in and out of her, prolonging her orgasm.

"I don't … fuck … I hate you."

Ren laughed, and stilling between her legs, kissed her again. This one was tender, reverent almost, as his cock swelled, and twitched inside her. He groaned as she clenched around him, and broke the kiss. Another gasp escaped her, as Ren pulled all the way out, only to slam back into her. The action ground his pubic bone into her clit, and Susie trembled around him. The just waning shock of her contractions seemingly flared anew, under his expert handling of her body, and try as she might she couldn't look away from his penetrating gaze.

"You might think you hate me, but your body tells me otherwise."

It was on the tip of her tongue to refute that, but then he set his thumb on her clit, while he started to pump in and out of her and in no time at all, she was falling apart around his cock again.

"There you go. You're mine. Don't ever forget that, girl, and in future, if you wake up before me, you won't sneak out without asking my permission, do you hear me? *Look* at me when I'm talking to you."

His tone of voice brooked no argument, and Susie forced her eyes open. She'd screwed them shut as her orgasm hit, and she tried her best to focus on what he was saying to her. With her body still shaking in delicious aftershocks, her breaths seesawing in and out of her, and her heart beat thundering in her ears it was hard to do so.

He smiled when their gazes connected, and Susie bit her lip when he pulled out of her. She felt bereft without his thick cock stretching her, and she swallowed hard when she saw him reach past her to the coconut oil he kept on the counter.

Her breathing grew even shallower when he proceeded to squeeze a generous dollop onto his hand and then lathered his cock, already slick with her arousal, in the oil. His grin turned sinful at her reaction.

"I'm still waiting for your answer, girl," he said, while getting yet more oil, which he spread across his fingers. Not once breaking eye contact with her, he grabbed her hips and tilted them upward more while half pulling her ass off the counter. A gasp escaped her when he slid first one, and then two lubed fingers into her asshole, and started to thrust in out of that tight place. Pleasure surged through her anew, especially when he added a third finger, stretching her until the sweet burn added that bite of pain guaranteed to send her over the edge again.

The urge to close her eyes, to give into the rapidly increasing need to let go consumed her, but his heated gaze still held her spellbound. A raw need reflected back at her, mirroring her own, and it made her blurt out the words she knew he wanted to hear.

"Yes, Sir. I'm sorry, Sir. I didn't think you'd mind, and I … oh…"

She bit her lip as Ren withdrew his fingers, and

lifting her off the counter, flipped her over until she lay across it. With her sensitive breasts squashed against the cool marble, and his body weight pressing her down, as he kicked her legs apart again, she had nowhere to go. Blunt pressure breached her hole, and she did her best to try to relax and breathe through the steady invasion of his thick shaft. The burn intensified, and she could have sworn she felt every vein on his cock, as he pushed in slowly, his harsh breathing in her ear telling her how much this affected him, too. Eventually his balls hit her clit, and his hair roughened thighs connected with hers, as he bottomed out inside her ass.

Ren bit her shoulder, before he withdrew, awakening all the sensitive nerve endings back in her butt, and making her groan in need.

"I fucking did mind. I had no idea where you were." He pulled almost all the way out, before he thrust back in, making her scream. Her hips hit the ledge, and her mound made contact with the marble. It sent delicious shockwaves of need through her pussy, and she pushed back against him, in a silent bid for him to do that again. Ren didn't disappoint. He set up an ever increasing rhythm, which meant she climbed the rungs of arousal at record speed.

Ren proceeded to berate her as he pistoned in and out of her, every word punctuated by another harsh thrust into her ass.

"I thought you'd run. I thought I'd have to fucking kill you. I don't want to have to do that, so fucking well do as you're told, girl. I can't … fuck … I'm coming … argh."

Heat flooded inside of her, and Susie lost all ability to think, to make sense of anything, as Ren pulled her to her feet. The action lodged him even deeper inside of her, and when he brought his hand round to her front and brought an openhanded slap down on her clit, she, too, splintered into a release so breathtaking she saw stars.

By the time she could breathe in anything resembling a normal rhythm again, Ren had withdrawn from her butt and maneuvered them both back under the stream of water. The careful way in which he washed her down, was such a stark contrast to his earlier behavior it brought renewed tears into her eyes. She winced when he washed her sore ass, and his murmured apology settled deep inside her psyche. This Ren, she could so easily fall in love with it scared her, not least because she very much suspected she already had. After all, why else would she respond to him like she was? Susie was no pushover. Even Brian hadn't managed to subjugate her. Not with his threats or his fists, and he'd tried both numerous times. She'd run the first chance she'd gotten, knowing full well that he would kill her if he found her again. Yet with Ren, it wasn't the threat of him killing her that kept her here. No, it was the man, who offered her a tender smile when he turned the water off, stepped away to wrap a towel round his hips, and then proceeded to wrap her up in a large fluffy towel before he picked her up and carried her out of the wet room. He didn't stop, despite her murmured protestations that she could walk, simply carried on, up the stairs, out of the cellar, and up more flights of stairs, past several of his laughing men, until he at long last shouldered open the door to a bedroom. His she assumed, as he deposited her in the middle of the huge bed. Taking his towel off, he proceeded to dry himself, before he strolled up to the wardrobe, and pulling out some clothes, proceeded to dress.

Susie's pussy clenched anew at the striptease in reverse. Ren really had the most amazing body for a man his age, and following that thought process through Susie blurted out her question.

"How old are you, Sir?"

Ren paused mid tucking his shirt into his jeans, and turning around looked at her. Something indecipherable crossed his harsh features, and he ran a hand through his still damp hair.

"Why does it matter?" he asked.

Susie shrugged her shoulders and shimmied further up the bed when he crossed the distance between them in a few long legged strides. Her heart beat faster when he brought his hand up and cupped her face. His thumb drew a far too arousing path across her lips, and he pulled in a sharp breath when she sucked that digit into her mouth and bit down slightly.

"Minx." He growled that one word, and everything south clenched in need. His amber gaze darkened as he seemingly noticed her reaction and withdrew from her.

"Behave yourself. I need to go out and take care of some things."

At her gasp in answer, he smiled grimly.

"You mean you're going to kill someone?" she asked, and he shrugged his shoulders.

"If it comes to it. There's a war going on out there, and it's my job to clean up." He paused and ran another hand through his hair. "It's what I do, pumpkin. I'm not ever going to pretend that I'm a nice guy. I don't do romance and flowers and all that shit you girls seem to lap up." He flicked her a glance, and his jaw tightened at whatever he read in her expression. "So don't expect soft words from me that don't mean shit in the long run, okay?"

He relaxed somewhat at her nod in answer.

"I mean what I say. You're mine. Not because

Huntly gave you to me, but because I want you." He paused when she couldn't help her gasp in answer. "That places you in danger, more so than you're in already. Folks will try and get to you, because you're with me, so for that reason alone, don't try and run. It wouldn't do you any good, because my boys and I would track you down, if the others wouldn't get to you first, and you've seen enough of how those fuckers operate, to know that wouldn't end well for you."

Again he paused as though to let his words sink in. Goosebumps broke out across her exposed flesh, and with a frown Ren reached across and rubbed them away.

"You're safe with me. With us, here."

Letting go of her he gestured around the room.

"I'll have your clothes and stuff brought up. This is my room, and now yours, too."

"Okay."

Ren flashed her a quick smile and crossed his arms over his chest.

"Okay? That's all? You're not going to berate me? Throw a hissy fit? Tell me how much you hate me again?"

Susie shook her head.

"Would it do any good if I did, Sir?" she asked.

Heat flared in his gaze briefly, and his grin grew positively sinful.

"Well, pumpkin, it would give me a perfect excuse to pummel that luscious ass of yours in punishment again."

She shook her head, and he laughed.

"Other than that, it wouldn't do you one iota of good, no, girl."

He moved to leave and stopped dead in his tracks at her murmured words.

"And for the record, Sir, I don't hate you."

He swung back round to study her, his expression a carefully controlled mask of indifference, but the swirling emotions in his eyes gave him away.

"I *should* hate you, but I don't, and I still want to know how old you are."

Ren shook his head, and just when she thought he wasn't going to answer her, he rumbled his reply.

"I'm forty-three, girl, which makes me almost twenty years your senior, I believe." He smiled at her sharp intake of breath, and Susie couldn't stop her smart ass response.

"Well that explains it then," she said. She giggled at the way his brows drew together in a frown at her actions. "My Gran did instill in me the importance of respecting one's elders, so … argh." She screeched and tried to get away, but he was faster than she was. In no time at all, she'd lost the protection of the towel, and found herself draped over his lap. The first openhanded swat to her ass took her breath away with the intensity behind it, and each succinct swat that followed further robbed her of any ability to protest. Ren pummeled her behind until it glowed and she'd grown pliant over his lap. Only then did he stop, and rubbed the abused flesh. Heat spread up from her bottom to every other part of her, and she moaned long and hard, when he brought his hand lower and swiped his fingers through her embarrassingly wet pussy lips.

"Such a naughty little girl, aren't you? I'll have to think of more inventive forms of punishments for you. You enjoyed this far too much." Pulling her back up by her hair, he kissed her. The intensity behind this further claim on her body left her breathless and tingling in need, and she slid onto the floor in an undignified heap when he got up again.

"One of the men will escort you the club later for

your shift. I'll see you there, and you'll come home with me. Don't even take the rubbish out, unless one of the guys is with you, understood?"

"Yes, Sir, but isn't that overkill? I mean, I'm not that important, surely."

A muscle ticked in his jaw, and Ren shook his head.

"Are you arguing with me, girl?" The step he took back toward her could only be described as menacing, and lord help her, if every feminine cell in her body didn't sigh in submission at his behavior. Fucked up in the head, that was her, for sure, but she couldn't bring herself to care about that right now, not when Ren looked at her as though he wanted to eat her alive.

"No, Sir, I'm not." She somehow managed to get her answer out past the huge lump of emotion lodged in her throat, and he nodded.

"Good, now, be a good girl, and do as you're told. I'll see you later."

Their interaction set the course for the next couple of weeks. While she was free to roam the house, she had her very own bodyguard every time she set foot outside. In truth, she was rather grateful for it, because the news was full of the unrest, and the apparent war between crime lords. No names were mentioned, but Susie could read between the lines well enough.

Huntly seemed to be in a round of never ending meetings at the club, and Susie lost count how many well-known figures she'd served drinks to in his private domain. More than one had taken an interest in her, but Huntly had steered each one onto a different girl with ultimate tact and discretion, while the cleaners adopted a more hands on approach on the club floor with any customer who tried to get too friendly.

All in all, Susie had never felt safer, which was an

oxymoron for sure, as Kim pointed out to her, when they found themselves taking a break together.

"Girl, you're positively glowing these days. I guess being shacked up with the Cleaners has its advantages, huh, though I wouldn't have had you pegged for enjoying being handed around them."

Susie choked on her orange juice, and Kim patted her back until she got her breath back.

"What do you mean? I'm not... Good lord, I'm only with Ren. He doesn't share me."

Kim's mouth fell open, and she whistled through her teeth.

"He doesn't? Then why on earth are all his guys watching over you as though they're mother hens? I mean, everyone knows they look after the girls who come to stay at their house, but they tend to come and go, and you've already stayed longer than any of the previous ones, and now you're telling me they're not even getting their dicks wet?"

Susie cringed at the crude words, but Kim wasn't finished yet.

"You do realize what that means, right?"

Susie had no idea what her friend was going on about and said as much. Kim rolled her eyes and literally hooted with laughter.

"It means, you ninny, that Ren has it bad ... for you. Never thought I'd see the day that man fell, but I reckon he has for you. Way to go, girl."

Susie almost choked on her refreshment again.

"Don't be ridiculous. He doesn't do love. He said as much. This is just..." She didn't know what label to put on their relationship, so she kept quiet, because like it or not, they did seem to have a relationship of sorts, at least. While Ren kept his distance at the club, he didn't seem capable of keeping his hands off of her in private, and as aloof as he was in public, when it was just the two of them he showed his tender side. And that side of him was irresistible. Ren cared deeply, in fact, about Huntly, his men, and it seemed increasingly so, Susie. Though she was still convinced that was more to do with the awesome sex they had than anything else.

That, and the deep seated, if somewhat twisted and fucked up code of honor he and the rest of the cleaners, for that matter, appeared to live by.

Put simply, they looked after Huntly interests, and by proxy that included her. They all held immense disgust for the human trafficking the Priestly brothers engaged in, and having met some of the girls the cleaners had rescued over the years, Susie could see why.

Huntly was knee deep in drugs and other illicit dealings, but he ran a tight ship, and protected the businesses under his care. Any girls who worked for him did so of their own free will and were paid handsomely in return. A far cry from the admittedly limited insight she'd had into Priestly affairs. All in all it meant her misgivings about being involved with a bunch of criminals took a second and fourth seat to her principles until said principles came crashing around her ears with the police raid.

Susie froze mid stacking the drinks delivery behind the bar, when the doors to the still shut club flew open and armed police burst inside, followed by a grim looking Ren and the rest of his team. Their gazes connected across the crowded room, and her heart broke when he openly turned his back on her, even as a plain clothed police officer made a beeline straight for her.

"Susie Elliot? I have a few questions for you."

Chapter Eight

Ren had known this day would come, but he hadn't counted on the insane urge to rip that police officer's head off, to grab his girl, and to simply run. Somewhere far away, where the ugliness of his life couldn't touch his pumpkin, and where he wouldn't have to see the adoration in her eyes change to disgust. He hadn't quite realized how much that meant to him, until their gazes connected, and her face fell when he forced himself to turn away.

Naturally the police would know her name. He'd known they were under surveillance—those fuckers were never that good at hiding themselves—and this particular officer was newly promoted and hungry for blood. Most importantly he wasn't on Huntly's payroll, and that could cause trouble for them all.

Sure enough Owen appeared, his face set in a rigid mask, as he approached the bar, where Susie was still polishing the glass in her hand. His girl was fucking terrified, not that she showed it outwardly, but Ren knew her responses inside and out. Her discomfort was there in every rigid line of her body and the fake smile she offered Detective Wonsan.

Not for the first time, Ren wished Huntly would have let him take that asshole out. He'd had plenty of opportunity, but that wasn't Huntly's style, especially when that over eager police officer had a wife and family at home. Sometimes principles fucking sucked. Mind you, being a family guy or not, if Wonsan gave his girl grief, then, Huntly's orders be fucked, Ren would make that asshole pay. Ty's hand on his shoulder made him swing round. The other man looked as on edge as Ren was. A lot was riding on this. If Susie squealed... That didn't bear thinking about.

"Detective Wonsan, to what do we owe this unexpected pleasure?" Owen held out his hand, while smoothly getting in between the officers and Susie. He flicked a glance to the semicircle of armed police guarding the exits, and smiled when Wonsan just glared at his hand, and didn't take it. "Why the animosity, Detective? Have I not been most reasonable in my help with your enquiries up 'til now? And how do you repay that kindness? By busting in my doors, and waving guns around. Shame on you, Wonsan. I hope you have a warrant for this nonsense."

Owen's voice, while perfectly polite, held an edge of steel, and his steel grey eyes drew together in a frown when Wonsan gave a short laugh.

"I can do without your so called hospitality, Huntly, or your *help*. It's a criminal offence to try to bribe a police officer."

Huntly's dark eyebrows drew to his hairline, and he flicked an imaginary speck of dust off his immaculate, tailor made suit.

"You wound me, Detective. Pride comes before a fall. You have a lot to lose after all. Your son's cancer treatment doesn't come cheap…"

Huntly's words seemed to enrage the Detective, because hands fisted he stepped right up to Owen.

"Stupid fucker."

Ty's murmured assessment behind him made Ren smirk. The Detective's partner, in the meantime, a pretty enough young blonde, pulled her boss back by his shoulders.

"Jim, this is what he wants."

Wonsan frowned and took a step back, while the pretty young thing shoved a sheet of paper at Huntly.

"Here's your warrant. It gives us leave to search the premises, and to interview any member of staff."

Ren's smirk deepened when Huntly didn't even glance at the paper. Instead he focused his attention on the woman in front of him. Ren knew that look. Huntly liked what he saw, and if the restless shifting the woman did under Owen's appraisal was any indication, she wasn't immune to the boss.

"And what's your name, my sweet?" Huntly asked, causing the woman to draw her shoulders back and glare up at him.

"Detective Marian Roots, not that it's any of your business."

Huntly smiled, and the voluptuous blonde took another step back.

"Well, Ms. Roots, if you ever get fed up with playing second fiddle to Wonsan here, I'm sure I'll be able to find you a much better paying gig right here in my club."

The woman's sharp intake of breath seemed far too loud in the tension filled room.

"I'm going to pretend you didn't just say that to me, Mr. Huntly. We're here on police business only, mainly the murder of one Myrtle Jones and Brian Monk. The former was one of your employees, and the latter Ms. Elliot's boyfriend."

"Ex-boyfriend." The words were out of Ren's mouth before he could temper them, and he knew instantly he'd made a mistake.

Huntly gave an infinitesimal shake of his head, Susie dropped the glass she'd been polishing, and Wonsan grinned. The man's eyes narrowed and a calculating smile spread over his pale face, as he looked from Susie to Ren.

Detective Roots sauntered up to Ren.

"You must be Ellis Reynolds. What would your interest be in Ms. Elliot's relationship status then?" she asked.

Ren clamped his mouth shut and shook his head.

Ty answered for him.

"How about you cut the bull and get on with it? If you've got something to say, then say it, or clear the fuck off out of the club."

Ren sensed rather than saw the rest of his team pull up behind him, and Marian Roots swallowed hard and lost some of her antagonistic stance.

Wonsan took up the conversation.

"Like Detective Roots stated, we're here on a murder investigation. Now we can do this the hard way or the easy way, but we have some questions for Ms. Elliot. I have no compunction to haul her up to the police station for questioning—"

"You'll have to get past us first, you cunt." Josh's deep rumble interrupted the other man, and as one the cleaners stepped forward. A small smile played around Huntly's lips, but he made no move to stop them, and some of his bravado left Wonsan. The police at the doors lifted their weapons, and Susie shot forward from behind the bar.

"I'll answer anything you want me to. I've got nothing to hide."

Ren tensed when she wouldn't look at him as she said those words, and Huntly frowned and inclined his head.

"If you're sure, Susie. You might want to wait until my solicitor gets here. They cannot force you to answer anything."

Susie wrapped her arms around herself and at long last looked toward Ren and his men. She smiled at each one in turn and shook her head.

"I won't need a solicitor, and you boys can stand down. I can look after myself."

It took every ounce of self-control Ren possessed to not grab his girl, fling her over his shoulder, and pummel her ass when she smiled up at Wonsan.

"Where do you want me, Detective?"

Wonsan regarded her through narrowed eyes, and Huntly intervened again.

"You may use my office for privacy, if you like. If you need any of us, all you have to do is press the intercom, Susie. We've got your back."

Ren didn't miss the undertone, and neither did Wonsan, because he puffed up his chest and glared at Huntly, who simply turned his back on the detective.

"Thank you, sir." Susie's quiet voice soothed the savage beast inside Ren somewhat, and emotions churning his gut, he watched her lead the two detectives away. Owen wrenched his head toward the back room, and taking the hint Ren followed him out, leaving the rest of his team to square up to the armed officers.

The minute the door shut behind them, Ren rounded on his friend. "What the fuck, Owen? What if she talks?"

Huntly adjusted his cufflinks and shrugged his shoulders.

"Have you given her reason to do so?" he asked, and Ren punched the wall in frustration.

"No, yes—fuck, I don't know. You should have stopped her from talking to them. God knows what she'll say even without meaning to. She's not used to this shit, you know that."

Ren fought the urge to swipe that smug grin of Owen's face and stuffed his hands into his trouser pockets instead. The knuckles he'd scraped on the wall protested that move, but Ren welcomed that pain. It was a distraction from the ache around his heart, after all.

"You should give your girl more credit. She'll do

just fine, I'm sure."

Ren snorted and swore under his breath, and Owen gave a short laugh.

"The rumors around this place are right then. You've got your balls all in a twist over this girl, haven't you?"

"So what if I have?" Ren countered. "That's my problem. If she squeals, however, that becomes your problem, and—"

"And I'll deal with it in the most expedient manner." Owen interrupted him, and cold sweat ran down Ren's shoulder blades at the menacing undertone. "You'll take care of her, if you have to, right?"

The crippling pain that shot through Ren's chest at that thought took his breath away, and Owen pulled him in for a one armed hug and pat on the shoulder.

"Let's hope it doesn't come to that. I've grown quite fond of seeing her bright smile around the place, too."

****

Susie's heart beat so fast she was afraid she might pass out. Bile churned her insides with every step she took away from the club and up the stairs to Huntly's office. Being able to look down and see the cleaners square up to the armed police in a silent battle of wills, didn't help calm her down one iota. Armed police, for fuck's sake. People could be killed, and it would be all her fault. While her heart had missed several beats and she felt the men's determination to protect her surround her like a security blanket, she couldn't let them do that. Besides, how bad could it be to answer some questions? She didn't know enough, anyway. Ren reappeared from the back room, a grim looking Huntly in tow, and when Ren looked straight up as though he could sense her gaze on him, she took a deep breath in to calm her nerves. She could do this, for Ren, for Huntly, who'd given her a job and his protection, when she'd had nowhere to run to, and for the rest of the men. She'd grown incredibly fond of them all, after all.

Wonsan stepped up right behind her, until the somewhat overwhelming scent of his aftershave enveloped her. Clearly the detective was one of those men who didn't get that less was more when it came to applying scent.

"Thank you for agreeing to answer our questions, Ms. Elliot. I must admit, I expected you to put up more of a struggle, considering you're living with Ellis Reynolds." Marian Roots clearly was going to adopt the good cop routine during this interview, while a scowling Wonsan was no doubt the bad one in this set up.

It would have been comical in any other circumstances, were it not Susie at the receiving end of their interrogation.

Squaring her shoulders and taking strength from Ren's unblinking focus aimed at Huntly's office, she forced a smile on her lips.

"I fail to see what my living arrangements have to do with anything," she said.

The other woman smiled.

"It all helps to create a picture of whom I'm dealing with here. After all, your file doesn't suggest you would be the kind of girl to end up working here, and being in a relationship with a killer like Reynolds."

Susie couldn't help her flinch at hearing Ren addressed like that.

"Don't you mean alleged killer, Detective? Otherwise, surely, he'd be under arrest already, and this whole interview would be a moot point." It gave her a small amount of satisfaction to see the other woman blink slowly.

Yes, put that in your pipe and smoke it.

"So, you like the bad boys then, Susie?" Wonsan took over, and Susie swung her attention over to him.

"That's Ms. Elliot to you, Detective. I don't know you well enough to let you call me by my first name, and my likes and dislikes are none of your concern. I suggest you get to the point as to why you singled me out to interview, or I'll simply return to my duties."

Wonsan laughed, and the disgusted look he gave her made her want to slap him. She did neither, of course, and glanced down on the main floor instead. Ren was now leaning against the bar, thick arms crossed over his chest, his focus still entirely on the office. He would know that she could see him, and she took immense strength from that. Not for anything would she betray him.

"Ah yes, your duties. Tell me, which one of them are you spreading your legs for tonight, or maybe it's all of them? Your grandmother must be so proud."

It was a low dig that hurt, which had no doubt been his intention. Susie blinked rapidly to push away her tears. She would not give him the satisfaction of letting him know how much that had hurt. Though deep down, she knew that come what may, her Gran would have had her back and would have respected her decision. Besides life wasn't a simple case of black and white. Good and evil, right and wrong. If she'd learned anything at all since she'd got dragged into this mess, it was that.

"Actually she would be, not that it's any of your business, either. If all you're going to do is hurl insults at me, I'm leaving." Her exit was barred by Marian Roots, and Wonsan's heavy hand on her shoulder forced her to take a seat.

"Sit down, Ms. Elliot, we are not done. Besides, I

very much suspect you'll lose your high and toity attitude, once I've shown you the evidence."

The female Detective passed him a file, and horror crawled up her spine when Wonsan flipped it open. Gruesome pictures spilled out, each one more horrific than the one before, and Susie swallowed hard to stop herself from being sick.

"Both bodies were fished out of the canal last week. It took us some time to identify them due to the damage inflicted by the water, but this," he tapped a particularly gruesome image of bloated body, barely recognizable as a black female and Susie knew instinctively that it had to be Myrtle. "This is Myrtle Jones, or what remains of her, once your boyfriends were done with her."

Susie shook her head and screwed her eyes shut, but the images were already ingrained in her mind.

I mustn't be sick. I mustn't be sick. She was a bitch. She had it coming.

Her internal mantra failed to work when Wonsan listed her injuries.

"They cut off her hands and tongue. A common thing to do for what they class an informer. She was also beaten into a pulp and raped repeatedly. We can't be sure if that was while she was still alive or afterwards." He paused, and Marian Roots passed her a glass of water from the carafe Huntly always kept on the long sideboard in his office

"Here, drink this. I know these are hard to take. You knew her, of course. I suspect you were quite close, after all—"

"We weren't close at all. Myrtle was a royal bitch, who didn't care about anyone but herself." Susie slammed her mouth shut, lest she said something she might regret and Marian pulled back in surprise.

"So, you're saying she had this coming? That she deserved this somehow? Wow, where is a little sisterly solidarity here?"

Susie bristled inside, and having taken a hasty gulp of the water in front of her, slammed the glass back on the table.

"Don't put words in my mouth. I'm not saying anything of the sort. I'm just not surprised she found a gruesome end. Besides, how do you know she was raped? That woman had more paying customers than you could throw a dick at. Who's to say that wasn't consensual?"

Wonsan gave a short laugh, and Marian shook her head.

"Be that as it may, I'm pretty sure she wouldn't have consented to having her hands cut off, though you don't seem too surprised at that. What did she do? Steal from Huntly and he had your boyfriends take him out?"

"They're not my boyfriends, damn you. Don't twist this into something ugly. I'm only involved with…" Susie bit her lip and scowled at the triumphant smile that spread over Wonsan's face at her almost admission.

"Oh don't stop there, you're involved with…"

"None of your fucking business." Susie ground the words out through clenched teeth, and flinched when Marian put a hand on her arm.

"I understand. You don't want to end up like Myrtle, but we can protect you. If you'll only testify against him…"

Susie reared away from the other woman's touch and shot to her feet with so much force her chair cluttered to the floor. Sidestepping Wonsan, she stepped up to the one way glass, and rested her forehead against it. Ren was smiling at something Ty said to him, and her heart gave a flip.

Even if she wanted to, the police wouldn't be able to keep her safe. Ren or one of his men would find her, and besides, that man owned her body and soul, and had done almost from the minute she'd laid eyes on him. She could no more betray him than she could stop breathing.

"If you're worried that we can't, then—"

"Spare me." Susie interrupted the other woman. "I wasn't born yesterday. Even if I had something to tell, which, by the way I haven't, you could never protect me. I have no wish to end up as the next lot of fish food, so whatever you're going to throw at me, it won't work. You clearly have no evidence at all, and are fishing for answers with me. Well, babe, you're not going to get those answers from me, so save your breaths and go after the real bad guys. Like the Priestly brothers, maybe."

"Funny, you should say that, especially as you seem to have switched alliances so recently."

Wonsan pinned her in place with his gaze, and Susie frowned at him.

"I'm sure I have no idea what you mean," she said and promptly flinched when Wonsan slapped another gruesome picture right up next to her on the window.

"I know he's in bits here, but surely you recognize one of your boyfriends?" The Detective's smirk made Susie feel ill, as did the image. They seemed to have pieced his body parts back together. Neither his head, nor his limbs were still attached to his body, his face was almost unrecognizable due to the beating he'd received, and the next picture Wonsan shoved in her face made Susie retch.

It was his severed penis and balls.

"Rather a coincidence that he was done over like that, when you've shacked up with the cleaners, wouldn't you say? This was a personal attack, a jealous new boyfriend maybe, going by the name of Ren, by any chance?" He paused in seeming effort to let his words sink in, and when she didn't react he shouted loud enough to make her jump. "Damn it, all hell is breaking loose out there, and it all traces back to you, Ms. Elliot. That's not a fucking coincidence. You're going to cooperate and help me put these monsters behind bars or—"

"Jim, stop." His partner's sharp command stopped the man mid angry diatribe, and Susie took a few steps away from him. "What my partner means to say is that we would value your cooperation in this matter. We will be able to keep you safe and you would protect countless innocent lives by speaking up."

The woman frowned at her when Susie couldn't hold back her laughter. Slightly hysterical laughter, for sure, but really, it was laugh or cry and rock in a corner somewhere.

"You've got this all wrong. If there are any monsters here, it was Brian. He groomed me for fuck's sake, like he did to countless women before me, and would no doubt have done to countless women after me. Whoever killed that bastard did society a favor. He was never my boyfriend. He was a sick, sadistic monster, who tried to control me with threats to my life and the use of his fists. He ran up debts in my name with loan sharks who threatened my life and the house I called home, trying to force me into prostituting myself for the Priestly brothers. I ran the first chance I got, and Huntly was kind enough to offer me a job as a waitress, and his protection. If you think for one minute that I am going to repay him by ratting on him, then you're deluded. You want to go after the bad guys, go after the Priestly scum. And no, I'm not going to testify against them either, so save your breath." Susie paused, and glared between the two detectives, before she stepped over to the desk and pressed the intercom.

"I want out of here, please."

Wonsan swore, and out of the corner of her eyes she saw Ren jump into action. It took a matter of moments before he wrenched open the door, and not caring what anyone thought of her, Susie threw herself into his arms.

"There, I've got you, baby." His deep rumble in her ear soothed her internal horror, and taking his beloved scent deep into her lungs she clung on for dear life, oblivious to what else was going on, until she was forcibly wrenched out of his grasp.

"Your girlfriend has proven most cooperative to us, and you, Ellis Reynolds, are under arrest for the murder of Myrtle Jones and Brian Monk. Anything you will say will be taken in evidence…"

Susie didn't hear the rest of the arrest spiel, too horrified by the look of betrayal she glimpsed in Ren's eyes, before he pulled down the proverbial shutters, and he became a man she didn't recognize.

"You can't do that. I didn't say anything. I … umph."

Ty clamped his large hand over her mouth to stop her from talking, and even though she fought him, she was no match for his superior strength.

In truth she could hardly breathe, as he also cut off her air supply, and the world grew fuzzy. Through the ever narrowing light of her fading consciousness she was dimly aware of Huntly's solemn promise to get *Ren out of this mess,* before the world faded to black.

Susie struggled back to consciousness, and she blinked in the bright lights of the locker room. Kim's concerned face appeared in her vision. Her friend helped her to sit up when she struggled.

"Here, take it easy now. You've been out a while. Drink this." She pressed a cold bottle of water into her hand, and Susie dutifully swallowed. The cool liquid felt heavenly as it slid down her bruised throat, and she blinked away tears of relief at being alive.

"Tell the boss she's awake, will you, Ty?" Kim's words brought Susie's head up, and she swallowed hard when she saw Ty approach. He didn't look happy, and neither did Josh, who pushed away from the wall and took off, presumably to tell Huntly that she was awake.

Bile threatened to come up, and she struggled to her feet, as Ty stopped in front of her.

"I ... I didn't say anything to the police. I didn't." She flinched when Ty raised his hand to her throat, and his deep sigh ghosted across her face. Instead of choking her anew like she'd been expecting him to, he stroked his thumb along the bruised flesh and clucked his tongue.

"Relax, we know that. I'm sorry I was so hard on you, but you were going to drop us all in it in your distress, and this was the quickest way to shut you up. I hope it doesn't hurt too much?"

Susie blinked in confusion. It took her scrambled brain a while to catch up with the meaning behind his words, and when she did, she sank back down on the bench she'd been sitting on.

"Oh, but I thought, you thought ... Ren looked so angry, and why did they arrest him, when—"

"Mind games, sweet thing." Huntly's deep tones interrupted her warbled words, as he strolled through the doors to the locker room. "They think by arresting him, they'll get him to talk. Make him believe that the woman he loves betrayed him, and he'll lose his cool."

"They don't fucking know him very well, if they think that's gonna work," Alex said, and his brother hooted in laughter. Ace smirked, and Josh crossed his arms over his chest and shook his head. Susie had no idea how they all came to be there. Maybe they had always been there. Her mind was still stuck on the L word.

"But that's ridiculous. Ren doesn't do love."

Huntly seemed to find her croaked protest most amusing, and the rest of his men all sniggered. Even Ace, which was most disconcerting, especially when he strolled over to her and flicked her nose.

"He doesn't do love, but he certainly *does* you, girl." Ace grinned, and the rest of the men all dissolved into laughter, which rang round Susie's hurting head like clanging cymbals and she winced.

Kim urged her back to her feet.

"Sir, with your permission I'd like to take Susie home. She's in no fit state to work tonight, especially not with all these cops still sniffing around."

Susie tried to protest, but it all fell on deaf ears.

"I don't want to go home, and what about Ren? I need to be here when he gets back. I need to explain."

Kim sighed, and Huntly grasped her chin to make her look at him.

"Listen to me, girl. You're exhausted. There is nothing you can do, and they'll keep Ren in for twenty-four hours to try and wring a confession from him." At her horrified gasp, he nodded. "They'll try for an extension, but my solicitor will make sure they won't get one. They have no real evidence against him. Ren is too good at what he does."

That simple phrase brought those terrifying images she'd seen back to the forefront of her consciousness, and wrenching free from the loose hold Huntly had on her, she made a dash to the toilets, afraid she would bring up the contents of her stomach. Kim, like the good friend she was, followed her, but there was no need as Susie managed to get a hold of herself in time. Kim smiled at her over the sinks as she freshened up.

"This seems to be becoming a habit of yours, girl," she said. "Glad that passed, because you're gonna have to work on that constitution of yours if you're gonna stick around, you know. Now, let's get you back to my place for a bit. I'll promise I'll bring you straight back here if we hear anything from Ren."

Exhausted after all the events of the last few hours, Susie allowed herself to be led away. Josh drove them both back to Kim's, and despite her friend's protestations that they didn't need a bodyguard, the big guy stayed.

Much to her surprise Susie did sleep. And it was an even bigger surprise when she encountered a half-naked and sheepish looking Josh emerging from Kim's bedroom the following morning. She sure hadn't seen that coming.

Despite Huntly's assurances, twenty-four hours turned into forty-eight, and Ren still hadn't been released. The not knowing when he was going to be was slowly driving Susie 'round the bend, and she threw herself into her work at the club with renewed vigor. It was the third evening following his arrest that she felt his stare on her ass. As she looked up, her heart stopped and then turned into a jackhammer when their gazes connected in the mirrors behind the bar.

Something hot, hard, and dangerous flashed across Ren's expression as he strode toward her with a single minded determination that made her whole body tingle in anticipation. He had never looked more dangerous than right now. He hadn't shaved, and the thicker than usual stubble, combined with the creased, dirty clothing, and the way he ignored all greetings aimed at him made her feel like the prey about be devoured. His thick forearms came round her trapping her against the bar, and with his body heat against her back, she had nowhere to go. All the previous days' tensions left her body, and she sagged against him when he nuzzled into her neck.

"What are you doing here, pumpkin?" he asked.

One of his hands grasped her chin and lifted her head up, until his intense gaze bored into hers in the mirrors. The rest of the crowded club faded away at the wealth of emotions she read in his eyes.

"Waiting for you, Sir."

Ren drew in a sharp breath at her whispered reply and the hold on her chin grew painful.

"You shouldn't. I'm no good for you. Besides, I'm setting you free." He stepped away, and Susie was sure the whole club ought to hear her internal scream. It certainly rang around her head with the force of a banshee.

"No." Only a whisper escaped her lips though, as she turned around and looked up at him.

"No?" he asked. Susie frantically shook her head and breathed a sigh of relief when he stepped toward her again and yanked her to him. Her arms went around his neck, and she rose on tiptoes, pressing her full length against his. The feel of his cock hardening against her lower belly made her moan, and Ren's amber eyes darkened to the deepest, darkest molten chocolate, as he bent his head and brushed his lips across hers.

"Last chance, girl. I'm not so fucking noble that I can keep my hands off of you, if you stay."

Susie drew back and closing his eyes, he tried to push her away, but Susie jumped up at him. With a curse, he grasped her ass cheeks steadying her, while she wrapped her legs around him and clung on like a monkey.

"I don't want you to, Sir." His eyes widened, and a slow grin spread across his harsh features. "In fact, please, Sir, I seem to recall you saying I need to beg for your cock, so, please, Sir, I want your cock."

Ren froze, and she couldn't even begin to guess what was going in his head right now as he studied her.

"Is that so, girl? Is that all you want from me?"

Susie swallowed hard and smiled at him.

"If that is all you can give me, then that's what I'll take." She paused and wriggled against him, loving the way his dick jumped against the fly of his jeans. Ren swore under his breath and digging his hands in held her still.

"Stop that now, minx. It's been three long days. I'm likely to come in my jeans like a fucking teenager if you keep that up. My street cred would never survive it. It's bad enough that I seem to have saddled myself with a missus."

He flicked her a glance, and Susie marveled at the uncertainty that she could read in his eyes now.

"Missus, huh? Aren't you jumping the gun a bit here, Sir? After all, it is customary to ask first." She grinned and gave a mock pout when Ren pinched her butt cheek hard enough to leave a bruise.

"I'll ask when I'm good and ready, which isn't now, pumpkin. Fuck, I'm no good at this shit, but you must know what I'm saying here."

Ren dropped his head and claimed her mouth in a kiss so intense it stole her breath and left her in no doubt as to what he meant. Her Sir, her very own killer, and the last man she ought to be feeling like this about might never say the words out loud, but she knew anyway.

When he eventually let her come up for air, they were both breathing heavily, and Susie knew her grin was in danger of splitting her face in half.

"I'm just going to have to keep telling you then, Sir. I love you."

It was almost comical to see Ren flinch as though it was the worst thing ever she could have said to him, so she said it again, and again. All the way through the crowded club, until Ren pinned her against the wall of one of the private lap dance rooms.

"Shut up, woman, and kiss me. You're mine now, and I intend to have you any which way I can, starting right now."

Susie gasped at the rip of her knickers, and seconds later, Ren did what he did best. Fuck her to oblivion and back.

The End

DEDICATION

With thanks to the fabulous team at Evernight, in particular my editor Karyn.

THE CLEANERS

HIS TO PUNISH

The Cleaners, 2

Doris O'Connor

Copyright © 2016

Chapter One

Ty Mason pulled his earbuds out and flicked off his music, as he approached La Masquerade. He nodded toward Ace, one of his fellow Cleaners, on watch duty. Ever since things kicked off in a turf war with the Priestly gang, security had been tightened, and even though the club didn't open until later that evening, they always had at least one man on alert at all times. Ty stretched to soothe muscles cramped by his five mile jog, and Ace rolled his eyes.

"Better ways to get rid of your excess energy, man, than pounding the streets. I'd have thought pounding the fresh cunt in there right now would be far more enjoyable."

Ty flipped him the finger, and the other man laughed.

"Just saying, man. You've been living like a monk since Ren hooked up with his bird. The guys are talking. It ain't natural."

Ty gave a humorless laugh and wiped the sweat out of his eyes.

"Just because some of us know how to keep it in our pants, doesn't mean jack shit. Besides, maybe I'm just fed up with casual hookups. Can't tell me even you cold hearted bastard don't smile when you see the boss and his missus."

Ace shrugchapged and pulled a face.

"She's all right as far as bitches go, but there's far too much pussy in this world for me to confine myself to just one bird. Just wouldn't be fair, to keep my cock all to myself."

Ace winked, and Ty shook his head, hard pressed to contain his amusement. Instead he punched the other guy in the shoulder and pushed open the door to the club.

"One of these days that ego of yours will make you trip up big time, and I, for one, look forward to witnessing it." He threw the words over his shoulder, and Ace's laughter followed him into the club. The man's reply was cut off by a new dance track starting up, as the next wannabe dancer gyrated her wares in front of Huntly. The club owner did not look impressed, and who could blame him? This bird was far too skinny, and even though she tried to look alluring, her make-believe sex acts with the pole just looked awkward.

"Enough, girl. Next!"

Owen Huntly's terse command stopped the girl.

Turning his back on the spectacle playing out on stage, Ty approached the bar, where little Susie was stacking the drinks. She smiled when she spotted him approach, and Ty murmured his thanks, as Ren's submissive passed over a sports bottle of ice cold water. He drank half of it and tipped the rest of it over his head. The cool liquid felt heavenly on his overheated skin, and when he opened his eyes again, it was to see Susie stare at him. With her mouth slightly open, heat rose in her cheeks when she noticed he'd caught her checking him out, and Ty smirked.

That look would land her in hot water fast.

Ren was nothing if not possessive over his woman, and sure enough the older man bristled.

"When you've finished tripping up over your own tongue, pumpkin, you might notice my glass is empty."

"Sorry, Sir, I didn't mean... Here." She quickly refilled his glass and worried her bottom lip with her teeth. She couldn't seem to help glancing shy looks at Ty's chest, and Ren growled his disapproval.

If that was possible her blush deepened, and chuckling, Ty sat down on the stool next to Ren.

"I take it the auditions aren't going too well then?" he asked.

Ren reached across the counter to run a finger down Susie's cheek, and the way the redhead leaned into Ren's touch while mouthing another silent *sorry* made Ty feel as though he was intruding.

Turning his back on the loved up couple, he watched the next dancer perform for Huntly instead. She was better, but Huntly stopped this woman, also, before her track was up.

"Yeah, the boss is in a foul mood," Ren said. "Think he's looking for another Myrtle, and that's nigh on impossible. The bitch was a lying, cheating cunt, but she sure could dance."

Ty nodded his agreement. The whole Myrtle episode had been regrettable and messy, to say the least, but it *had* brought Ren and Susie together. It had, however, left a big hole in the dancing girls. Huntly only employed the best, and had been looking for a replacement ever since.

It didn't look as though the owner of La Masquerade was having much luck replacing her today either. Ty let his gaze roam along the few remaining wannabes, and the skin on his neck prickled when he clocked the last one. Curves in all the right places, this one seemed nervous, and pissed off. She'd chosen an odd outfit for her dance. The blouse and pencil skirt were more suited for an interview at the office, even if they did hug her curves, and made a man salivate, imagining what she was hiding under there. The six inch stiletto sandals on her feet were sexy as fuck, however. The blonde wig she was wearing—and it had to be a wig—made a startling contrast to her flawless mocha skin. Tall and breathtakingly beautiful, it was the expression on her face that made Ty take the most notice. While her body was swaying in tune to the current track in that subconsciously fluid way only a born dancer could bring to the table, it was the sheer hatred burning in her almond shaped eyes which gave Ty pause for thought. Not aimed at him, but Ren and Susie. As far as Ty knew, there could be no reason for this, because she was definitely a new face. Ty would have remembered seeing her before. He nudged his boss and long-time friend.

"That one might have potential?" He nodded toward the woman, whose gaze now connected with his. Her eyes widened, and Ty grinned. He was no stranger to women's reaction to him, and he couldn't deny the instant tightening in his groin at the knowledge that this cute piece of ass liked what she saw. Ace had been right in one assessment. It had been way too long since he got his dick wet. Besides, if this bird had some hidden agenda for being here, then getting her under him was a surefire way of getting to her secrets.

If Ren knew her, he gave nothing away as he let his gaze roam over the girl.

"Hmm, maybe. I'll reserve judgment until I see her dance. She'll do, I guess."

Ty had to laugh at the carefully phrased words, especially as he saw Susie frown and put her hands on her hips. Submissive she might be, but she was just as possessive of Ren as he was of her. Again, that general feeling of unease spread through Ty, not helped by seeing the woman's now careful avoidance of looking toward the bar. Something was up, and he didn't like it. And he certainly didn't like the urge he had to go up there, and get close and personal. What was that about, for fuck's sake? So she was pretty and just his type, didn't mean a thing. Not if she presented an undetermined threat to those he cared about.

He kept an eye on her, as the dancers in front of her did their piece and were summarily dismissed by Huntly. When, at long last, it was her turn Huntly sat forward in his seat, hands stapled in front of his face, and Ty, too, moved closer to the stage. Huntly glanced at him and smirked.

"What happened to you?" he asked.

Without taking his eyes off the woman nervously smoothing non-existent creases out of her grey skirt, Ty shrugged.

"Jogged here, that's all and I needed to cool off."

Huntly shook his head and laughed.

"We do have showers, you know."

"Yeah." Ty smirked, and stepping closer to the woman who found the study of the stage floor most interesting all of a sudden, jumped up next to her. She flinched as he stepped right into her personal space and grasped her chin to make her look at him.

"True, but I didn't want to miss this."

He flashed the girl a smile and flicked the blonde strands hanging into her cleavage behind her shoulders.

"Why the wig, sweetheart? The boss won't stand for disguises, so I suggest you lose it."

She threw him a mutinous look from under her naturally long eyelashes, and Ty fought his growing erection. It would be too damn obvious in the low slung joggers he was wearing, but *fuck*.

That look made him want to bend her over his knee and spank her insolent ass until it was glowing a nice shade of red, and she was begging him to fuck her.

"That's none of your business, mister, and if you don't let go of me, I'll be forced to put you on your butt. I'm here to audition, not to be manhandled by..." She wrenched her chin out his grasp, and Ty let her with a smirk. He did like his women feisty, and the way her toffee-colored eyes spat fire at him was a huge turn-on.

"I'd like to see you try, sweet thing," Ty said. A huff was his answer, and Ren's laughter joined Huntly's as Ty jumped back off the stage and sat down next to Owen. It would afford him a perfect view up her tight skirt once she started to dance, and something told him that this woman would blow their minds.

Huntly seemed to have come to a similar conclusion, because he leaned back and smiled at the bristling woman.

"Put your claws away, girl. While it would be most amusing to see you try and put Mason in his place, it wouldn't end well ... for *you*. You're here to audition, you say, but you're hardly dressed for it."

The woman on stage pushed her shoulders back, and dropped her hip, an action that reminded Ty instantly of Myrtle, and that itch on his neck returned tenfold, especially when she threw another murderous look toward Ren. Crossing his arms over his powerful chest, Ren quirked an eyebrow at her, and after murmuring something to Susie, the head of the Cleaners made his way toward them.

"Do I know you from somewhere, girl?" At her hasty shake of her head, Ren ran a hand through his shoulder length hair, and he sighed. "Then I would appreciate you not giving me dagger looks, if you want to seek employment here. You'll find attitude like yours is not appreciated around here."

"And who are you to tell me what to do?" Instead of being subdued, this woman appeared even angrier, as she continued to stare Ren down, and Ty shook his head in wry amusement.

"His name is Ren, girl," Huntly said. "And you'd do well to heed his words. Now, if you're here to dance, then by all means, dance, or stop wasting my time. And lose the wig. I want to see the real you."

There was an edge of steel to Huntly's words, and some of her bravado left the woman on stage. Ty groaned under his breath when she unclipped the wig and acres of dark, shiny hair tumbled halfway down her back. Fuck knew why she'd decided to hide it under that contraption, but the curly mass made him want to give into his original instinct.

Come what may, he would claim this one, even if he had to kidnap her. After all, that plan worked out well enough for Ren.

He glanced at his friend to see him sit down on the other side of Huntly, seemingly determined to give his input into this dancer.

The girl in question nodded toward the sound station, which set her chosen dance track into motion, grasped the pole with both hands, closed her eyes … and Ty's tongue stuck to the roof of his mouth.

"Hot damn." Huntly's murmured assessment of her dancing skills said it all. The sultry tones of Rihanna's song, "Skin", filled the air, and all three men sat entranced as she did things to the pole that should be illegal and probably were in some places. Her blouse came loose during her dance, exposing her toned, smooth abdomen, and a stunning butterfly tattoo down one side, as she hung upside down off the pole. Her skirt rode up, giving far too arousing glances of the tiny, purple, thong which covered her pussy, and Ty gave up all pretense of hiding his erection. By the time the song faded out, he was so hard he could pound concrete. She slithered to the floor to end in a split with her arms above her head and her head thrown back, an action that exposed the curve of her delicate neck where her pulse beat a staccato rhythm, and Ty groaned under his breath.

Ren and Huntly seemed to be in a similar predicament, because Huntly adjusted himself, and Ren rose wordlessly, stalked over to Susie, and dragged her away out back. No doubt to fuck her brains out, the lucky bastard.

"What's your name, girl?" Huntly's voice sounded hoarse, and Ty didn't miss the brief look of triumph in the woman's eyes, as she opened them and rose back to her feet. Oh, yeah, she fucking knew the power she exuded in her dance, and that made Ty want to … well, what he wanted to do would get him put up for an assault charge faster than you could say *bad idea,* but he wanted her.

****

Jeanette tried to catch her breath, and not give away how much she'd enjoyed dancing like that. Who knew what a fucking turn-on it would be, however? The practice sessions she'd put in at the studio had not prepared her for the reality of dancing in front of three virile men. While every instinct screamed at her to scratch Ren's eyes out, she couldn't deny the man's charisma. Just like his reputation foretold, he had a *presence.* Danger, aggression, and strength literally poured off him, and as for his dark haired second in command…

Hells bells! The pictures had not done him justice, not when he was hot, sweaty, wet, and dressed in his running gear, stood in front of her. It had taken every ounce of willpower she'd had to not take a deep sniff of his far too arousing scent. Earthy, primal, with a hint of left over cologne, his very aura had wrapped itself around her, and far from thinking him a domineering asshole, she'd had to fight the urge to simply do as she was told.

Which was a completely alien concept for her. Jeanette McArthur didn't bow to any male not after having witnessed both her mum and little sister fall into that trap. It had turned her mother into a drunken crack addict, and as for her sister…

The old hurt, which had been ripped wide open with recent events, made breathing even more difficult, and Jeanette forced herself to concentrate on what Owen Huntly was saying to her. He'd asked her a question, hadn't he? She wanted, no, needed this job, if she was to accomplish what she had come here to do, and pissing off the influential owner of La Masquerade any more than she already had with her prickly attitude would not get her a job and the *in* she was looking for.

"Jeanette … sir." Belatedly she added that respectful title, and Ty Mason swore under his breath. Jeanette had to grab hold onto the pole, because seeing him adjusting what looked like a sizable erection in seeming reaction to her words, did strange things to her equilibrium. Not for the life of her would she give him the satisfaction to know that he was getting to her, but, judging by the sinful smirk which kicked up the corners of his mouth, he already knew. Damn it all to hell and back. This would just complicate things even further. Belatedly she realized she was still staring at his groin, and fighting the hot blush creeping up her neck, she wrenched her gaze away from Ty's brooding presence and looked toward Huntly indeed.

Seeming amusement crinkled up the corners of the club owner's steel grey eyes. They lost most of their earlier frostiness as a result of that devastatingly charming smile, and against her better judgment Jeanette found herself smiling back at him. She didn't have the immediate, visceral reaction to this man as she had to Ty Mason, but there was no denying that Owen Huntly was sinfully attractive and charismatic in his own right.

And deadly, don't forget that. He's a criminal. They all are, and you've entered the lions' den.

Her mother's warning, given in one of her rare lucid moments, rang in Jeanette's ears, and she forced her raging hormones back into submission. At least now she understood why her little sis had thrown away her promising career in the Royal Ballet to pursue her pole dancing. Even if she had followed a man and got tangled up in the criminal underbelly as a result.

"Jeanette who, girl?" Huntly asked, and she swallowed hard as he leaned forward to study her.

"Jeanette McArthur, sir."

Huntly's eyes drew together in a frown, and he stapled his hands in front of his face again, while he leaned his elbows on his thighs. It was disconcerting to be under such close scrutiny, and when he smiled, seemingly having come to some form of conclusion, she pulled a much needed breath into her constricted lungs.

"You remind me of someone. Well, your dancing does. She was classically trained. I am guessing you are, too?"

This was dangerous territory to get into, because

if Huntly drew the obvious conclusion, then lord only knew what he would do to her.

Not trusting her voice to not give away how nervous she was, Jeanette simply nodded.

"So, why are you not pursuing a career in that field, if you don't mind me asking?" As politely phrased as that question was, Jeanette recognized the inherent threat. Lying would never do. Besides, she didn't have to about this, at least.

"I grew too tall, and I became a dance teacher instead, but it doesn't pay well."

Huntly's smile in answer didn't reach his eyes, and a cold shiver ran down Jeanette's spine as he let his gaze roam over her body in a leisurely appraisal that made her feel as though she was standing naked in front of him.

"You do realize that the real money in my club doesn't lie in just dancing, right? Are you prepared for that?"

"No... I mean yes ... maybe." Jeanette corrected herself, as Huntly's eyebrows rose, and Ty shook his head. He didn't look pleased with her answer, and for some strange reason that bothered her.

"Which one is it, girl. Yes? No? Or maybe? It'll affect the terms of the contract I'll offer you, so I need to know a definite answer."

Hope swelled in Jeanette's chest at those words.

"Does that mean I passed the audition and you're offering me a job?"

Huntly smiled again and nodded toward Ty.

"What do you think? Is she good enough to dance in the club, Mason?"

Chapter Two

Ty barely hid his amusement as Jeanette's head spun round toward him with a speed that should have put her at risk of whiplash. She tried to stare him down, but eventually dropped her gaze to his collarbone. It clearly cost her to do so, because a deep frown creased her forehead, and she wrapped her arms around herself in a defensive move, which pulled at his heartstrings.

She'd exuded sex appeal and confidence when dancing. Right now, however, she looked nervous, if not to say frightened stiff, her body held rigid, as though she was afraid to break down.

Ty exchanged a glance with Owen, and he read the same puzzlement in the club owner's eyes.

"You're leaving this up to me, boss?" Ty finally said. "Not wanting a taste yourself?"

That brought the girl's head back up, and her sharp intake of breath seemed far too loud in the stillness of the room.

Owen smirked and shrugged.

"Not after the last time. No point getting attached, and besides, I've got my hands full with other things."

A shadow crossed Owen Huntly's features. It was a mere flash of emotion, so brief Ty would have missed it, had he blinked, but it made Ty wonder just how far Huntly's attachment to Myrtle had reached. Everyone knew he'd plucked her off the streets and made her into the success she had been, before he'd given the orders to kill her, but maybe … just maybe that cost him more than he'd let on.

"If you're sure, boss."

At Huntly's curt nod, Ty smiled and turned his attention back to the woman on stage.

"In that case, I'd say we have to test the theory."

One effortless jump meant he was back on stage, and Jeanette swallowed hard, taking several steps away until the pole stopped her. Using his superior body height to his advantage, he crowded her against the shiny object. Her eyes widened when she appeared to notice his erection digging into the juncture of her thighs. It made him smile, because with her killer heels on she was just the right height to fuck.

His cock twitched at the thought, and a gasp escaped his prey. It was a matter of moments for him to grasp her delicate wrists, and pin her arms high above her head. The action pushed her impressive rack further out and into his chest, her nipples hard little points, digging into his chest. He dipped his head to lick across the rapidly beating pulse point in her neck, and her sweet and far too addictive flavor exploded on his taste buds. She tasted of caramel, with a hint of sweat and coconut oil, which conjured all sorts of images. It was, after all, his favorite kind of lube to use.

"Please, don't."

Her breathless plea stopped him from exploring the far too enticing curve of her neck further. He inhaled deeply and then brought his head up to study her.

"Don't what, titch?"

He smirked at her reaction, because that frown was back and she did her best to glare at him.

"What did you just call me?"

Ty tightened his hold on her wrists when she pulled against him, and she glared some more at his laughter.

"What? Titch?"

"Yes, that. I'm not small. Were you not listening when I told your boss I got too tall for ballet?"

Ty smirked and threw a glance toward Huntly.

"Oh, I was listening all right. You also said you

knew what the other side of being one of his dancers entails, so it's time to test the theory. Can't let you loose on our clients, without ensuring you're up to the task, *titch*."

She blanched under her mocha skin and shook her head.

"I'm not a titch."

"Well, you are to me. Stop struggling, girl, you'll only hurt yourself. Then again, maybe you'd like me to hurt you?"

Instead of succumbing to him, Jeanette struggled more. He blocked her move to bring her stiletto down on his toes, by simply picking her up and swinging her over his shoulder.

Owen laughed, and his prey screeched like a banshee.

"Let me go, you can't do this, damn you. I'm not one of your whores."

Ty brought his hand down on the delectable ass next to his head, while maintaining a firm clamp on her legs to stop her from flailing about. Nothing he could do about the fists pummeling his back. She packed quite a punch, too, and his dick hardened further at the thought of taming all that passion. This woman would be a hellcat in bed, of that he was sure.

"Not yet, you're not, you mean, and perhaps you won't ever be. After all, you might be no good at it. Now stop hitting me, girl, or I'll be forced to tie you up. As much as I'd enjoy that, I don't want to be drawing too much attention to ourselves when we leave. Usual protocol, boss?"

He swatted Jeanette's ass a few more times, and while she continued to struggle, the sweet musk of aroused woman also hit his nostrils. She might act all outraged, but she wanted him, that was for sure.

"Yep, take her to the Cleaners' house and report back when you're done. Unless the lady has changed her mind about dancing for me?"

Owen's amusement showed in his voice, and Jeanette gave an exasperated huff.

"I haven't, but I object to being manhandled like sack of potatoes by your goon … *sir*."

The pause before she added that title made it sound anything but respectful, and Ty chuckled to himself, while he ran his hand slowly over the curve of her butt and pinched the crease where her ass met her thigh.

"Ow, that hurt. Put me the hell down."

At Owen's nod, Ty slowly slid her down his front, enjoying the feel of her soft curves sliding along the hard planes of his body. She was all soft and round, and judging by the blush that darkened her skin, she enjoyed that sensual slide as much as he did.

"That, titch, was a mere kiss compared to what I have planned for you," he said.

Jeanette bit her lip, her pearly whites a delightful contrast to her dark skin, and Ty indulged his need to keep on touching this woman by tracing his thumb across her jaw. He then pulled her full, succulent lips away from danger. Ty let that digit linger, again fascinated by the softness under his calloused pad, and he didn't miss the shiver of awareness that made goosebumps appear on his girl's skin. And she so was his, regardless of what she might have to say about it.

This chemistry they shared was too potent not to explore, and then there was the underlying current of animosity he sensed, directed at Ren. The man himself had reappeared from out back. When he seemed to notice her reaction to him, he stopped in the middle of tucking his shirt back in his jeans. Ren crossed his arms over his chest, leaned back against the wall and quirked a silent eyebrow in query.

That earlier itch crawled back up Ty's spine, and he turned his attention to the woman in front of him.

"I promise you'll enjoy yourself. After all, if I went to investigate that sweet cunt of yours, I bet I'd find it nice and juicy."

Jeanette swung her gaze back to his, and if looks could kill he'd be six feet under already.

"Don't flatter yourself," she said.

Ty slid his hand down to her throat, and she stiffened when he tightened his hold. Not enough to cut off her air supply—yet—but it was a silent warning nonetheless. One she heeded beautifully, because she went very still.

"Good girl." Ty whispered the words and leaning in closer, dropped a kiss on the tip of her nose. She went cross eyed trying to keep her focus on him, and her breathing grew shallow.

"Besides, I can smell how wet you are for me, so be a good girl and stop fighting this. I'll take you one way or the other, but it will be much easier on you if you simply comply."

Having made his point he released her, satisfied to see her make a grab for the pole, as though her legs couldn't quite support her weight right now. She groaned when Owen addressed her.

"So, let me ask you this again. It is a yes, no, or maybe still, to the other duties which will be required of you in my club, girl?"

****

Damn it all to hell and back.

Jeanette inwardly cursed a blue streak any sailor would have been proud of while she desperately tried to keep her composure on the outside. She forced herself to let go of the white knuckled grip she had on the pole, and pulled a much needed breath into her oxygen starved lungs. Why, oh, why did she have to meet someone like this Ty here? Like it or not, he made every feminine cell in her body sing, and rather than be disgusted by this caveman possessiveness he exhibited toward her, she w*as* turned on beyond measure.

It wouldn't do, this insane attraction. For all she knew he'd had a hand in her sister's demise, and she should want to scratch his eyes out, not fall at his damn feet.

"Answer me, girl."

Startled by the club owner's harsh tone of voice, Jeanette told her brain to *shut the fuck up.*

"It's still a maybe, sir, sorry, and I fail to see why I have to go anywhere with *him.*"

She risked a glance up at Ty Mason, and instantly wished she hadn't. The glittering intensity in his dark eyes, his entire focus seemingly on her, was most disconcerting. It made her want to throw caution to the wind, and to simply take what he offered. Besides, this was the *in* she needed, wasn't it?

It took immense effort to break their stare, and shaking her head, she addressed Owen.

"Why do I have to go someone's house? I have my own home. I don't need to—"

"The job comes with live-in accommodation here at the club. If, and I say *if* Ty deems you worthy, then here is where you'll be expected to live and *entertain.*" He paused as if to make sure his words sank in, and when she simply continued to stare at him, he smiled.

"It's for your own safety, girl. I look after the girls who work for me, and experience tells me this is the best way. There are exceptions to that rule, of course, especially, once you've proven your loyalty to us. Until that point, you'll be assigned to one of the Cleaners." He nodded toward Ty. "As Mason wants you, you're his. Those are my terms. Accept them or walk out and never darken my club doors again."

Ren moved closer, seemingly intent on helping to evacuate her from the building, and the words tumbled out of her mouth before she could stop them.

"If this is all to keep your girls *safe*, as you put it..." The club owner's eyebrows rose at the intonation she'd unwillingly put on that word. She knew she shouldn't carry on, but seeing Ren strut his stuff, made her want to hurl something at him, and meant she threw caution to the wind. "Then why did that dancer end up as fish food in the canal, if you don't mind me asking, that is ... I mean?" She couldn't continue, because Huntly grew tense, and she realized she was so overstepping the mark here.

Ty stepped closer to her, and she winced at the iron band his fingers formed around her elbow. He yanked her back against his solid frame, and when she looked up at him, his expression had turned into a closed off mask. His dark eyes glittered with dangerous intent, and for the first time she truly felt afraid.

What are you doing? These men are killers. Why are you antagonizing them?

The little voice in her head taunted her, only to be interrupted by the club owner's cool voice.

"Which dancer would you be referring to, girl?"

Jeanette tried to push away from the quiet menace Ty presented right now, but she should have known that would prove a useless exercise, because her other elbow was grasped in a viselike grip, which would surely leave fingerprint bruises behind on her skin.

"I'd answer him, girl."

Ren's deep, commanding drawl brought her

attention back to him, and she swallowed hard. Standing perfectly still, his head cocked to one side, he was watching her every move. Coiled, ready to strike like a deadly snake stalking its prey, he looked as though he'd earned every one of the rumors surrounding him. Unwittingly her gaze strayed to his large hands. Held loosely next to his denim clad thighs, they brought her reality home more than anything could have done. Everyone knew Ren killed with his hands, and Jeanette swallowed convulsively to stop herself from being sick.

Ty's fingers dug deeper into her arms, and his hot breath ghosted across her jawline as he spoke to her.

"You're testing our patience, titch. Start talking, or so help me, I'll make you talk."

The inherent threat in those softly delivered words for her ears only shouldn't make her heart beat faster in excitement. It really shouldn't. Yet, held up by the strength of the male, hard body surrounding her, his scent invading her nostrils, and the stubble on his jaw creating delicious shivers of awareness to chase each other across her skin, that's exactly what was happening. All of her senses seemed heightened by the dangerous atmosphere she found herself in. It was crazy. That's what this was, but in a strange way it helped her understand the path her sister had chosen a little better. Myr had always gone for the bad boys, sought the next adventure, and it had driven a wedge between them when they were growing up.

Now, well now it was all too late, but Jeanette could do this small thing for her to make amends. To right a wrong, and to seek revenge.

"I don't recall her name now, but she was all over the papers a while back." The lie came surprisingly easily, and Jeanette forced herself to hold Huntly's searching gaze.

"Let me refresh your memory then. Her name was Myrtle, and she was indeed my top dancer..." A shadow crossed his features. The act was so brief that Jeanette wasn't entirely sure she hadn't imagined that flash of emotion. "Until she decided to leave my employ, and thus, my protection. I'm glad you brought her up, actually, as Myrtle's unfortunate *end*..."

A grim smile played across his features when he said that, and it took all of Jeanette's willpower to not scream at him, *unfortunate, my ass. She was murdered!*

She didn't do anything of the sort, of course, mindful of the fact that her own life was at stake here, so she gritted her teeth instead, and forced a smile, of sorts, on her face.

"Like I said, as unfortunate as that was, it demonstrates my point quite clearly. Myrtle brought her demise on by herself. Had she stayed loyal and thus under my protection none of that would have happened." He paused, and this time his smile was pure evil. It made Jeanette step back and seek the solid warmth of Ty's protection, which should have been an oxymoron, but right now it made sense to her. She certainly would not get any help from Ren or Huntly, who studied her again as though she was an interesting species of microbe under the microscope.

"I see."

Ty's sigh behind her raised the fine hair on her neck, and belatedly she realized that he was resting his head on her shoulder.

"Titch, do you have a death wish?" The murmured words made her turn her head slightly, so that she could see his expression, and she shook her head.

"Could have fooled me," Ty said, and straightened up again. He also released his hold on her, and Jeanette felt strangely bereft without his body surrounding her. She wrapped her arms around herself instead, and kept her gaze on Owen Huntly' shiny black Italian loafers instead, as she murmured her apology.

"Sorry, I'm just trying to get this straight in my head, that's all. You say you protect your girls, but what happens when they've had enough and want to leave?"

"Nothing, they leave." Ren replied instead of Huntly, and when she risked a glance up at the club owner, she saw him give a sharp nod.

"Just like that?" she asked.

"You heard Ren. I see no reason to repeat myself here. Now, like I said, give me your answer or leave—"

"Yes."

Ty sighed again, Ren shook his head, and Huntly smiled. It didn't reach his eyes, and he addressed the man behind her instead of her.

"You'll have your hands full with this one. I expect a report on her *abilities* when you're done with her. Depending on what that says, I'll have a contract drawn up for her to sign."

Owen dismissed her with a wave of his hand and gesturing for Ren to follow him, left the club floor. It placed her on her own with Ty Mason, and her heart turned into a jackhammer, when he stepped around her and held out his hand.

"Let's go, titch."

She grimaced at that word he insisted on calling her, and amusement twinkled in his dark gaze.

"Get used to it, girl. Now, how did you get here? Public transport or…"

Jeanette shook her head.

"My car is parked in the multi-story round the corner. Why?"

Instead of answering her Ty looked toward his hand. Taking the hint, Jeanette took it and immediately wished she hadn't. The jolt of connection that shot up her arm at the innocent enough contact was hard to take, made ten times worse by Ty's sharp intake of breath, as though, he, too, had felt that. He tightened his hold on her hand and drew lazy and far too arousing circles over the back of it with his thumb.

"That wasn't so hard now, was it, girl? As to why I asked after your car, I would have thought that was obvious. I jogged here today, and we'll need transport to get the Cleaners' house. I'd have had to have nicked one of the boy's cars to take us there, but we can take yours, so it's all just fine and dandy."

"He wasn't kidding about that then? I'm expected to live with you?"

Ty surprised her by pulling her hand up to his mouth and dropping a kiss on back of it.

"*Au contraire,* my fair lady. You will be living with me, Ren and Susie, and the boys." Having clearly judged her incredulous expression correctly, he winked at her.

"Ordinarily speaking, I'd be expected to share you with the boys, but I'm gonna pull rank and keep you to myself."

"That … that is … *what*?"

Jeanette could hardly hear over the blood rushing in her ears, and when Ty pulled her close she gratefully leaned on him. It was that or fall down. What in the hell had she let herself in for?

"You do that?" she finally asked, when she managed to project her voice with some semblance of its usual cadence.

"Usually speaking, but, if it makes you feel any better, Ren set a precedent with his Susie, one I aim to shamelessly exploit, so relax."

"Precedent?" Jeanette was painfully aware that

she was giving her best parrot impression here, and she wasn't usually lost for words, but really, what was she supposed to make of this?

Ty flicked her nose with his index finger and laughed.

"Don't worry about it. I'll make sure the boys know you're mine."

Something twisted inside her at those possessive words, especially as he'd dropped his voice on the last one. It made the imp in her rebel, and she stalked back to where she'd left her bag and car keys.

"I'm not *yours*," she said, once she'd retrieved her bag and turned to glare across the stage at him. Not that it had any effect on the infuriating man. Arms crossed over his impressive chest, he was leaning against the pole with an insolent smile on his lips. He made no move to disguise the fact that he had clearly been checking out her ass, bent over as she had been in the process of gathering her belongings. Judging by that sudden flare of heat in his dark gaze, he'd liked what he'd seen. "I'm not." She reiterated her earlier statement, and Ty laughed and ran a hand through his mop of black hair. It made it all stand up in disarray, and gave him that just out of bed look, which made him even more edible.

Like it or not, her body wanted this guy, as much as he wanted her if the long, hard outline of his cock, clearly visible in his joggers was any indication. Ty had pulled his vest top out of his waistband, but the action did little to hide the evidence of how well hung he appeared to be.

Jeanette fought another blush at her wayward thought processes. They were most unlike her, after all. According to her last few unfortunate encounters with men—she refused to call them boyfriends—she was a frigid, unresponsive bitch.

More like they hadn't come even close to revving her motor like this guy did with just one heated look.

He moved toward her now, all stealth and intent, and for the life of her Jeanette couldn't move a muscle, or look away from the glittering intensity in his dark eyes. They weren't completely black, as she'd first thought, because flecks of amber showed in them now, as he grasped her chin with one hand, and pulled her right into his hard frame by grabbing her ass.

She had a second's warning before his mouth crashed down on hers with a growl.

"Mine."

Chapter Three

Ty expected her to fight the kiss. Instead, Jeanette melted against him. With a small sigh she opened to the insistent strokes of his tongue along her full lips. It meant her sweet breath mingled with his, and Ty brought his hand around to fist it in her hair. A whimper escaped the woman in his arms, and when she brought her arms around to lock them around his neck, he threw all caution to the wind.

Just like he'd suspected she would, Jeanette gave no quarter in the kissing department. She kissed him back with ever bolder flicks of her tongue against his, while she pressed her tits into his chest, and he ground his rock hard dick into her pussy. Even through the layers of clothing separating them, her wet heat called him. The sweet musk of aroused woman filled his nostrils. When he massaged her ass cheek on the way down, she moaned into his kiss again, and spread her legs of her own accord to give him better access.

It was Ty's turn to groan into the kiss, as he encountered the sodden wet fabric of her thong covering her slit.

Wrenching his lips off hers, he pulled her head back by her hair, and the fabric under his fingertips grew even wetter. What an interesting development that was.

"Like I said, you're mine. And this," he pushed his fingers into her pussy as far as he could with the fabric still covering her hole, and smirked at her sharp intake of breath. "This sweet cunt knows the truth."

Jeanette tried to shake her head, but he tightened his hold on her hair further. Her eyes widened and filled with tears at the pain he knew he was inflicting on her sensitive scalp, and the dark bastard he hid inside reveled at the tiny yelp she clearly didn't want to make.

"That's just a physiological response." She went a little cross-eyed while saying that. When he flicked the hard nub at the top of her slit with his thumb, her hips bucked at the lazy circles he drew around her clit, and her breathing sped up further.

"Doesn't mean anything. You'll never own my soul." The gasped words pissed him off, because he could read the sincerity in her eyes. She truly believed that, and while that shouldn't bother him, it damn well fucking did.

"Is that so, titch? We'll see about that, shall we? You'll be begging me for my cock before the day is out, girl."

To prove his point, he nudged the elastic of her underwear out of the way, and sank two fingers knuckle deep into her cunt, while keeping up the gentle pressure on her clit. Jeanette was so wet that he encountered no resistance, and when he curled those digits, exerting pressure against the fleshy mound he was looking for, her whole body jerked in need. Perspiration broke out on her skin, her fingernails dug into his shoulders, and she rocked herself against his hand in tiny, jerky moves, she didn't seem aware of making.

Incomprehensible sounds spilled from her lips, as he pushed her toward an orgasm he had no intention of letting her have.

She was breathtaking as her arousal amped up. Eyes screwed shut, mouth open, skin flushed, she looked like a woman on the edge, as confirmed by the wetness coating his fingers and hand, and the way her internal muscles clenched and released around his digits.

It made Ty wish it was his cock her cunt muscles were squeezing to death, but he'd meant his earlier words. She would damn well beg him for his cock, and he would only fuck her once she'd lost the fucking attitude and admitted she was his.

"God, I'm ... fuck ... don't stop, please ... I'm..."

Ty didn't need to hear the words to know how close she was, and without warning withdrew his fingers. They left her body with a squelch, and giving her a shove away, he licked his fingers clean, while Jeanette stumbled and moaned her denial.

It was utterly delightful to see her so on edge, and when she tried to pull her skirt up, seemingly determined to finish herself off, he grasped her by the shoulders and slammed her body against the wall.

"Ow, damn you." Bringing his hand around, he clamped it over her mouth so hard he would leave bruises, and her sudden fear was an almost palpable force in the room. It made him even harder, and he ground his erection into her ass.

"That's Sir to you, titch, and you'll only come when I give you permission to. You haven't earned that right. Try and get yourself off again, and so help me, you won't be able to use that hand for a while. Broken fingers are not that easy to dance with, are they?"

"No, please..."

He smirked at her strangled reply and stepped away from her.

"Now that we've established some ground rules, tidy yourself up. You look a mess, girl."

He had to give it to her, she had spunk, because her eyes flashed fire at him, as she turned around and did her best to straighten her disheveled clothing.

"And whose fault is that ... *Sir*?"

The intonation she put on that title made it sound like an insult, as was no doubt her intention.

"Yours clearly, girl, for not obeying the rules. Now, be a good girl for five minutes, and let's get to your car. The sooner we have your stuff, the sooner we can get started on your training."

She snorted at that, and Ty crossed his arms and raised an eyebrow at her.

"For your information, I'm keeping a tally on all these infractions of yours, and once I've got you in our cellar, your ass will be lovely shade of glowing red, I reckon."

Jeanette swallowed hard.

"Cellar?" she asked, and he had to wonder at the wobble in her voice. "I'm not ... I can't ... please, Sir, I'll behave, no cellars."

She wrapped her arms around herself, and he frowned at the way she tried to hide her trembling.

What the fuck?

"It's not really a cellar, at last not if you're thinking dark, wet, and creepy."

"Oh, thank God. I have never liked cellars. They give me the creeps."

Her heartfelt sigh of relief made his chest feel tight with a surge of emotion and the need to protect the shivering woman in front of him. Giving into the instinct to soothe her, he put his hands on her shoulder and stroked the delicate skin of her neck with his thumbs.

"We have those too, of course, but you'll only end up there if you've pissed off Huntly."

A tear rolled down her cheek, and he frowned at the silent misery she seemed to be caught up in.

"Tell me," she finally asked. "Is that where Myrtle ended up? Did she piss him off that much?"

That warning itch returned tenfold, and Ty took his time answering her.

"I'm sure I don't know what you're implying, and talk like that will not be good for your health. I'd have thought you'd learnt this by now." He took his hand off her and picked up her bag off the floor.

"Why the interest in Myrtle, girl? And don't even think about lying to me. I can spot a lie a mile off."

She flicked him a glance and instead of answering him, fiddled with her car keys. The resulting jangle ground on his last nerve, and she jumped when he put his hands over her fingers to stop that frantic, nervous movement.

"I'm replacing her as far as I can tell. Surely, it's reasonable of me to want to find out what happened to her. After all, I don't want to end up like her … Sir."

She yanked her hand out of his grasp, and Ty frowned.

"That's simple enough. Don't lie, cheat, or steal, and you'll find Huntly to be a very accommodating employer."

Another one of those silent tears rolled down Jeanette's cheek, and she swiped it away with a rather angry hand move.

"Are you saying that's what she did?" she asked.

Ty shook his head.

"I'm saying this subject is closed, until you're ready to tell me the truth." Ty grasped her elbow and started walking, giving her no choice but to follow him. Ace smirked at them when they walked past him, and the way he ran his gaze all over Jeanette made Ty want to swipe that grin off the other man's face with his fists.

"Ah, fresh cunt for us all. How utterly delightful," Ace said.

"Find your own whore, man. This one is mine." Ty's reply meant the woman at his side tensed.

"I'm no one's whore," she said, and Ace laughed.

"Not yet, sweet thing, but you soon will be, and then, my dear, you and I will have some fun."

"Fuck off, Ace. She might decide she wants out

before that." Ty's reply just seemed to make Ace laugh more. He did step out of the way, however, and Ty breathed a silent sigh of relief when they left the club behind. A quick scan of his surrounding showed there to be nothing suspect, and Ty nodded at Jeanette.

"Which one, left or right?" he asked.

"Left."

Ty flashed her a quick smile and resumed walking, and in no time at all, they were standing next to her little car. The ancient mini had seen better days, and Ty grimaced to himself as he folded himself into a pretzel trying to get into the passenger seat, and that was with the seat sat as far back as it was.

Jeanette smiled at him, when he hit his head on the roof for the third time.

"Sorry, I know it's not very big, but I love it. Mustang was my first car, and I'm loath to let him go."

"Mustang?" Ty shook his head when Jeanette grinned at him. The first genuine smile he'd seen from her today, and one that made his insides itch with foreboding. Because that smile, fuck, yeah, he wanted to see more of that, and that should probably worry him a great deal.

"Yeah, as in my trusty steed. I know he doesn't look like much anymore, but he hasn't let me down yet." Sure enough, the rust bucket started on the first turn, and the engine positively purred along.

Ty whistled through his teeth.

"Someone's looked after the engine, all right," he said, and, again Jeanette shot him one of those open smiles. She really did look beautiful when she did that, and Ty found himself hard pushed not to grin back at her. "You'll have to give me his number. We're always on the look-out for a good mechanic."

Jeanette's smile slipped to be replaced by a

frown, and she hit the steering wheel, while muttering something under her breath.

"Don't mumble, girl. If you have something to say, then say it to my face, at least."

When she shook her head, seemingly intent on ignoring her, he swatted her thigh hard. The action made her jump, and the car jerked to a stop at the red traffic light they were approaching.

"Damn it, what was that for?" She glared at him while she turned the key to restart the engine. "Look what you made me do. Sorry, Mustang." Ty's amusement increased when she stroked the dashboard.

"A man could get jealous at the attention you bestow on this rust heap."

Her head swung round, and he was at the receiving end of another one of those cock hardening glares. Ty's hand itched to put her over his knee, and to teach her some respect. To have this woman freely submitting to his will would be a heady aphrodisiac, and he realized with sudden clarity, that that was exactly what he wanted.

It was a sobering thought indeed. Ty would never take a woman against her will, not that there had been ever a need to even chase one. Most women in his acquaintance were only too eager to spread their legs— for anyone. Maybe that's what was niggling at him.

He wanted something more, had done for a while, but finding anyone untouched by the darkness the Cleaners surrounded themselves with on a daily basis, proved nigh on impossible.

Ty shook his head to clear it of his maudlin thoughts. He was thirty-eight next week, for fuck's sake, not fifty-eight, and there was plenty of time to settle down, as he'd told his dear mama only the other week. A smile played on his lips as he thought of her.

His earnings kept her well looked after in a top notch nursing home, and she had no idea what he really did for a living. The worry would kill her faster than her failing heart.

"For the last time, Mustang is not a rust heap." Jeanette's answer made him look at her, and he was surprised to see her studying him. As was typical for this time of day, traffic was diabolical, and they were in a long slow moving queue of cars. "I would have thought you'd never be short of female attention," she said.

At his laugh, her flawless mocha skin darkened in a blush, and his gut churned at the ugliness she was signing up for.

It really shouldn't bother him, and besides, he got to taste the goods first. All in a day's job and move on, that was the Cleaners' motto after all, but the mere thought of using this young woman like that left a sour taste in Ty's mouth.

Subsequently his reply came out much harsher than he intended it to be.

"No, usually your sort fall at my feet."

The instant hurt that flashed up in her expressive eyes made him want to take the words back. The fact that it did, made him angrier, and he swore softly under his breath.

"Anyway, like I said, I want your mechanic's number. Huntly will be able to use him."

"Huntly will do no such thing. Besides, I'm employed for servicing other parts, I believe."

Jeanette pulled her shoulders back and stuck her chin out in a defiant gesture, while they crawled forward a few more car lengths.

"Jeez, this traffic is doing my head in. I should have taken the tube, and walked the rest."

Ty conceded that she had a point there. It was one

of the reasons why he liked to jog, and the Cleaners' house was in the opposite direction, and the route less prone to congestion than the one Jeanette was taking.

"You're the mechanic?" he asked, and she shrugged and threw him a coy glance.

"Yes, so? Just because I'm a woman and a dancer I can't get my hands dirty?"

Ty looked toward said body parts, and clearly following his thought processes, she held her left hand up. The long, ruby red, perfectly manicured nails made him doubt that statement, and when he made a point in looking from them to her, she smiled.

"They're fake. A friend did them for me, yesterday. I wanted to make a good impression for the audition, and broken, greasy fingernails don't exactly scream seductive." She bit her lip as though she was worried she'd said too much, and Ty laughed.

"Maybe not. So, tell me, which is the real you? The one with the wig and the fake nails, or the one with your hands covered in mechanic's grease?"

A gap appeared in the traffic, and Jeanette put her foot down, to cut across oncoming cars and into a side road.

Ty braced himself against the dashboard and swore as his head hit the damn roof again.

"Fucking hell, woman, you *do* have a death wish, don't you? What the hell was that for?" he asked.

"Shortcut, and stop moaning. We'll be there soon."

Ty checked his surroundings and frowned as she sped through a myriad of side streets, taking them closer and closer to...

"Where exactly is there?" he asked. "You best not taking me on a wild goose chase, girl." That itch was back, making him feel like an army of ants was crawling underneath his skin.

Grasping the opportunity when she had to slow down to take a bend, he grabbed hold of the steering wheel, and yanked the hand brake up. The car slid to a screeching stop, narrowly missing a row of parked cars. Jeanette cried out in surprise, and Ty pulled her head round by her hair.

"Who the fuck are you, Jeanette?"

****

Her scalp stung, and her heart was all but ready to beat itself out of her chest with the fright she'd just had, not to mention her poor little car. Mustang's tires must be smoking after that abrupt and painful stop. Her seat belt dug into her body where it had locked on her, and it made breathing difficult, if not nigh on impossible. She was well and truly trapped.

Someone drove past honking their horn at them, not that the angry man who held her hair in a death grip took any notice of them. No, it might have been just the two of them on their own, because the rest of the world faded into insignificance under his intense regard. What on earth had happened to cause that change in him? One minute she was happily driving along, having a somewhat reasonable conversation with him, the next he almost killed them with this crazy ass stunt.

She knew better than to give voice to those thoughts, however, because right now, in this moment, this Ty Mason scared the crap out of her. He looked ready to tear her apart with his bare hands, and sure enough, when she didn't answer his question, he brought the hand not painfully buried in her hair, 'round to her throat. Panic seized her anew as he cut off her air supply for a few precious seconds, before the pressure loosened and he smiled at her.

A far from reassuring smile, because it didn't

reach his eyes, and his voice held a dangerous edge when he addressed her again.

"I asked you a question, girl. Answer me."

Lord help her, that deep menacing growl made every nerve ending in her body tingle. This shouldn't be a turn-on. He frightened her stiff right now, and yet, her pussy was soaked with a fresh wave of her completely inappropriate response to this man's brooding dominance. It made no sense at all whatsoever. She was losing her fucking mind here, clearly.

"Jeanette MacArthur, Sir. I told you that at the audition. I ... ow ... please."

The plea came out on a sob, because Ty pulled her hair so hard she had to be missing a clump of it. As abruptly as he'd done that, he let her go, and punched the roof of her poor little car instead. The force behind that move rocked the suspension, and she wouldn't be surprised if she didn't have to beat out a fist shaped dent out of the roof, if she lived long enough to do so, that was.

"Stop fucking lying to me. Who the hell are you?"

"I'm not lying, Sir, truly I'm not."

Her voice rang with sincerity, because she wasn't, not about this bit anyway.

"I don't believe you."

For some reason that reply stung, and ignoring the ache in her scalp, Jeanette leaned back to loosen the seat belt. Once it unlocked and she could breathe easier, she swiveled round to glare at him.

"Why not? What could I possibly gain from lying? I am Jeanette MacArthur, dance teacher, sometime mechanic, and down on my luck, which is why I sought employment with Huntly. I need the money, all right? I wasn't lying. I live in a fucking tower block, okay, and

I'll never get out of that area unless I make some more money, so—"

"Which tower block on which estate?"

Jeanette blinked at the curt question with which he'd interrupted her.

"Priory Court on the Densen Estate. What does it matter? I…" She jumped when Ty punched the headrest right next to her head, and leaned in until his nose almost touched hers.

"What does it matter? Jesus, girl, I can't make up my mind if you're really this stupid, or a conniving bitch with her own agenda."

The words stung. Not as much as they should have done, because she *did* have her own agenda, just not whatever one Ty suspected her of.

His black eyes searched hers, the amber swirls of fire around his irises utterly mesmerizing. Their breaths mingled, and she didn't dare move, too caught up in this strange spell surrounding them.

"I don't understand," she finally whispered, and Ty's sigh of frustration blew his hot minty breath across her face.

"The Densen Estate is right in the Priestly gang's territory, girl."

Jeanette blinked again and frowned.

"So?"

Ty reared back as though she had physically struck him.

"So?" He stared at her as though she'd grown another head, but before he could say anything, blue lights filled the interior of the car, and a police siren blipped once.

"Shit." Ty's attention shifted to the police car which had pulled up behind them, and he fixed a somewhat forced smile on his face, when the uniformed traffic cop tapped on the window on Jeanette's side.

"Open up, Miss, and let me see your papers."

Jeanette hastily wound down her window, and reaching across a silent Ty fumbled in the glove box for her driver's license and insurance papers.

"Here, Officer, is there a problem?"

The grey haired traffic cop scanned her papers, and said something into his radio that she couldn't quite catch over the roaring in her ears. Ty must have done, however, because his thigh muscles tensed in her peripheral vision, and he made an effort to uncurl his hands.

"I should ask you that question. Any particular reason why your vehicle is causing an obstruction?" He flicked a glance at a stoic looking Ty, and lowered his voice.

"Anything I can help you with, Miss…" He glanced at her license again, before he handed it back to her with a smile. "MacArthur?"

Ty bristled next to her, and the cop stepped back slightly.

"Do I know you from somewhere, son?" he asked, addressing Ty.

"I have no idea, Officer, do you?" Ty replied. "I apologize if my girlfriend's actions caused any upset. She was avoiding a cat, and the car stalled. We'll be on our way."

The cop studied Ty for what seemed like ages, but could only have been minutes before he addressed Jeannette.

"That what happened, Miss MacArthur?"

Not trusting her voice to not give away her agitation, Jeanette simply nodded.

"You have your answer. Like I said we'll be on our way now. Thank you for your concern, Officer."

Ty's tone of voice sounded anything but grateful, and sure enough, the traffic cop frowned.

"Got any papers on you, son?" he asked and Ty spread his legs and arms wide and gave a humorless laugh.

"Does it look as though as I do? I was jogging, and Jeanette is giving me a lift home. Tore something, see." He screwed his face up as though he was in pain, and massaged his calf.

"Is that so?" the cop asked, and once again Jeanette was under his close scrutiny.

Forcing a smile on her lips, she nodded.

"I keep telling him he's overdoing it, but will you men ever listen?"

"Watch it, titch, I heard that. Tell her not to fuss, Officer. I'm fine, just need to rest it."

Ty's grumbling answer brought a genuine smile on the copper's face, and he nodded.

"Very well, make sure you do. And Miss MacArthur, try not to cause an accident in future. Avoiding cats is all well and good, but not at the expense of human life."

The irony in those words forced a laugh from her, and she hastily restarted the engine, and drove off. It was only when they turned the corner, and she couldn't see the police car in her rear view mirror anymore that she dared to breathe again.

Ty's warm hand cupped her nape, and she heard the smile in his voice.

"Good girl, you did very well back there. Just keep on breathing now, nice and steady and concentrate on the traffic. Let's get you to that godforsaken place you call home in one piece, shall we?"

Jeanette gave a tight nod and slowly unfurled the white knuckled grip she had on the steering wheel.

The closer they came to the estate and home, the more she relaxed, and Ty tensed. His mood swings were enough to give a woman whiplash, and she daren't question him about his off behavior. His jaw was clenched so tight, she could almost hear his teeth grind together. The furtive glances he swung around as they entered the estate made her nervous. Ty slid down into his seat as far as he was able to.

When he pulled his phone out and fired off a series of text messages, while muttering to himself, she had to ask.

"You never explained why living where I do is such an issue." Her tower block loomed large in front of her, and she sighed when she spotted the gaggle of hooded youths by the bin area.

"Damn it, they're out early."

"Of course they fucking are. Park as close to the entrance as you can, will you, and when I say get out, make a run for it Whatever happens don't stop until you're in your flat, got that?"

"Yes, but why?"

"Don't argue with me, which number are you?"

"75, but—"

"Hush, woman, do as you're told."

The clipped command did little to soothe the army of butterflies which seemed to have taken residence in her belly. Usually the youths didn't pay her comings and goings too much attention, bar the usual wolf whistles and crude suggestions, but this time, they jumped to attention as soon they spotted her little car. She put her foot down and swerving around them went 'round to the back entrance.

Screeching to a halt outside, she grabbed her bag and ran as instructed, with Ty hot on her heels.

"Oi, fucker, we'll have ya."

The shout from her back made her screech in fright, because two youths came through the door she needed to use to get in the building. One pulled a knife, and Ty swore and promptly shoved her out of the way. He disarmed the knife-wielding thug with a quick flick of his wrist and a knee shattering kick to the guy's kneecap, which made bile rise in Jeanette's throat. The youngster went down screaming in pain, and the other guy got a knuckleduster punch right into Ty's kidney.

Ty went down to his knees briefly with a grunt of pain, before he swung his fist into the youth's groin, and hollered at Jeanette to *fucking move.*

As the other gang members approached, Jeanette flew through the door, and took the back stairs at a run. She didn't stop running until she was safely in her flat. Never had she been so grateful for the solid fire door than when someone pounded against it.

"Open up, bitch. You can't hide in there forever. The boss wants to see you. You wanna spread your legs, you're fucking well gonna do it for us, cunt."

Chapter Four

Ty was outnumbered seven to one, which would normally not have been the greatest problem, but he didn't even have a knife on him, and that punch he took to the kidney still hurt like a fucking bitch. No doubt he'd be peeing blood for a few days. He'd broken that asshole's neck, once he'd doubled over in front of him, and now stood with his back against the wall, trying his best to fend off the fuckers.

He deflected one knife aimed at his throat, but the slicing pain in his side told him he took one anyway. A hot sticky mess trickled down his hip. Ty swore and head butted one guy, while he kicked the other away. A punch to the side of his head he hadn't seen coming made his ears ring, and he shook his head to clear his fuzzy vision, while automatically blocking a few more punches.

A kick to the back of his legs brought him down, and an uppercut to his chin threw his head back to connect painfully with the wall. Blood filled his mouth, and he caught the glint of a red stained knife. He put his hand up to stop that weapon from slicing his throat, and pain cut through his palm instead.

Fuck it. He needed to get up. He was a sitting duck down here, staring at dusty boots, and he wasn't going to fucking snuff it now. There was Jeanette for starters. No way would he let these fuckers get their filthy hands on her. Ignoring the kicks and punches aimed at him, he lunged in the air with an ear splitting roar, which earned him a second's respite.

The seeming leader of the gang laughed and drew his gun. The shot missed Ty's head only because he'd ducked out of the way of another fist aimed at his chin. Even so, the heat of the bullet singed his cheekbone. Ty ducked his head and shoulder charged through the fuckers in front of him to get to the asshole with the gun. The momentum gave him the upper hand and he managed to tackle that piece of scum to the floor, while scrabbling for the gun. This guy's goons tried to pull him off their leader, but Ty wasn't letting go of the fucker. Throwing his head back he heard the satisfying crunch of a nose breaking, and then the gun went off. Heat shot through his belly and through the roaring in his ears, he could hear Ren holler.

"Let's clean this mess up, boys."

Ace's trainers appeared in his vision, as around them bodies started to fly through the air, and the concrete turned crimson. It gave him a certain amount of grim satisfaction to hear the blood filled gurgles of the men who attacked him. No doubt, their cohorts were banging Jeanette's door down even now. He hoped she had the sense to lock herself away, and the boys could get her out before the Priestly scum could get to her.

Ace pulled him to his feet by the scruff of his neck ,and Ty swallowed a painful groan, when their resident medic clamped his large hand over Ty's hurting side.

"Fuck, you took a knife. Hope that bitch is worth it, man. Should have bailed the minute you knew she was a Priestly cunt."

Ty glared at the slightly smaller guy, and Ace flashed him a grin.

"Watch your fucking mouth about her. Besides, we don't leave girls at those fuckers' mercy, you know that."

Ace shrugged and shoved his shoulder under Ty's armpit when his knees buckled, and Josh grabbed his other side.

"We need to get him to the van, man. He's gonna pass out," Josh grumbled.

Ty shook his head and tried to dig his feet in, to stop his friends from pulling him away from the scene. Sirens could be heard in the distance, and he knew they had to get away, but not without his *titch*. He didn't even question the possessive nature of his thought.

"No, fuck you. Ren, flat 75, go get her for me."

Josh swore, while Ren kicked the lifeless form of the guy he's just beaten into a pulp, and wiped his bloody hands down the side of his jeans.

"There isn't time, Ty. She's not worth it."

With superhuman effort Ty shook off the arms holding him up, and somehow limped over to his longtime friend. He tripped over one of the bodies, and Ren caught him before he face-planted at the man's boots.

"What if it was Susie?"

Ren swore and growled low in his throat while nodding to Alex and James.

"Fuck, you heard him. Let's get the girl. You, Ty, let Ace take care of you, 'cause I swear, if you snuff it because of that piece of pussy, I'll kill her myself."

Ace clamped his hand over Ty's side again, and the intense pain meant he finally blacked out.

****

Her longest kitchen knife held in front of her, Jeanette stood at the end of her tiny hallway, ready to gut anyone who stepped through her front door. At least that's what she told herself, as she swallowed down bile and clamped a hand over her wrist to stop the knife from shaking so much it was a mere blur in her vision.

How on earth had she ended up in the middle of a gang war? They always left her alone, so why were they banging on her door saying those vile things? It made no sense, and frightened out of her wits as she was, she couldn't get her befuddled brain to grasp the obvious. An almighty bang shook her front door, and she screeched at the pool of dark blood that seeped through under the bottom and onto her cream carpet. When the handle turned she did scream, because that shouldn't be possible. As though in slow motion the door opened, and Ren stepped through. His eyes widened when he saw her, and throwing all caution to the wind, Jeanette made a run toward him, knife held up high, determined to do him some harm. This was all his fault, after all.

He'd killed her sister and now he was here to finish her off.

Instead of shoving the knife into his gut, however, as had been her intention, Jeanette cried out in pain, as her wrist was caught in a crushing grip, and she was spun into a wall. No, hang on, not a wall, but a laughing wall of male muscle.

Amber eyes crinkled up at the corners, as this guy cupped her chin to study her, while someone else twisted her arms back up high against her back, until she couldn't move.

"Feisty little thing, isn't she, bro?" The amused baritone at her back made her turn her head, to see who got hold of her. Slightly taller and bulkier than the guy in front of her, there was no mistaking the family resemblance. These two had to be brothers.

The guy at her back winked at her, and despite the situation, or maybe because of it, her stomach flipped over. Jeez, was there a law that stated every Cleaner employed by Huntly had to be any woman's wet dream?

"She sure is. I can see why Ty wants her."

The mention of Ty made her struggle against them.

"Ty, how is he?"

"What do you care, girl?" Ren's dark voice sent shivers of dread down her spine, especially when he took the picture of her and Myrtle off the wall and studied it with a frown. It had been taken years ago, when they were teenagers, but Ren wasn't stupid. He would figure this out, and she was *so* dead.

Sure enough, he stepped closer and holding the frame next to her head, studied her. If that was possible, his expression grew even more forbidding, and she flinched when he murmured to himself.

"Well, I'll be damned."

The approaching sirens got louder, and Ren shook his head.

"Take her down, boys. I'll be there in a minute. Just gonna find out who this bitch really is."

He turned on his heel and disappeared into her bedroom.

"No, you have no right, you ... umph." Her protest was cut off by the guy at her back clamping his large hand over her mouth. She bit down on the thick digits, and he swore softly, before the world tilted and she found herself flung over his brother's shoulder.

"No, dammit, put me down. You can't do that. You have no right."

A stinging swat to her ass was her reward, and she narrowly missed banging her head against the doorframe when the man-made mountain turned abruptly. He stepped over the prone bodies of what had been two hooded youths, and Jeanette's protest died in her throat, when she looked straight into the glassy eyes of one of her neighbors.

Good lord, she knew his mother, and now he was dead, because of her. She blinked back tears and tried her best to carry on breathing, as the guy whose shoulder she was slung over like a sack of potatoes jogged down the stairs.

They narrowly avoided the uniformed police

officers coming up the stairs, and slipped out of the building via a side entrance in the laundry room. She hadn't even known there was an exit there, but a quick fumble of the lock later by man-mountain's brother—which sure explained how they got past the locks to her front door so easily—and she was glinting in the bright sun, reflected off the police cars parked at all angles.

She ought to scream, do something to alert the two officers, who had their backs turned to them, she knew that, but the soulless eyes of her neighbor's son haunted her. She had no doubt that these guys would kill the cops as easily as they had killed everyone else so far, and she really didn't want that on her conscience.

Besides, even if, by some miracle, she managed to get away from them, where would she go? She would never be able to go back to her flat, because she was as good as dead now. Jeanette might not be all up to date on the latest crime gang etiquette, but it didn't take Einstein to figure out that they would be looking for revenge. And that revenge would be aimed at her for bringing the Cleaners to their estate and causing all those deaths.

So, instead of screaming her head off, Jeanette bunched her hands into the shirt of the man carrying her to steady herself, and bit her lip so hard she tasted her own blood. The guy holding her turned and twisted in so many different reactions she started to feel dizzy and lost all sense of direction as they ran down the alleyways that made up the estate.

They encountered no one else, and for that she was grateful, at least, while fervently wishing she was the sort of woman who could faint. It sure would make things easier, especially when Ren joined them, one of her hold-alls flung over his shoulder.

She swallowed hard at the thought of this killer rummaging through her things.

"This way, boys. They're waiting round the corner for us. The place is swarming with fucking coppers, and I sure as fuck hope those cameras aren't working."

"Doubt they will be, boss. That scum wouldn't wanna be caught on them any more than we would," the guy carrying her said.

"Let's hope you're right, James. I don't wanna go down for this bird."

James gave a dry laugh and shifted her to her feet. Before her head had even stopped spinning at the sudden move, his brother grabbed her wrists in crushing grip again, while Ren regarded her through hooded lids.

"Ty's girl or not, you'll be spending some time in the cellar, girl, and we'll talk."

The ice cold hand of fear squeezed the air out of her lungs, making it impossible to talk. Not that the arrogant asshole expected an answer out of her right now, and Jeanette tried her best to glare at him.

"Go easy on her, boss. Ty must like this one to put himself out there like that."

Ren's attention shifted to the man behind her, and Jeanette pulled a much needed breath into her lungs.

"So it would seem, Alex, but we'll see how much he likes her when he finds out she's Myrtle's sister."

Ren smirked at her involuntary gasp, and his two compatriots both swore.

"Ain't that a fucking turn up for the books," Alex said, and tightened his hold on her. His brother swung round and glared at her. He brought up his fist, and for one awful second she thought he was going to hit her. Instead he punched the nearby tree instead, flexed his fingers with an ugly grimace and reaching in the back pocket of his black jeans pulled out a couple of cable ties.

"Best put those on her, bro. Can't trust the bitch in that case."

Jeanette opened her mouth to protest, but all she achieved was to have a foul smelling gag shoved into her mouth. A hood of some sort followed and her world went black, as the cable ties drug cruelly into her wrists and ankles. For the second time that day, the ground lifted away, and through the misery and sheer terror filling her lungs, she heard the screech of brakes, the metallic crunch of a sliding door. When she hit something hard, it knocked the wind out of her. Cruel male laughter reached her ears, even as rough hands pulled her into an upright position until she leaned against what she assumed must be the wall of the van.

Sure enough the vehicle started to move, and something warm collided with her foot. A pain filled grunt reached her through the hood, and then a voice she recognized as Ace, the guy who had been at door duty at the club earlier.

"Take it easy, up front, Josh. I don't want him to bleed out, and with your crazy ass driving, he'll do that before I get him to the house to stitch him up."

He had to be talking about Ty, and shifting sideways, she blindly groped until she encountered a naked male chest, sprinkled with hair. She swallowed hard at the sticky mess she found, and unseen fingers yanked her bound wrists away and up. The sudden move hurt her shoulders, and she whimpered around the gag in her mouth.

"Move her away from him. She's done enough damage for one day." Ace's voice didn't hold an ounce of compassion, and the world shifted again until she, presumably was on the other side of the van. A heavy hand clamped around her thigh, holding her in place, and this time Jeanette didn't even try to hold in her tears.

They wouldn't be able to see them, hidden as she was under this godawful sack they'd put over her head, and it was that or scream. As she couldn't do that crying as silently as she could would have to do.

"You can fix him though, right?" Ren asked, and Jeanette flinched when she realized it must be his hand on her thigh. He didn't try anything remotely sexual, and for that, she was grateful. From what she'd seen of him and his woman in the club, she knew she was at least safe in that regard. He seemed smitten with the redhead, the tenderness she'd witnessed him exhibit toward her a direct contrast to the way he was treating Jeanette now. To what he'd done to Myrtle.

The horrific images that police detective had shoved under her nose would forever haunt her. She had sworn there and then, that she would get revenge for her little sister somehow, but, instead she had become another victim and had caused God only knew how many deaths today.

It was too much to wrap her head around, and she shrank in on herself as much she could. The hand on her thigh lifted when she pulled her knees up to her chest, no doubt giving the men in the back of the van the perfect view up her skirt, but she couldn't bring herself to care about that now.

"I'll do my best, boss." Ace's curt reply shook her out of her morose thoughts, and she held her breath. Why was she this worried about Ty anyway? He was one of *them*. So what if he'd fought those guys for her? Didn't mean a thing. No doubt he had his own agenda, and besides, they would kill her now anyway.

"Why's she trussed up like that, anyway?" Ace asked. "Ty won't be happy when he comes 'round. He went through a lot of trouble for that bird."

"She's Myrtle's sister," Ren said.

A collective chorus of male swearing rang in her ears, and Jeanette stopped breathing, when Josh, at least it sounded like him, seemed to speak from somewhere right behind her. She must be sitting against the partition to the driver's cab.

"If that's the case why is she still alive?"

"Reckon Huntly will want some answers from her," Ren said to the other side of her, and Jeanette frantically shook her head. She couldn't breathe, dammit. That blasted gag seemed lodged in her throat. Spots danced in front of her eyes, and her heart beat far too fast making her feel faint. She didn't want to hear any of that, and besides she didn't know anything, other than what Detective Wonsan had told her, *off the record*.

She could still see his face, the smile that was supposed to be sympathetic, yet seemed to be anything but, and the frown on his partner's face as he told her Reynold Ellis was to blame for the death of her sister.

"But don't you worry. We'll bring those bastards in sooner or later. He got off on a technicality. Eventually he'll slip up. Now, if we had a person on the inside, an informant, if you will, that would bring justice for your sister so much sooner." He'd glanced at her certificates on the wall and smiled. "Huntly will be looking for a new star dancer…"

His partner had rallied at him, and Wonsan had thrown his hands up in a conciliatory gesture.

"Just saying. That would help the case immensely."

With sudden clarity of insight, Jeanette realized one thing, before the stress of the day got on top of her and she slipped into the blissful oblivion of unconsciousness.

She had been played.

Chapter Five

Ty willed his way out of the heavy quagmire his mind and body seemed to be caught up in and groaned. Ace must have pumped him full of drugs to help him stave off infection from the myriad of injuries he'd sustained. His left hand and especially his side hurt like a fucking bitch, and there was a dull ache in his lower back. All things considered, however, he didn't seem to be in too bad shape. He was alive for starters, which was something of a miracle, considering the shit that had gone down. *Fucking Priestlys.*

Swallowing a groan, he forced his heavy eyes open, and Susie jumped to attention. He forced a smile on his cracked lips for her benefit, because the curvy redhead looked worried sick.

"Hey, sweet thing, smile. I'm all right. Takes a lot more than that kerfuffle to knock me out, you know."

"I know, but, here … goodness, take it easy." Her sweet flowery scent teased his nostrils as Ren's girl leaned in and helped him to sit up more. Ordinarily, he would have protested that he didn't need any help, but Susie, here, would see right through any bullshit. Besides, all the Cleaners had a huge soft spot for her, and if she was here it would be at Ren's orders, and Ty had no wish to get the lovely woman into trouble. Ren was volatile at the best of times, and his friend and boss would be pissed as fuck at the latest developments. Susie handed him a glass with a straw, and he gratefully accepted the proffered drink. The cool liquid got rid of the god-awful taste in his mouth, and he took several sips. With a smile he handed it back to her.

"Thanks, I needed that. I also need a shower, I must stink."

Susie's frown changed into a giggle, and she

wrinkled her nose.

"Well, I've smelled worse…" She winked and continued. "In a pigsty anyway."

Ty shook his head at her.

"I take it Ren isn't around, or you wouldn't be that sassy, girl."

Ty regretted those words almost immediately, as Susie's amusement dissipated instantly.

"He's had his hands full. What were you thinking, going into that estate by yourself, Ty? You almost got yourself killed, and from what I can gather, she's Myrtle's sister. That can't be good."

This news made him sit up straighter, and his various injuries protested loudly. Ty glared at the bandage on his hand and the one covering his side.

"She's what?" he asked, and Susie blinked.

"You didn't know then. I reckoned you couldn't or you would have left her to it…" She bit her lip and didn't quite look at him. Ty cupped her chin with his uninjured hand to make her look at him.

Her blue eyes swam with unshed tears, and Ty frowned.

"You're worried about Ren?" It was a statement more than a question and Susie sighed.

"Well, yes. She's her sister, and she lives on Priestly territory and she tried to get a job at the club. Why would she do that, if not to cause trouble? I saw the way she looked at Sir at the audition, and I know Huntly gave her to you to check her out, but I don't like it." Susie crossed her arms under her impressive chest, and Ty's gaze wandered to her rack. He couldn't help it. She might be Ren's and thus completely off limits, but he could still look.

A slight blush stained her cheekbones when she noticed, and she hastily uncrossed her arms, and stuck her hands on her hips instead. Everyone in the Cleaner house knew that gesture. Little Susie meant business, and Ty forced his gaze back to her face.

"I swear, if she causes any more trouble, then I'll … well, I'll think of something. It grates enough that she's here, and I have to cook for her. And then she doesn't eat it. What the hell is that about? I tried talking to her, too, but she completely blanks me. I'd say she's scared. God knows I was when Sir brought me here, but no one has freaking touched her. Jesus. Ignore me, it's just … why is she here?"

Ty smiled at Susie in an effort to reassure her, while inwardly breathing a sigh of relief that Jeanette was not only alive, but safe here at the house. He would wonder about why this was so important to him later.

"Where is she?" he asked.

"In the cellar, of course. Hardly punishment. That place is better equipped than a hotel, and while she's down there, none of us can use the equipment." Susie stuck her bottom lip out, and Ty laughed. The action hurt his ribs and jarred his side, and Susie glared at him.

"This isn't funny, Ty. Sir says she's yours to punish, and I know she's chained, but she can still move around, and … oh just ignore me. I'm worried, that's all. What if the police come looking for her here? You've been out two days as it is, and to all intents and purposes she has just disappeared. That blasted police officer was at the club again last night. That man gives me the creeps. I don't like it, and if she's a threat to what we have here, then, well I'm gonna kill her myself."

Ty's eyebrows rose at that vehement statement, and Susie stared him down, as though daring him to disagree with him.

"Sweet thing, you couldn't kill a fly, and besides," he put his hand up to stop her from talking, when she looked all set to interrupt him. "Ren would never let you do such a thing. You don't need blood on your hands, Susie. Jeanette is my problem, and I'll deal with her."

"Will you though?" Susie asked. "I mean, you've risked so much already and for what? For all we know she's a spy sent to infiltrate us and ... what?" She glared some more. "I have ears, and the men talk. Having her in this house is making everyone uneasy, so I wish you would deal with her one way or the other."

Ty smiled.

"I will, but for that I need to get out of bed, and as I'm naked under here, perhaps you'd like to leave? No skin off my nose, if you stay, but Ren might have a thing to say about that." He swung his legs off the side of the bed, and despite the resulting ache in his back, he laughed when Susie blanched and backed away.

"I'm gone. Come and find me in the kitchen when you're decent. I've made some of that chicken soup you like, and I'll heat it up for you. You must be starving, and best to deal with contrary females on a full stomach, right?"

Ty nodded his approval, and Susie scarpered from his room. In truth he was glad she wasn't here to witness his shit ass struggles to simply get to his damn feet. He was as weak as a fucking kitten, and utterly confused.

What Susie had imparted about Jeanette did not come as a complete shock to him. He'd known there was something she was hiding, and at least that explained why she'd seemed so familiar to him. She looked very different from Myrtle. She was a whole skin tone lighter, for starters, but certain mannerisms were the same, and Jeanette exhibited the same fluidity and inherent sensuality that had made Myrtle's dancing such a success.

As he hobbled to the adjacent bathroom to relieve himself, he could only hope that's where the similarities ended. If she turned out to be conniving bitch liked her sister had been, it would fall to Ty to end her, and for some reason that made his gut twist.

Like it or not, his *titch* had gotten under his skin. Time would tell what that meant in the long run, and no doubt, once he had actually fucked her, those conflicting emotions would crystallize for him.

They had better, one way or the other.

The hot spray of the power shower did a lot to revive him, even if the water stung like crazy on his various abrasions. Staring at the bruising on his face in the mirror, Ty sighed. He would have to postpone his visit to the nursing home. There was nothing at all wrong with his mother's eyesight, despite her advanced age and fragile overall health, and she'd read him the riot act for sure, if she saw he'd been hurt.

Thought of his mum made him smile. She was an excellent judge of character, and once he didn't look as though he'd had been involved in a boxing match and lost, her reaction to Jeanette would tell him a lot.

Was he actually considering bringing a girl to see his mother? Ty shook his head and grimaced anew at his reflection. The drugs must have addled his brain. Mum would jump to the obvious conclusion that he was serious about this girl. Then again, would it hurt to let her think so? His mother did not have long, and if she thought he'd found someone to settle down with, it would be a lot off her mind.

Ty had planned to borrow Susie for the task, when the time came, something Ren had reluctantly agreed to, if need be. After all, he'd spent many happy days at Ty's parents' place when they'd both been on leave from the Army, and Dad had still been alive.

Running a hand through his still damp hair, Ty forced his thoughts to the here and now. It did no good to dwell on the past. Ren and he had both chosen this path, after all. Ty, being younger than Ren, had stayed in longer, but once he'd left civilian life had held no appeal. He'd seen too much shit to ever just be able to slide into civvie street, so when Ren offered him the job as second in command to the Cleaners, he'd jumped at the chance. It kept the demons at bay and meant he could make a difference. Cleaning the world of scum like the Priestly brothers and the misery they inflicted on those in their territories made him feel good—most days.

It certainly brought him considerable satisfaction when they rescued some hapless girls who'd been caught in their human trafficking scheme.

Spreading your legs for money was a valid career choice, if the girls did so of their own free will, and were protected from the scum that preyed on working girls. It was an entirely different matter when that choice was taken away from them.

The Priestly gang excelled at grooming young impressionable women—women like Ren's Susie—who'd barely escaped from their snare, and that was far from all right in Ty's eyes, which brought him neatly back to the woman currently chained up in their cellar. He hovered outside the locked door, on his slow painful progress toward the kitchen

Which camp did Jeanette fall into? She'd seemed genuinely puzzled at his reaction to her living in Priestly territory, and why that should be a problem. No one was that naïve, surely, not with Myrtle as her sister, and living where she did. Ren's deep rumble galvanized him into action. The boss was back then and would no doubt be able to answer some questions for him. The kitchen door opened, bringing with it the most enticing smell of chicken, and Ty's stomach made its presence known.

Ace smirked as he held the door open for Ty.

"Good to see you up at last, man, and hungry, too, from the looks of it. I was coming to check on your wounds. How you holding up there?"

"I'm fine, all present and correct. That's some neat stitching."

Ace shrugged and gestured to the chair he must have just vacated, and Ty gratefully slumped down.

"Ty."

Ren's concerned gaze ran over him, and Ty mustered a grim smile for his oldest friend.

"I'm good. Like I said to Ace, no need to fuss. Ouch, that hurt." He swung round to glare at the medic, who'd pulled up his shirt, and was probing the wound in his side.

"Stop being a pussy. Just making sure this holds. You ought to be all right to keep the bandage off it, now, but I'm gonna redo your hand."

Ty frowned at the zigzag wound winding across the fleshy part of his palm. That, too, had needed stitches.

"Flex your fingers for me," Ace said.

Ty flipped him the finger instead, and everyone in the room laughed.

"Smart fucking ass. You're lucky it didn't cut the tendons." Ace stepped away to grab the first aid kit they kept in the kitchen, and with sure, deft movements proceeded to bandage his hand up again.

"There, only a light dressing, to protect it, and come to think of it. Let me do that to your side, too. Lord knows what you'll get up to when you actually get to see the cunt in the cellar, so…"

Ty glared at him, but, before he could say anything, Susie plonked a steaming bowl of soup in front of Ty with so much force the contents slopped over the side.

"Pumpkin." Ren's voice held a note of censure, and, sure enough, Susie blanched, dipped her head, and grabbed a cloth to mop up the spill.

"Sorry." Ty almost didn't catch that murmured apology, and Susie froze when he grasped her wrist with his uninjured hand.

"Let it go, sweet thing. I said I'd sort it."

"If you can't be civil about this, I suggest you leave, pumpkin."

Susie bit her lip and shook her head, and sighing, Ren held out his arms and Susie rushed into his embrace.

Ace rolled his eyes at the display, and Alex and James grinned around their last mouthfuls of soup. There was no sign of Josh, who was presumably on door duty at the club. Huntly had employed more bouncers since things kicked off with the Priestly Brothers, but at least one of the Cleaners was usually there to supervise.

"Have you decided what to do with her yet?" James asked, while getting up and putting his empty bowl in the sink. "That was delicious, Susie, as always." He smiled at the woman huddled in Ren's arms, and she offered him a wobbly smile.

Little Susie was so not happy, and that made Ty's guts twist anew. He hated being the cause of any distress to her, but the whole lot of them had to realize and accept that Jeanette was indeed his to do with as he pleased, and that he'd had his reasons for going into that estate with her.

He sipped his soup slowly, to give himself time to formulate an argument that wouldn't come across as though he was being led around by his dick.

Ace and Ren had both been at the club, after all, and had witnessed the chemistry between him and Jeanette firsthand, as had Susie, of course.

Crossing his arms over his big chest, James waited until Ty had finished his soup, before he pounced.

"So, how are you going to deal with the Jeanette being Myrtle's sister issue, then?" He smirked when his brother pushed his chair back and shook his head at him.

"Subtle as always, bro. Let the man's food go down, at least. He's been out of it for two days. I highly doubt he has a plan yet," Alex said.

Susie tensed in Ren's arms, and Ty barely suppressed his irritation.

"What would you all have me do? Whether she's Myrtle's sister or not isn't really relevant right now. You all know what that scum would have done to her, had I not been with her when she got back to the estate. She crossed the lines, coming to Huntly and asking for a job. He made her my responsibility and that meant I couldn't just let her walk to certain doom."

"If that is what would have happened. For all we know she was sent by the Priestlys to infiltrate us. At the very least to draw us out into their territory." Ren dropped a kiss on the top of Susie's head as he spoke, and she snuggled in even more. "You made yourself a fucking target, Ty."

"And like I said to you then, what would you have done had it been Susie?"

The redhead blanched, and Ren looked ready to murder him.

"She needs her lunch, pumpkin. Go and take it to her, while I have this out with the idiot."

"No stay, Susie," Ty said when she made to leave. "I'll be taking it down to her, and you have as much right to hear my reasons as the boys."

Ren frowned, but he didn't insist on her leaving further, and pulling out a chair, Susie sat opposite Ty.

"I would have gone in for any of our girls, and I

know damn well you would have done the same. Yes, I know, strictly speaking she isn't one of us yet, but she did come to Huntly, and he offered his protection. I hazard a guess that's why he hasn't ordered her killed yet. Besides, we need to know why she did what she did. So, you want to know my plans? I tell you what they are. I'm going to do my fucking job, that's what I'll do. If she turns out to be cheating, lying bitch like her sister was, I'll kill her myself."

Susie gasped at that, and Ren nodded with a grim smile.

"You saw her at that audition, boss. She was nervous as fuck. And really pissed at you, which makes sense if she's Myrtle's sister, but my gut tells me there is more to that then the obvious. She didn't appear to have any grasp of the danger she was in when we were heading back to that estate, and had she wanted to, she could have shopped me to the police there and then."

A collective murmur went around the room, and Ren swore under his breath.

"What the fuck happened?" he asked.

Ty shrugged and instantly regretted that move, as his sore side smarted.

"Got stopped by the cops. Not gonna bore you with the reasons. Suffice to say she went along with the cover story I made up, instead of getting me arrested for assault."

Ren's eyebrows shot to his hairline at that statement, and Ace chuckled.

"Hell, that's more like it. Manhandled her a bit, did you?" he asked.

"Something like that. I'd just found out where she lived, and … yeah…" He gave a short laugh. "It didn't go down well with me, as you can imagine. Anyhow, like I said she kept quiet then, so for that reason alone, I had to go with her, and that's why I'm asking you all to give her the benefit of doubt for now. I admit I have no fucking clue what her game is, but instinct tells me she's not with the Priestlys. Just let me do this my way, okay?"

The boys all exchanged a look, and nodded as one. Susie looked less happy as he got up and held out his hand.

"If you'll give me her portion, I'll take it down for her."

He had to smile at the disgruntled way Susie ladled the steaming soup into a dish, covered it with a plate and tore off a chunk of bread. Freshly baked by her fair hands that morning, no doubt. They had all lucked out when Ren claimed Susie for his own, because the Cleaners had never eaten better.

Having put it all on a tray, she handed it to Ty with a frown.

"There, though I don't know why you bother. She hasn't eaten a thing since she got here."

"Oh, trust me, sweet thing, I'll get her to eat, and talk."

Susie swallowed hard at whatever she read in his expression. If he looked as murderous as he felt at the news that Jeanette seemed intent on starving herself, then it wasn't perhaps surprising that she took a step back into Ren.

The head of the Cleaners smiled.

"Welcome back, Ty. Have fun with that, and holler if you need help. She sure is a spitfire that woman of yours."

Ty grinned and hobbled out of the kitchen.

Hearing Jeanette being referred to as *his woman* had a far too nice ring to it. He could only hope his gut wasn't letting him down and she really was a somewhat innocent in all this.

Chapter Six

The locks at the door of her luxurious prison clicked open, and Jeanette roused from her slumber. Her butt had gone to sleep sitting on the hard floor, where she had more or less collapsed earlier. The lack of food was getting to her, but there was no way she was eating anything. She kicked the tray holding the uneaten pancakes Ren's woman had brought down this morning, and the chains around her ankles clanged.

Chained like a fucking dog. Who did these assholes think they were? Okay, so she could move, thanks to the long chain attached to the runners to the ceiling. It afforded her enough movement to make it to the toilet, and back into this ... whatever the hell this was. Her prison held a very comfortable bed, and the attached wet-room was state of the art, but the cellar also held a myriad of BDSM equipment, half of which she couldn't even put a name to. She'd recognized the free standing X shaped structure from her reading material. The St. Andrew's Cross was well padded and clean, as was the spanking bench.

She had to give it to them. They clearly looked after this place. The door opened and shut, and the delicious smell of chicken assaulted her nostrils. Bringing her knees up under her chin, she hugged her arms around her legs and willed her growling stomach to stop.

There was no way she would give whoever was coming down those stairs the satisfaction of knowing how hungry she was. She might not have any control over her surroundings, but she *could* stop eating. Jeanette stubbornly ignored the little voice of reason in her head which told her that she was only hurting herself. Knowing these Cleaners they'd quite happily let her starve herself to death down here.

"I don't want it, so you can take that right back up there, or stick it where the sun doesn't shine."

It was somewhat disappointing to not get a response from Susie. Not even a gasp. Maybe the woman was simply getting used to Jeanette's outbursts. Then again, those approaching footsteps were much heavier than Susie's, and the fine hair on Jeanette's arms rose when she got a whiff of far too familiar spicy cologne. It made her stomach cramp anew, and not from hunger this time.

Looking up into the mirror on the wall, she flinched seeing her expression. What little makeup she'd had on, had long since disappeared, her hair, devoid of the smoothing products and heavy duty straighteners she used to tame the willful curls, resembled a bird's nest, and her bloodshot eyes looked too big for her face.

Not to mention her torn, dirty blouse and skirt. In short, she looked like she felt—fucking awful. Not that the man now standing behind her with a clit clenching scowl on his face looked much better. Jeanette gave out an involuntary gasp when her gaze finally connected with his face. Even the much heavier stubble covering his jaw couldn't hide the bruises on his skin, nor the swollen, cut lip and black eye. Steristrips held together a cut on his left cheekbone, and the white bandage on his left hand made a startling contrast against his tanned skin.

"You're alive then." She inwardly grimaced at both the inanity of her comment and the far too breathy quality of her voice, but, really, God almighty. No man had any right to look so damn sexy. The injuries just added to his bad boy appeal, not least because he'd sustained those in his efforts to let her escape to her flat. His hair was still slightly damp, as though he'd only recently showered and fell over his uninjured eye in a jaunty wave, which made her fingers itch to swipe it back for him.

"So it would seem." Ty's reply, accompanied as it was by a smirk, made everything south clench in need, and try as she might, Jeanette couldn't look away from his searching dark gaze. Like it or not, she responded to this man's presence on a deep, instinctive level. It wasn't something she could explain with any rationality, it just was. Which only served to make her angrier. She didn't want to want him. She didn't want that overwhelming feeling of relief which flooded her system just by being in his presence, by breathing in his scent, and to know that she was safe—for now, at least. He was just as much a criminal as the assholes who'd chained her up, had killed her little sister. Thoughts of Myrtle brought hot tears to her eyes, and she tried her best to blink them away. She'd cried enough to last her a lifetime, and tears never did any good anyhow. Ty's harsh expression softened slightly, and stepping around her, he put the tray of food down on top of the spanking bench. When he held out his hand in a silent demand it seemed the most natural thing in the world to take it and to let him pull her to her feet.

The sudden move made her head spin, and when she grasped onto Ty's side to steady herself, his grunt of pain rang in her ears.

"Sorry, I—"

"It's okay, titch." Ty's husky reply interrupted her apology.

What the fuck am I apologizing for, exactly?

His strong arm came round her waist supporting her, and as the world was still spinning, she gratefully leaned into his warm, solid body. She hadn't really realized how cold she'd felt, until she was in his arms.

"Here, lean on me, and let's get you over to the bed. What on earth were you doing on the floor?" Ty grasped her chin with his bandaged hand, and a pang of something suspiciously like regret at his injuries went through her. She really had to get a grip of these emotions. It had to be Stockholm syndrome or something, or maybe she was just too starved of not only food, but also human touch to be reacting to his small act of kindness with such intense longing.

The hold on her chin grew painful when she didn't reply, and her stomach dropped at the sound of his voice.

"I asked you a question, girl. Do me the courtesy of answering it. I really do not want to get heavy with you, but I need answers. They," he nodded toward the ceiling, leaving her in no doubt, who he was referring to. "They want answers, if you want to live."

He smiled grimly at her sharp intake of breath at that statement, and when he traced his thumb over her lips in a gentle caress, Jeanette fought the urge to simply let go. It would be so easy to let her walls down, and she couldn't do that.

"They're going to kill me anyway, so why should I?"

A short laugh was her answer this time, and she blanched when Ty slid his hand down to her throat.

"I could snap your neck right here, if I wanted to." His digits dug into her skin in silent affirmation of that fact, and Jeanette didn't dare move. Not that she could have done so anyway. There were her chains, for starters, and the small fact she was so weak from lack of food, she would probably disgrace herself and faint at his feet any minute now. As it was she was seeing two of him. Her vision was blurry, and she shut her eyes from that far too disorienting sight.

The tight grip on her neck loosened, and before she could grasp his intentions, Ty had hoisted her up in his arms. Another grunt of pain made her open her eyes. He stumbled, and she brought her arms round to hang on to him as much she could. Ty had gone very pale, his face a mask of intent, and they both breathed easier when he put her down on the soft comforter of the bed she'd so far refused to sleep in. Ty sat next to her holding his side, breathing heavily. Against her better judgment she reached out to touch him. The process made the chains, which linked her to the ceiling, clank.

"Are you okay?" she asked.

"I will be. I've had worse."

"Can I see?"

Wordlessly Ty lifted up his shirt, and Jeanette swallowed down bile. His entire side and torso was covered in bruises, with several clear boot marks visible, and she traced her fingers over the dressing. Spots of blood marred the pristine white, and her stomach churned anew.

"What is…"

Ty swatted her fingers away and stood up abruptly. The instant dismissal stung, and the resulting movement of the bed made her feel dizzy all over again.

"It's nothing, girl. Like I said I've had worse, and I'm not here to talk about my injuries, but to talk about your reason for being here. For wanting a job at the club, and to discuss the demise of Myrtle Jones, and so help me you will give the answers, and you *will* tell me the truth, or everything that has happened to you so far will seem like a picnic in the fucking park."

Jeanette flinched, and when Ty stalked back to the bench, and brought the tray over to set it on the nightstand, she shook her head.

"I told that Susie I'm not eating anything, and

don't you dare mention my sister. You and that Ren killed her. I saw the fucking pictures." She wrapped her arms around herself, yanking hard to get the hated chains to cooperate, and the cuffs chafed her skin. Ty's large hands closing over her wrists and uncrossing her arms made her look up at him.

"If I take these off you, will you promise me to eat something?"

****

Jeanette blinked in surprise, and in truth Ty had shocked himself by uttering those words. Seeing her yank the chains around, the delicate skin on her wrists looking angry and red, coupled with the fragile mental state he sensed from her had made him angry, however. Irrationally so, and Ty had no answers for this overwhelming drive inside of him to take care of her.

She clearly hadn't made use of any of the facilities here since Ren and the boys had dumped her in the cellar. She was too gaunt, too desperate, yet still with that indomitable spirit, which had first attracted him to her.

Despite her disheveled appearance and his injuries, his dick was getting harder by the minute, especially as her torn clothes afforded enticing glimpses of mocha skin he wanted to run his tongue all over. She would taste delicious, of that he was sure.

Ty loosened the hold he had on her wrists, and using just his thumbs, stroked the reddened area of skin visible under the heavy cuffs. He inwardly frowned at the unpadded cuffs. Whoever had chained her up wanted her to hurt.

"What does it matter to you if I eat or not? If I starve myself it saves you the job of killing me, after all," she finally said. Jeanette lifted her head up in a defiant gesture, but he caught the wobble in her voice, and the glance of sheer longing she allowed herself in the direction of the steaming bowl of soup.

"I can't stop you from starving yourself, if that's what you want to do, but it would be a damn waste." Her mouth fell open, and Ty bit back a laugh at her astonishment. "Susie made that soup herself, and the bread. Pissing her off is a surefire way of getting Ren on your back, and, trust me, titch, you ain't seen his bad side yet. So, be a good girl, and eat Susie's food. Whatever you think of Ren, me, or the boys, whatever you think happened with Myrtle, and I can assure you, you'll have the wrong end of the stick, especially if these pictures you saw came from the source I suspect." He paused to let his words sink in for a minute, and when she didn't react he continued. "Susie is not to blame for any of this, so do not take it out on her."

This time Jeanette yanked her hands out of his, and not wanting to hurt her wrists further than they were already, he let her.

"What makes her so damn special, other than the fact she sleeps with you all?"

She glared up at him, but Ty swallowed the immediate, angry retort he wanted to make, when she swayed. Instead he grasped her by the shoulders, and shoved her further up the bed, until her back rested against the headboard. He picked up the bowl, dipped the spoon inside and held it up to her mouth.

"I won't dignify that with an answer. Eat, girl."

Biting her lips so hard she was surely in danger of drawing blood, Jeanette shook her head.

"Suit yourself," Ty said, and ate that mouthful himself. Her eyes flashed fire at him, and he made a big show of licking the spoon clean while making appreciative noises. When he held the filled spoon up to her lips this time, she hesitated, before shaking her head.

It took three more attempts, before she swore under her breath and all but attacked the spoon he held out.

Ty murmured his approval, and his chest felt a little tighter, when she closed her eyes to savor the next mouthful.

"It's good, huh?" he asked.

Jeanette nodded and tried to take the spoon off of him.

"No, titch, I'm feeding you. No argument. Open up."

With a resigned sigh she complied. When the spoon scraped the bottom of the bowl, Ty handed her the hunk of bread.

He had to smile again at the way she tore bits off it and stuffed them in her mouth.

"Easy now, girl, take it slowly. You don't want to make yourself sick. Here have a drink."

Ty was half expecting her to kick off in protest again when he held the bottle of water to her mouth, but she dutifully sipped it, and then gave him a surprisingly timid smile, before she dropped her gaze and resumed eating the bread at a more sedate pace.

A comfortable silence fell between them, while she finished her food, and Ty took the time to study her.

She was badly in need of a shower and fresh clothes, but he still had to fight the urge to not just grab her, and fuck her senseless. His dick jerked against his zipper, in silent affirmation of those plans. He could simply do that. No one would come to her aid if she struggled, and besides he doubted she would resist him for long. That simmering attraction, the sexual chemistry which had been there from the first moment he'd touched her was still very much there. Like it or not, this woman got to him, and judging by the way her breathing sped up and she licked her lips, when his gaze came to rest on the full flesh of her mouth, he got to her just as much.

A breadcrumb stuck to her chin, just under the fleshy swell of her bottom lip, and she didn't pull away when he reached out to flick it away. It took tremendous effort on his part to not lean in and kiss her. Instead he forced himself to let go of her soft skin, and he crossed his arms over his chest.

"So, now that you've eaten, and will hopefully not pass out on me, I ask you again. Why did you want the job at the club? And tell me the truth, titch."

She blinked, threw him a glance from under her long lashes and murmured her answer.

"I was there for my sister."

"And?" he asked.

"I wanted … needed revenge. She was killed by…" Not looking at him, Jeanette hung her head and swiped away fresh tears.

Ty's chest ached anew at the grief he was witnessing. Lord knew he knew how much it hurt to lose a sibling. He would always miss his big brother. Sam had been the sole reason Ty had joined the army. And when the brother he'd always looked up to had been killed by a motherfucking mine, Ty would have gone stir crazy, had it not been for Ren.

He would always have the man's back, which was why Jeanette's next words winded him completely.

"That bastard Ren killed her. Butchered her, and I want him dead."

She flinched as though she was expecting him to hit her when he brought a hand up to scrub his face.

"Look at me, titch." When she shook her head he lowered his voice and grasped her chin. "I said, *look* at me."

The sheer hatred burning in her dark eyes when their gazes connected was another proverbial punch to his solar plexus.

"Ren is my friend, and even if you could kill him, trying to do so would mean I will have to end you." She gasped and tried to wrench out of his grasp, but Ty grabbed the back of her head to keep her in place instead. "As I don't particularly like either of those scenarios, let's explore a solution, shall we? You mentioned pictures earlier. Who gave you those?"

He tightened his hold on her hair when she hesitated, and he could tell the precise moment the fight went out of her.

Her muscles went slack, and she swallowed hard.

"I hate you."

Ty smiled and kissed her nose. An action which made her pulse rate go into overdrive, and made him wish this conversation was behind them already.

"Of course you do, girl. Now tell me, the pictures?"

Jeanette's sigh skittered over his jaw, and he pulled back a little, lest he gave into the instinct to kiss the frown lines of her face.

"Does it matter? I know what he did. All I want to know now is who helped him. Did you?" She looked up at him, a myriad of emotions chasing each other across her face as she studied him.

"Did I what, titch?" he asked, and she blinked away fresh tears.

"Did you have a hand in killing my sister?"

Chapter Seven

God, why had she asked that question, and did she really want the answer to it? Ty didn't look inclined to answer her, his face once again an expressionless mask. He pulled further away, letting go of her hair in the process, and Jeanette felt the loss of his warm strength surrounding her keenly. She wrapped her arms around herself as best she could to hide the shivers, she didn't seem able to stop. She was just so damn cold.

"Would it matter if I did?" Ty finally asked. The deep sigh which accompanied that question made her feel even more wretched. Her stomach churned, and it took every ounce of willpower she possessed to hold his gaze. From somewhere deep down inside of her she dredged up her rightful anger, and thus she managed to project her reply with the force needed to make her feelings clear.

"Of course it bloody matters. She was my sister, my little sister, and you lot, you..." She ran out of words, when his harsh expression softened, and something like compassion crossed his features. He reached out as though to touch her, and then balled that hand into a fist, and shook his head.

"How close were you?" he asked, and Jeanette frowned.

"What has that got to do with anything? She was *my sister.* My little sister at that, and I should have been there to protect her, to ... damn it." She bit her lip and took deep breaths in and out to calm her emotions. It wouldn't do to break down and bawl her eyes out in front of Ty. She got the distinct impression that it wouldn't achieve anything, and besides she didn't want to give him the satisfaction. This man saw far too much as it was. She had to keep thinking of him as the enemy, and not be swayed to let the rare moments of tenderness he showed her, to influence her thinking. Therein lay madness, and certain ruin for her. It would be too easy to lose herself and to simply give in to the silent dominance which oozed out of this man's pores.

She had to avenge her sister, *had to*, and nothing and no one could get in the way of that.

"I reiterate, how well did you know her?" Ty's question demanded an answer, his voice having dropped to that deep, commanding growl that settled straight in every one of her erogenous zones. Maybe that online test she had participated in ages go had been right after all, and she was submissive, because, lord help her, that voice made her want to do everything he asked and more.

When she didn't answer he wrapped his hand in her hair and pulled her so close to him that their breaths mingled. Jeanette couldn't move, could barely breathe, truth be told, because Ty looked furious right now.

"Let's get one thing straight once and for all, girl. You *will* answer my questions, or so help me, I'll get the boys in here and let them loose on your insolent ass." He smiled grimly at her sharp intake of breath and her attempt to shake her head. "Trust me, once you've had a good flogging at all their hands strapped to that cross you'll sing like a fucking canary, because they *will* make that hurt, especially Ren."

She flinched at the mention of his name.

"That man is a fucking monster. You all are."

Ty pulled back to study her, and his smile in answer didn't reach his eyes. He looked disgusted with her right now, and that really shouldn't bother her. Who cared what he thought of her, what any of them thought of her? They were nothing more than a bunch of murdering scumbags.

"Why?" Ty asked, and she blinked in surprise.

"Why what?" Her voice rose to a shrill squeak in her agitation, and Jeanette took a swing at his belly. Not that it had a huge effect on him. Ty paled, and grunted, but he didn't release her, and Jeanette was pretty sure her ineffective punch only registered on his radar due to his previous injuries. Thoughts of those bruises she'd seen instantly squashed her anger.

"I'm sorry, I shouldn't have done that. You're hurt already. Jeez, I don't know what … I'm not normally this…" She stopped babbling when Ty smiled. A genuine smile this time, which lit up his features and intensified the amber flecks in his dark eyes.

"Yet you've come to the club with the intention of revenge. Tell, me, how exactly where you going to achieve that? Creep up on Ren and stab him in his sleep, perhaps?"

Jeanette dropped her gaze, that statement being far too close to the truth, and Ty swore under his breath.

"And you call *him* a monster. That's rich, girl."

He shoved her away and stalked away from the bed. Every line of his body screamed of his anger, and she jumped when he punched the St. Andrew's Cross with so much force the entire structure wobbled.

"He butchered my sister. He deserves to—"

"Shut the fuck up, girl, and let me enlighten you about this sister of yours." His growled words stopped her response, and had she been able to, Jeanette would have run away and never come back. Hands fisted by his sides, head down, and with his whole attention focused on her, Ty looked murderous, and far too damn sexy, which made her fucked up in the head, for sure. She ought to feel nothing but disgust toward this man. Instead the crotch of her knickers was soaked through with her arousal, and if he chose to take her right now, she had no doubt she would come like a freight train. As it was it took every ounce of self-control she had to not clench her thighs together to relieve the insistent pressure building between her thighs.

What in all that was holy was that about? She didn't understand her body's visceral response to this man at all. It made no sense, yet somewhere deep inside in that place that no other man had ever been able to reach it made perfect sense. The little devil sitting on her shoulder urged her to let go, to not overanalyze these conflicting emotions battering her soul.

Truth was she couldn't think straight when Ty was with her, let alone when he exhibited this raw masculinity.

So, instead of ranting at him, like she ought to have done, she kept quiet, allowing her gaze to roam over his muscled physique, while his deep voice broke through all of her defenses and shattered any illusions about her sister she might have still been holding onto. Tears of shame and disappointment gathered in her eyes, and she hastily blinked them away.

"Your little *sister* was a royal bitch, who threw everything Huntly did for her back in his face, and to top it all stole from him, and then sold it to the fucking Priestlys, the very kind of fucking scum Huntly's actions rescued her from in the first place."

Jeanette shook her head and whispered her denial.

"I don't believe you. Myr wouldn't do that. Sure, she was a wild child and she was led astray by that no-good-for-nothing-boyfriend of hers, but she never touched drugs. I don't believe you. She was a dancer. We look after our bodies, we don't abuse them. It doesn't make any sense."

The bed dipped as Ty sat next to her and taking her hands in his slowly uncurled her fists. He ran his thumb over the crescent moons her fake nails had left behind in her skin, and clucked his tongue.

"I ask you again. When did you last see her?" The gentle tone of his question meant she blurted her answer out before she could think about how wise that action was.

"She was sixteen."

Ty kept up the soothing massage of her palms, and Jeanette flicked him a glance. Seeing nothing but quiet expectation in his gaze she continued.

"Mum and she had another row. I'd managed to get Myr a scholarship at the Royal Academy of Dance, and she'd decided she didn't want to do that after all. She was gonna move in with her boyfriend, and he was gonna get her into more lucrative *dancing.*"

Ty's hold on her hands tightened for a few precious heartbeats, and a muscle ticked in his jaw, before he resumed stroking her skin in lazy circles.

"I see, and did he?"

Jeanette gave a short laugh.

"I'd always assumed he had. She sounded happy on the few occasions that she rang up. In fact, I recall when she told me about the job she'd landed at La Masquerade." Jeanette smiled recalling the excitement in Myr's voice.

"She sounded so happy, and it was a huge relief to hear from her. I hadn't heard from her in almost a year by then. She'd ditched the boyfriend, she'd said, and this was her chance to make it big. She tried to get me to sign up, and I'm afraid we had a row about it. I couldn't understand why she would choose pole dancing over a career in the ballet. She had the freaking talent, and she could have gone so far, where as I was … never mind."

"No, continue, whereas you were?" Ty let go of her hands and nudged her chin up to make her look at him.

Jeanette flashed him a smile and shrugged.

"I'd been booted out for being too tall, so, yeah, I was jealous of her, okay? Which makes me a horrible person, because who is jealous of their sister?"

Ty smiled, and some of her anxiety fled when he quirked an eyebrow at her.

"Sibling relationships are complicated at the best of times, especially same sex ones. We tend to compete for everything, and feeling jealous is a normal, human emotion."

He looked lost in thought for a minute and incredibly sad, so much so that Jeanette blurted out her question without thinking.

"You have siblings?"

Ty shook himself, and studied her for the longest time as though to weigh up his response to her.

"I had a brother," he finally said, and the odd undertone in his voice made her stomach cramp anew.

"Had?"

"He was killed by an IUD in Afghanistan. It left only parts of him to bury."

Ty smiled grimly at her sharp intake of breath.

"I'm so sorry."

"Why, titch? I mean really, why do folks always say that? You weren't the one to place that fucking bomb there, and besides, he died doing what he loved best. Mum and Dad took some small comfort from that fact at least. For myself, I killed as many of those fuckers as I could, but it left a sour taste in my mouth. Ren had resigned out to work for Huntly and eventually convinced me to do the same. Besides, not much scope in civvie life for men with our unique skill set, shall we say."

Jeanette swallowed hard at the images that conjured up.

"You could have started work for a security firm or something? I mean, you didn't have to turn into a criminal?"

This time Ty's smile in response chilled her to the bone, and his reply did nothing to reassure her.

"I could have done, but you're missing an important fact here. I enjoy killing, especially bastards like the Priestlys. There is an awful lot of scum out there that cannot be reached by legal means. That's why you need the Cleaners. If that makes us monsters in your eyes, then so be it."

He sat back and crossed his arms over his chest, and Jeanette licked her lips and swallowed hard to get her dry throat to work. The way Ty's gaze dropped to her lips and stayed there made her heart miss a beat.

"So, you did have a hand in killing my sister then?" Her voice broke on the last word, and she raised her head to see his reaction.

Ty didn't look happy, but he didn't deny it either.

"I was there, and I helped apprehend her if you like, but I didn't kill her, no."

"Thank God."

Ty shook his head at her heartfelt response.

"No, titch, God had little to do with it. The Myrtle we know, the bitch we ended, had it coming. Her actions placed us all into danger and were a direct slap in the face for Ren and Huntly. Ren was the one who rescued her from the clutches of her abusive boyfriend in the first place. You call him a monster, and I will freely admit, he can come across as such, but one thing Ren is, is fair. He would never stand by and see a woman abused in a non-consensual context. Besides, there was only one place Myrtle was heading, and that was into human trafficking. That asshole boyfriend of hers was grooming her. When he got heavy with her in front of Ren, who was at that particular private party enjoying the show thus far, the boss intervened, which made Myrtle his responsibility. He took her to Huntly, and recognizing her potential, Huntly put her to work in the club. He offered her the same choices he offered you."

Ty paused when her mouth fell open at that news, and smiling, shut it for her.

"Unlike you, Myrtle wanted it all. Guess she was so used to spreading her legs at that point, it didn't make much difference to her who she was doing it for."

Jeanette shook her head, not recognizing her sister at all, but she couldn't deny the sincerity in Ty's voice. He was telling the truth as he saw it, and, really, what reason did he have to lie to her? She was tied up in the Cleaners' cellar, with no one knowing her whereabouts. They could do to her as they pleased, and she had no means to stop any of it. For the first time since she started on this quest for the truth, she conceded that she might have been wrong about a few things. That knowledge sat in her gut like lead, but it did make her listen to Ty, and to swallow down her immediate denial. The sister she knew wouldn't have acted like that, but she hadn't seen her sister in almost ten years, and time changed people.

"Did you … I mean who *trained* her?"

She mimed quotation marks around that word, and the chains clinked, another far too audible reminder of her current predicament.

"Ren was going to, but Huntly took her on himself. I believe he grew rather fond of her, which is why her betrayal hit him hard. He certainly afforded her far more liberties than any of the other girls in the club. Toward the end she had unsupervised access to Huntly's office and his house. Guess that's how she managed to steal the crack from him."

"She did *what*?"

Ty smiled and shrugged.

"For what it's worth I don't think she used herself, but, yes, she stole the drugs and sold them onto the highest bidder. Which happened to be the Priestly brothers, Huntly's sworn enemies and the biggest lot of scum that ever walked on this planet. God knows what she was thinking, considering she barely escaped from their clutches the first time round."

Jeanette's head was starting to hurt from the information overload she was being subjected to, and she put one hand up to stop Ty from talking.

"You mentioned that name before. When we were going to my flat. Is that? I mean I've heard of them in passing, but ... is that why they were after me? Because I went to Huntly?"

Ty's gaze grew intense as he studied her, and cold sweat ran down between Jeanette's shoulder blades, while dread crawled up her spine.

When he at long last gave a sharp nod, Jeanette pulled a much needed breath of air into her lungs.

"I'm still not sure I understand," she said.

Ty sighed, stood, and started to pace to and fro in front of the bed with a speed that threatened to make her dizzy.

"You really don't, do you?" he asked

****

Fuck. That surge of relief which flooded his being brought him to his emotional knees. The sheer force of his feelings made breathing difficult, and schooling his features into a mask of indifference he turned to address the trembling woman on the bed.

Whatever sharp response he was going to say died on his tongue because Jeanette looked utterly done in. So instead of questioning her further, he shook his head.

"We'll discuss it further another time. I daresay this has come as a shock to you. I'm gonna leave you to digest it all, and I suggest you have a bath and change out of those clothes. You'll feel better for it."

Jeanette pulled a face and shook her head.

"Change into what? I haven't got any of my clothes, and if you think I intend to run about naked, then you've got another think coming."

The return of her sass made Ty grin.

"Watch it, girl. I like my women sassy, but too much of it will earn you a punishment. In fact, you've already earned several. I might not be up to deliver them right now." He pressed his aching side to relieve some of the pain, and Jeanette eyes widened as she followed his movements.

"I'm sorry you got hurt because of me," she said.

She looked as surprised as he felt hearing those words, and before he could formulate a response, she rushed on. "I mean, why did you do that anyway? You had no reason to do so, and once you knew I was Myrtle's sister I'd have thought you…" She shivered and ran her hands up her exposed arms. "All of you would have just left me to them."

"That was certainly an option Ren favored, but it's not the way we work. You would have ended up dead, or far worse sold on to some sick bastard. A beautiful, sensual woman like you would fetch a very high price indeed."

He grinned as her eyes widened, and she shook her head.

"You need your eyes tested if you think I'm beautiful. Myr was the beautiful one. I was always too tall and gangly, and when I'm not dancing likely to trip up over my own two feet at a moment's notice. And as

I've been told and you mentioned a few times my runaway mouth tends to get me into trouble."

She slammed said mouth shut, as though she'd said too much already, and Ty laughed.

"Yes, I did notice, and I can think of several inventive ways to put that mouth of yours to far better use." Predictably her eyes flashed fire at him, but he didn't miss the way her pulse jumped, and she surreptitiously squeezed her thighs together. He let it go for now and made his point verbally.

"It's that very sass which would make you a catch. There are plenty of sickos out there, who would love to beat you into submission, to break that beautiful spirit, until you're a mere fuck toy to be passed around their friends and business associates, and once you've fulfilled your purpose, or they deem you too old, you'd become another statistic, who died of an unfortunate overdose."

He paused to let his words sink in a bit, and all the color drained out of her face, leaving her beautiful mocha skin a mere ashen paste.

"Is that what would have happened to Myr, had … you know?"

"Yes, titch, she was heading that way, when Ren found her and Huntly gave her a job. You would not believe the number of our girls who've come from that route. Some decide to stay and work, others decide this life is not for them anymore, and others still, can't cope with their freedom and go back to the very ones who abused them. It's a sad cycle, for sure."

Silence fell between them, only broken by their combined breathing. Jeanette was breathing too fast, and she'd be in danger of hyperventilating soon, if he didn't put a stop to this. Acting on the need to touch her, he placed his hand on her nape to pull her closer, and rested his forehead on hers.

"Breathe, titch, you're safe here. In ... out ... come on, do it with me."

"Safe? I'm being held a prisoner, and you call this safe?" She struggled against his hold, but Ty kept her steady and murmured his next question.

"Would you rather I'd have left you to your fate at your flat?"

"No." Her strangled response brought out his need to protect her, and tightening his hold on her slightly, he kept on simply breathing. Eventually, her breathing evened out to match his, and the color returned to her cheeks. Only then, did he give into the urge to kiss her. Her gasp of surprise gained him entry as he licked along the seam of her lips, and taking full advantage he deepened the kiss.

A needy whimper escaped her, and when she started to kiss him back, Ty threw caution to the wind. He might not be able to fuck her right now, but he could claim her like this and he damn well would. Fisting both hands in her hair, he angled her to give him the best access, and his groan joined hers as the kiss grew ever more passionate. Just as he'd suspected, Jeanette gave as good as she got. He withdrew every time she attempted to take charge of the kiss, and her hands fisted in his shirt as she tried to close the distance between them. With a sharp tug to her hair he yanked her back, and her eyes flew open in protest.

"Please ... why?"

"Who's in charge here, girl?" he asked, and the little minx rolled her eyes at him.

"You are, but..."

Ty quirked his eyebrow at her, and she added a rather reluctant, "*Sir.*"

"Better, girl." Having dropped another kiss on her

lips, he released her and stepped back.

"I've got things to do, but I'll be back later with your dinner, and I expect to see you having taking care of yourself." Jeanette pulled a face and lifted her hands up, making the chains clink.

"That's not an excuse. You can still clean up, and there is a perfectly good bathrobe you can slip into in the bathroom, until I can get hold of some clothes for you, though I rather like the idea of keeping you naked." His dick jerked against his zipper, and reaching into his jeans he adjusted himself. When he looked back up it was to see Jeanette's gaze riveted on his crotch, and Ty barely bit back a smirk.

"If you want my cock, you'll have to ask me nicely, titch, remember."

A strangled groan escaped her, before she wrenched her gaze back up to his face and glared at him.

"I'll never do that."

Ty laughed, picked up the two trays of food and made his way up the stairs.

"I mean it, Sir. Put that in your pipe and smoke it."

Ty turned at the top of the stairs, and he wasn't at all surprised to see her sticking her tongue out at him.

"Oh yes, your mouth will be super busy, girl, don't you worry."

He stepped through the door, which locked shut behind him, and the thump against it made him laugh out loud. Josh, who was hovering by the front door, gave him an incredulous look.

"You're playing nursemaid to that cunt now, Ty? Why is she still alive?"

"Don't talk about her like that, Josh, if you want to keep that pretty face of yours looking right." Ty ground the words out through clenched teeth, and hands up in the air, Josh took a step away from him.

"Chill, Ty. Just saying, she's gotta be bad news, right?"

"That's for me to decide, not you. Stay away from her. She's mine."

Josh laughed and stalked off toward the stairs.

"Whatever you say, man. I swear there's something in the fucking water around here. Hi, boss." Josh nodded at Ren, and Ty sighed as Ren stopped at the bottom of the stairs and crossed his arms over his chest.

"So, are we killing her or not?"

Ty frowned and readied himself for a fight.

"Or not."

Chapter Eight

Jeanette frowned at the bouncy and surprisingly heavy ball which ricocheted off the door, hopped down the stairs and came to rest at her feet. Lord only knew why that thing was in here, but it was the first thing she had grabbed from the side cabinet, when she'd been searching for something to chuck at the infuriating man. She hadn't been fast enough, of course, so instead of colliding with Ty's broad back it had hit the door instead. Still, it had made a rather satisfying loud thump as it impacted, and would get her opinion across about what she thought of his high-handed attitude quite nicely.

It was also, no doubt, infinitely safer to hit the door rather than Ty. For starters she didn't really want him hurt more than he was already, and she was honest enough with herself to admit that she was turned on beyond all reason by his threats—or were they promises? Her befuddled brain couldn't quite make that one out. One thing was sure, however, a bath sounded heavenly right now. She glowered at the chains, but as Ty had promised they didn't get in the way too much. She had to rip her clothes get them off her, mind you. Exhausted from that effort, she sank into the depths of her lavender scented bubble bath, and soon forgot about the damn chains and everything really. Jeanette closed her eyes and simply relaxed.

How long she had been luxuriating in there, she couldn't be sure, but noise from the main area made her sit up with a start and bring her knees up to her chest. The water sloshed over the sides, and Jeanette frowned at her wrinkled toes and fingers. They would suggest that she had been in this bath for ages. She must have fallen asleep, because she certainly couldn't recall the passage of time, yet the water was still hot. A self-heating bath really was the lap of luxury, but then again, everything she'd encountered so far, served to reiterate the fact that being a criminal clearly paid well.

A knock on the open door stopped that particular train of thought. Jeanette wrapped her arms around her knees, and croaked a greeting.

"Hello? Who is this?"

"Only me, can I come in?"

Susie's voice rang out loud and clear, and Jeanette shrunk further into herself as guilt crawled up her spine.

She really hadn't been very nice to the woman, and, yet here she was being polite and courteous as always.

"Jeanette, are you all right in there? I brought you some stuff that you might need."

"Stuff?"

Jeanette swung her head round to see Susie stick hers 'round the door frame. If she'd blinked she'd have missed the brief smile on the redhead's face. Susie waved a cosmetic bag at her.

"I brought you some products. Not sure if they'll work on your hair, but they sure help me with my frizzy mess. If they don't and you tell me what you need, I'll make sure to get them for you. Ty has tasked me with buying you some new clothes anyway, so I need to know your size."

"He has?" Another brief smile chased across Susie's pale features, and she took a few tentative steps inside the wet-room.

"Why do you sound so surprised?" she asked.

Jeanette lifted her arm to show the ever present cuffs, and glared at Susie.

"Duh?"

Susie dumped the cosmetic bag onto the vanity with so much force, Jeanette jumped. Before she could blink, the other woman was standing in front of her, hands on hips, her blue eyes the frostiest she had ever seen them. It made Jeanette rather glad there were no weapons in easy reach, because, right now, Susie looked as though she wanted to murder her.

"For pity's sake, what do you expect? Drop the fucking attitude, and show some respect. You're only alive because of Ty. He got hurt trying to protect you, and he's been at loggerheads with Ren because of you. Those two never argue, but they have over you. I don't like it. I don't like you, and if you want any chance of getting out of here, you best buck up your ideas."

Jeanette opened her mouth to say something, but Susie wasn't done yet.

"No, you shut the hell up and listen to me. I get it. Lord, I get it. I was where you are now. Okay, I wasn't chained up, but I was a prisoner nonetheless. Not in the sense that I was confined to this room, but in that I held onto my misguided notions of what I thought was right and wrong."

"Misguided?"

Susie blinked and took a step back when Jeanette shot to her feet, sending yet more water flying everywhere. Not caring about exposing her naked self, Jeanette stepped out of the bath, and wrapped the oversized towel around herself. So much for using the bathrobe. Damn the infuriating man all over again. How the hell was she supposed to get dressed in anything with these blasted chains on her? Having managed to tie the towel up, she whipped back round to glare at Susie some more.

"They killed my sister. There is nothing misguided about that."

Susie took another step back and the look of sympathy, if not to say pity leveled at Jeanette was even harder to take.

"I'm sorry you lost your sister, but I'm not sorry that she died." The quietly uttered words held utter conviction, and Jeanette sat down on the edge of the bath with a thump. It was that or fall down.

"Are you that fuckin' brainwashed that you can't see how wrong that is?"

Susie shook her head and gave a short, humorless laugh.

"Believe it or not, I'm here of my own free will."

Jeanette shook her head, and after a moment's hesitation, Susie sat down next to her. The wide edge of the bath made a surprisingly comfortable seat.

"I am, and you can't tell me that this whole thing isn't a huge turn-on for you."

Jeanette whipped her head round to glare at her, all ready to dispute that notion, but her gaze snared on her knickers left on the floor. Heat rose in her cheeks, and she kept quiet.

"It's okay, you know. That's what I meant earlier, when I said I'd been there. Finding yourself aroused in these sort of fucked up circumstances feels wrong, but it isn't really. I saw the way you and Ty sparked off each other back at the club. That sort of chemistry is hard to find, and you don't throw it away on a whim."

Jeanette made a strangled sound at the back of her throat, and Susie gently squeezed her hand.

"Ty likes you, a hell of a lot, if you ask me, to put up such a fight for you. Don't make him regret sticking his neck out for you. Besides, it won't do you any good. You're one of the Huntly girls now, and that's not ever going to change, so deal with it."

Jeanette snatched her hand out of Susie's and immediately regretted that action, because Susie rose stiffly and all of her previous sympathy vanished in a flash.

"Anyway, I'm guessing you're what? Size 8 to 10, slightly bigger in tops?" She didn't wait for Jeanette's reply, simply nodded and turned to leave.

"So, I'm just to forget about what they all did to my sister?" Jeanette aimed the question at Susie's departing back, and the other woman tensed. "I've seen the pictures of her body, they're—"

"So have I." Susie's curt statement interrupted Jeanette. "I'm guessing it was Detective Wonsan who showed them to you."

"How do you…"

Susie turned slightly so that she could fix her expressive gaze on Jeanette.

"I know, because he did the same to me. Tried to use me to turn in Sir and the rest of the Cleaners. Needless to say it didn't work. Even if I hadn't already fallen hopelessly in love with Sir by then, I never would have ratted on them. It's not conducive for one's health for starters, and, besides, Huntly helped me out of a bind. Say what you will about him, he looks after the people working for him."

Jeanette snorted her disbelief.

"Like he looked after my sister."

Susie swung fully round and shook her head.

"Yes, because he did, right up until she betrayed him. Do I think she deserved to die for that? Yes, actually, I do." She nodded grimly at Jeanette's sharp intake of breath. "She knew what she was signing up for, just like I did, when I sought Huntly's protection, just like you did when you applied for the dancing job." She paused to study Jeanette. "Ty says, you didn't really know what you were letting yourself in for, and maybe that's true, but Huntly made his terms perfectly clear, and you were given a choice. Just like I was. I chose to be just a waitress, and that's still what I am. Huntly is a man of his word, which is more than can be said for others. Detective Wonsan being a point in question. For Christ's sake the man is married with a sick kid, yet he's looking to score. Did you know he's been sniffing around the club? Not in his official capacity. Oh no, this is for his *personal* entertainment." Susie pulled a face as she said that. "That man gives me the creeps. My friend Kim danced for him the other night, and Josh had to tell him to back off. Had he been any other punter, he'd have been thrown off the premises there and then, I tell you. Kim doesn't do extras." Susie added the last bit, clearly interpreting Jeanette's surprised expression correctly.

"Anyway, like I said Huntly looks after us all."

"He's still a criminal," Jeanette said more to convince herself than anything else, and Susie laughed.

"You've got a lot to learn. Life isn't black and white, you know."

Jeanette struggled to her feet, glaring at the clinking chains.

"Can you honestly say it doesn't bother you? All the violence? Your lover killed my sister, damn it."

She swallowed down the hot, angry tears burning in the back of her throat, but if she'd expected Susie to show remorse for that then she was disappointed.

"Yes, he did. It's what they all do." Susie said. "They're the Cleaners. Someone has to do it. Do I sometimes wish things were different? Yes, sure I do, but wishing for something doesn't make it happen, and besides I love Ren, all of him. You see him as nothing but a monster, but there is so much more to him than that. To them all, and if you just let go of your preconceived notions, open your heart, and follow your instincts, you'll see that I'm right."

Jeanette laughed. It was a slightly hysterical

laugh to be sure, but, really, this had to be the most bizarre conversation she'd ever had.

"And if my instincts tell me to kill your precious Ren next time I see him, what then?"

Susie paled and took a step back. When she spoke the frost behind her words could have turned the Sahara into a glacier.

"Then you'd be dead faster than I can say deluded cow."

With that, Susie swept out of the room, leaving Jeanette to her thoughts.

That surreal conversation set the pace of things to come over the next few days. Ty turned up for the next meal, as promised, but he seemed preoccupied, and once he had reassured himself that she was indeed eating, he left. Not before he'd unchained her to enable her to get dressed in the clothes provided by Susie. The simple jogging bottoms and t-shirts were nothing special, but the fact that Ty took the time to enable her to get dressed, meant the world to Jeanette.

"Thank you, Sir."

His harsh features had lit up in a dazzling, toe-curling smile, which had shot straight to her clit.

"You're welcome, titch. You remain cooperative and I'll get you out of here soon enough."

He'd dropped a kiss on her nose and left, leaving Jeanette to feel strangely empty inside. The only interaction she had with the outside world, if you could call it that, was through Susie, and as the days wore on she looked forward to seeing the redhead. Not that the other woman spoke to her much, if at all, but she was courteous, and without her help, Jeanette would be stuck in the same clothes day in and out. As it was Susie unchained her morning and night to enable Jeanette to wash and change her clothes.

After a week of this, and no sign of Ty or any of the other cleaners, Jeanette had had enough. When Susie came down with her breakfast things, Jeanette held out her wrists.

"What do I have to do to get rid of these for good?"

Susie smiled and looked up toward the top of the stairs.

"You had to ask, titch."

****

Jeanette's reaction to his words was truly priceless, and Ty suppressed a grin as he made his way down the stairs. In the week since he'd kept away, his titch had lost the gaunt look. She looked ready to take on the world, but far more importantly she had lost some of her antagonistic stance. He wouldn't go as far as to say she'd mellowed. The fire sparking in her dark gaze as she glared at him was certainly proof of that, but she'd had plenty of time to think, and to adjust to her situation. Even a few days ago, she wouldn't have asked that question. She'd have demanded to have the chains removed, had, in fact, done so on numerous occasions.

Susie had ignored her every time, as instructed. Jeanette hadn't known it, but one of the Cleaners, more often than not Ren, had kept watch behind the open door, lest Myrtle's sister try anything when Susie took the chains off to enable Jeanette to change her clothes.

It had been a hard-won concession, Ty knew, and he'd breathed a sigh of relief that Jeanette had always just disappeared into the wetroom to get changed in private, rather than trying to overpower Susie. That wouldn't have ended well for Myrtle's sister.

"Just keep her fucking naked, that'll solve the issue." Josh's suggestion had been met with a chorus of approval when Ty had first brought up the subject. It had been Susie who had volunteered to fulfill the task, taking everyone by surprise.

"What? I don't like the woman much, but I bring the cow her meals, and I really don't need to see all that flesh on display." She'd pouted when the men had laughed, and continued under her breath. "No one should be allowed to have such a stunning figure. Damn it."

That outburst and the inherent self-criticism had earned her a hard spanking from Ren, which had meant she had winced every time she sat down for days.

Fun times. Such treatment was long overdue for his own unruly woman. And fuck it, Jeanette *was* his, whether she realized that yet or not. Ace had declared him healed enough, so Ty wasn't going to waste one more minute. Especially as all the background checks the Synn brothers and resident tech gurus had carried out on her had proven what Ty had instinctively known. Jeanette was exactly who she'd said she was. Myrtle's half-sister whose connection to the Priestlys started and ended with living on that estate. While she had clearly sought employment at the club with a view to get revenge for her sister, it had been her own personal demons driving her, not a Priestly engineered attack.

Jeanette seemed an outstanding citizen, in fact, and thus far too good to be getting involved with him, which of course made him more determined to claim her. His titch was what he'd been looking for, and he wouldn't let her slip through his fingers, even if he had to keep her tied up forever.

It wouldn't be the best solution, because she would be missed. Not by her one remaining relative, mind you. No, her mother was a hard-nosed crack addict, too involved in getting her next fix to worry over her daughter. No wonder Myrtle had turned out to be the way she was. Jeanette seemed the total opposite.

She volunteered at the local community center teaching underprivileged kids to dance for a minimal fee, and she'd left behind a steady job at dance studio in Leeds, when she'd come to London in search of her sister six months ago. Apart from a couple of ex-boyfriends, where both times she had ended the relationship pretty quickly, she hadn't even been very active in the sex department. A delightfully open book with kinky edges, as Ty had found out when a laughing James had called him over, after he'd hacked into her Amazon account. Her Kindle held an interesting collection of dark erotica, and BDSM stories.

"You're gonna have fun with this, right?" James had laughingly slapped Ty's back. "And, you know, if you need help breaking her in, Alex and I are always happy to oblige."

"Fuck off." James had laughed even harder at Ty's curt response.

Fun times ahead indeed.

"You *what?*" Jeanette spat that question out at him now, as he reached the bottom of the stairs, and Susie hastily stepped out of the way.

Ren's sub rolled her eyes at him and threw her hands in the air, as though she was exasperated with the other woman, and Ty nodded toward her.

"Thank you, my sweet, I'll take it from here."

Susie's eyes widened as she recognized his slipping into Dom mode, and dropping her gaze, she made a hasty exit.

Ty took his time answering the bristling woman in front of him, who held her arms out in a silent bid for him to remove the chains.

"No, I don't think I will. I don't like your attitude much, girl," he said, and Jeanette groaned and stamped her foot.

He wouldn't have been surprised had she stuck her tongue out at him, too, but one look at his expression stopped her in her tracks.

Uncertainty flitted across her expressive features, and she threw a longing glance at the pancakes Susie had brought down.

Liberally smothered in golden syrup, they confirmed not only Jeanette's sweet tooth, but also Susie's innate generosity. She'd made savory pancakes for the men this morning, so this must have been a batch specially made for Jeanette. Susie had made no qualms about the fact that she didn't like Jeanette, yet she still looked after her.

Ty crossed his arms over his chest and quirked an eyebrow at his unruly submissive.

"Acting like a spoiled brat will simply earn you yet more punishment, so I suggest you ask me nicely."

Jeanette opened her mouth to no doubt give him another verbal dressing down, but whatever she read in his expression stopped her. He could almost see the two sides of her warring with each other. There was the fiercely independent, sassy woman, used to making her own way in life, the one who never relied on anyone, and kept men at arm's length.

And then there was the submissive streak, which ran much deeper than she no doubt realized herself. That hidden part of her which automatically responded to his dominance, the very part which meant that this whole situation fed into her deepest, darkest fantasies, and judging by the sheer number of capture books on her Kindle, that particular need was strong.

Ty was only too glad to give her what she needed, but they had to establish the ground rules first. Not least, because they would keep her safe in his world.

At long last she hung her head with a sigh.

"Please, I've had enough of these. Please take them off."

Ty wrapped the chain leading to her cuffed wrists around his hand and yanked her to him. Her soft curves collided with the hard planes of his body, and damn him, if she didn't fit against him as though she was made for him.

A gasp escaped her lips, and when he brought his other hand down to her ass, and squeezing the luscious globes pulled her hips further against him, her breathing sped up. Rapid puffs of air ghosted across his jaw, and her hard nipples poked into his chest, almost as much as his hard-on was digging into her abdomen. Dipping his head just slightly, he bit the soft lobe of her ear, earning himself another gasp from the woman in his arms.

"Take them off, what?" he asked.

Jeanette tensed, and he tightened his hold on her, as he rubbed his jaw along the rapidly beating pulse point in her neck. Her sensitive skin reddened under his heavier than usual morning stubble, taking on a much darker hue than its original mocha skin tone. It simply begged for him to mark that soft flesh, and giving into that instinct Ty bit her neck.

A needy groan came from her, and she sank into his body as he licked the half-moon imprint of his teeth left behind. The inherent caveman in him strutted in triumph, seeing her thus marked, and his fingers itched to strip her naked and to further mark her as his.

He pulled back slightly to see her expression, and her dark eyes held a desperation that tore at his heart strings. Now was not a time for tenderness, however. That would come later, when he'd put his point across, and she'd accepted her fate.

Ty wanted, needed her submission, and he would damn well have it, before she left this room.

It took a while, but eventually Jeanette dropped her gaze to his collarbone and murmured the words he needed to hear.

"Please, Sir, will you take these chains off me?"

"No, I won't. Not yet."

Chapter Nine

Jeanette's head whipped up, and she opened her mouth to give the bastard what for, but stopped the angry tirade ready to spew from her lips at the last minute. That was what he expected her to do, after all, judging by the amused twinkle in his eyes. They darkened further as she continued to look up at him, and when she very deliberately bit her lip, the hot hard cock digging into her belly jumped. It meant she had to swallow her groan, because another surge of arousal dampened her knickers.

This close to him, his raw masculinity was overwhelming. The faint shadows left over on his face from his previous injuries were a far too visible reminder of how dangerous and deadly this man was, which should have turned her arousal dead, but it had the opposite effect on her.

Susie's words bounced in her brain.

It isn't wrong ... just let go...

It was so very tempting to do just that, if she didn't fear that she would lose herself completely in the darkness contained in Ty's soul. A darkness which she ought to run from, not be drawn to like the moth to the flame. Instead she had that burning desire to taste said flame, to let it set her alight, until she knew she would never be the same again.

"As you wish, Sir. May I eat my breakfast?" Lord knew how she managed to get those words out. They certainly didn't sound like her. It wasn't just what she'd said, either, it was the breathy, shaky quality of her voice she didn't recognize.

She'd surprised him, because he blinked and released her.

"As you ask so nicely."

It took an extraordinary amount of willpower to

step away from him. Somehow she managed it, and pulling deep on her years of dance training, she took a surreptitious breath and slid to the floor in a sinuous move, or as gracefully as she could manage with her chains hindering her movement. She might well look like a stranded whale. Joggers and an oversized t-shirt were hardly seduction material, after all. Still, as she spread her legs out, to bring the plates of pancakes right up between her splayed legs, she risked a quick glance up at him, while pushing her rack out. Unfettered as her boobs were, her hard nipples were clearly visible through the thin fabric covering of her top, and she made sure to give them a little shake, while she stretched her arms above her head.

"Ah, that's better," she said, not even trying to disguise the sexual purr in her voice, which would have done any porn star proud.

Ty's eyes narrowed, and she swallowed hard as he tensed. She'd forgotten how quickly he could switch from easygoing to super intense, but at least she knew she had his attention now. Forcing herself to continue in this silly game of one-upmanship she had initiated, she ran a finger over the back of one of the sticky pancakes, gathered the syrup, and brought it to her lips.

Ty's gaze never once wavered from her actions, and he stepped closer as she made a big show of licking her finger clean.

A growl erupted from his chest, the sound so animalistic that her hormones sighed in submission. Hands fisted by his sides, Ty came closer still, until his groin made up her view. Her pussy clenched in helpless need, seeing the long, solid imprint of his cock challenging the denim of his jeans. He looked enormous, far bigger than her previous boyfriends, and her breathing sped up, imagining his taking her.

"If you want your breakfast I suggest you fucking eat it, before I give you a different breakfast entirely." Ty's voice had dropped an octave, and the delicious deep growl settled straight in her clit. If she got any wetter, she would disgrace herself, that was for sure. It was utterly insane, this hold he had on her, the sexual energy coursing around and through them. It was small comfort to see him as much in thrall of what was happening between them as she was, because when she picked up a pancake and bit into it, Ty groaned. Out of the corner of her eyes, she could see him stroke his erection through his jeans, and she could swear she could feel his hot gaze follow the trail of syrup, down her chin and into the V-neck of her shirt.

When she made no move to swipe it away, Ty swore under his breath, and in the next instant she was on her feet.

Hand fisted in her hair, he angled her head, so that he could lick that sticky trail away, and all pretense went out of the window. The remains of the pancake fell to the floor, creating a sticky mess on her bare feet, and the world narrowed to the feel of his tongue on her overheated skin. It sent shivers along her spine and a fierce longing into her pussy, which meant her next words came out far too husky.

"I thought I had to beg to get your cock, Sir."

The hold on her hair grew painful, and Jeanette gasped as Ty shoved her away. His dark eyes glittering in silent fury, he reached in his back pocket for the key to her chains, and before she could draw another breath into her constricted lungs, her restraints fell away.

Oh, I've done it now.

Jeanette ought to run, she ought to scream, do something, yet all she was capable of was to stand there. The sheer force of his will held her spellbound, unable to move, those restraints far more effective than any chain could ever be.

Ty looked furious, and so damn sexy, it was hard to breathe.

"Remember you asked for this with your behavior, girl. Now strip and face the wall."

The edge to his voice brooked no argument, even if she had been capable of it, as Ty grasped the neck of his shirt and yanked it over his head. Muscles rippled, and her gaze followed the enticing trail of dark hair. It covered his pectorals, and arrowed into a happy trail disappearing under the waistband of his jeans. Her gaze lingered on his side, where the stitches remained in his wound. The all too visible reminder of how close he'd come to losing his life sent shivers of dread down her spine, because it brought it home more than anything else could have done that she had feelings for him. Convoluted ones, for sure, but feelings nevertheless.

Ty's hands went to his belt, and she jumped when he spoke again.

"I said strip, girl, *now.*"

Jeanette complied with shaking hands, and another one of these deep, dark growls rumbled from Ty's chest, when she stood before him naked. Try as she might she couldn't bring herself to look at him, had to fight the insane urge to sink to her knees, in fact. Lord only knew what was happening to her. She was losing the plot, because she could swear she could feel Ty's intense gaze like a physical touch, as he ran it over her naked body.

She jumped again when he cracked the belt through the air like a whip, the resulting snap far too loud in the quiet room. He stepped around her, running one finger along her skin. From the tip of her nose, around her mouth, down her neck, and along her collarbone into the valley between her breasts, he continued the silent exploration, the contrast of his much paler flesh next to hers a heady aphrodisiac indeed. When he cupped one of her breasts in his hand and lifting it, bent his head to suck her hard nipple into his mouth, Jeanette couldn't stop her whimper of need. Unbidden her hands tangled in his hair, to keep him there, as every hard suck made her pussy quiver in need. She could smell her own arousal in the air, as her juices slowly trickled down the inside of her thighs.

Ty bit down hard on the breast in his mouth, and the sharp pain of his bite made Jeanette cry out. Not in pain exactly, because she was far too turned on and already teetering on the edge of an orgasm.

"Please…"

Ty soothed the leftover ache from his bite by licking it, before he abruptly withdrew.

"I haven't given you permission to touch me, girl." He reached up to grasp her wrist, and Jeanette immediately let go of his hair. She caught a glimpse of his stern expression before he swung her around.

"Face the wall, and spread your legs, girl."

It didn't even occur to her to disobey, and when he joined her moments later his clean male musk enveloped her. He crowded her against that wall, the coolness of it against her skin a direct contrast against the heated male body pressing against her from behind. The feel of his chest hair against her back made her hyperaware of his harsh breathing. She closed her eyes against her shame, when he reached around and between her legs. There was nowhere to hide now, as confirmed by his next words.

"So fucking wet for me. You're mine now, girl."

A bite to her shoulder followed that possessive claim, and Jeanette cried out in surprise when he shoved two fingers into her pussy at the same time. Wet as she was they slid right in, and her internal muscles clamped down on the invaders. Ty thrust those digits in and out of her channel and adding another one, finger-fucked her with merciless precision. His cock was a hard, solid ridge against her hip, and he groaned into her neck again, when she spread her legs wider for him.

"Yeah, that's it, baby, your body knows who you belong to, doesn't it?"

Jeanette tried to respond, but nothing but a keening sound came out, because Ty curled his fingers to massage her G-spot. Pleasure surged through her hard and fast, and her hips took on a life of their own as she rocked herself against his hand, desperate to gain the friction she needed to her clit to get over.

Before she could get there, however, Ty withdrew his fingers, and slapped her ass hard. Jeanette moaned her denial and shoved her ass back into him in a silent bid for him to continue, but she should have known that was a useless exercise.

"No, your orgasms belong to me now, and you will not come without my permission."

One hand fisted in her hair, he pulled her away from the wall and marched her across to the cross. Jeanette's heart missed a few beats, and then turned into a jackhammer when she caught side of their reflection in the mirror on the wall.

She looked like she felt, a woman on the edge. Her eyes were too wide, her mouth, still swollen from his earlier kisses slightly open, her breasts swaying from side to side, and shaking with every harsh breath she managed to draw into her lungs, as he half dragged her along. Her skin already showed the marks of his possession, his bite marks clearly visible, and she groaned when his arm came round her waist, and he kicked her legs apart. It meant her swollen most intimate parts were clearly visible. Jeanette ought to be ashamed at how wet she was, at the needy sounds that immediately spilled from her lips, when Ty yanked her head back further, and rubbed his jaw along her neck. His breath singed her skin, and their gazes locked. His dark eyes flashed with dangerous intent, and Jeanette's internal muscles clenched in response, sending more moisture to her swollen lips. Ty smiled when he noticed, and his voice had dropped even further, sending yet more shivers of dread, or was it anticipation, down her spine. Her clit quivered, the usually tiny bud clearly visible at the top of her hood.

"Take a good look, titch. Your body doesn't lie. You want this, need it, even, and I'm just the man to give you what you need. All you have to do is ask."

He shoved his thigh in between her legs as she spoke, and Jeanette closed her eyes and gasped in helpless delight. The friction his thigh created against her sensitive pussy lips, torture and pleasure all in one. Torture, because it wasn't enough to send her over, just enough to keep her teetering on the precarious ledge between pleasure and the fall into an abyss so deep, she wasn't sure she'd survive it.

"Tell me you're mine, baby." Ty's whispered the words in her ear, while he nibbled along her earlobe, and delivered tiny bites along her neck.

She wanted to give in so badly, but Myrtle's face swam into her mind, and she sobbed her denial.

"I—I can't. Let me go."

Ty's immediate withdrawal from her didn't bode well. She cried out in pain, because he yanked her across to the padded, wooden structure by her hair. A shove sent her flying into it, and her breath escaped her lungs in a shocked whoosh at the force of the impact. She caught a glimpse of his closed off, angry expression, before he was on top of her. Using his considerable bodyweight he crushed her against the frame, and only let her go once her arms and legs were fastened to the thing. A blindfold followed, robbing her of her vision, and Jeanette started to fight, while calling him all the names under the sun.

A short laugh was the only response to her outburst.

The crack of his belt gave her a second's warning before the leather made contact with her ass, and Jeanette cried out at the strip of white-hot pain left behind. Before she could draw another breath, a second even harder strike happened, followed by a third. She dimly registered that he hit a different place on her butt every time, before the pain morphed into one big ache.

All the fight went out of Jeanette as he continued to punish her ass, varying the tempo and force behind the lashes of his belt. As abruptly as he started, he stopped, and Jeanette gasped when he molded his body against hers. His hard cock dug into her abused ass, and she winced as he rubbed his hips across them.

"Why did I punish you, girl?" he asked, his voice surprisingly tender as he stepped away and ran his hands over her shoulders, and down her back. She tensed anew, when he stopped just above her tender backside, and breathed a sigh of relief when he didn't go further.

"I would suggest you answer me, titch. As much as I enjoy making this ass glow, I don't think you're really up for anymore strikes. More's the pity. You did very well, taking your lashes, sweetheart."

The unexpected endearment further screwed with her state of mind, because he sounded as though he meant it. She read regret in those words laced in with pride, which made no sense at all. Neither did the tight feeling in her chest that came with the knowledge that she had pleased him.

A buzzing sound reached her ears seconds later, and before she could process what that was, she gasped as something cool slid along her exposed pussy lips.

"Relax, sweet, now comes the pleasure."

Ty's dark voice had the desired effect, helped along by the sudden vibrations against her clit. A long, drawn out moan came from her lips, one that Ty caught in the kiss he gave her, as he pushed that toy deep inside her pussy. Jeanette tensed and then shuddered as the egg shaped object settled against her G-spot. The vibrations kicked up, reigniting her earlier denied orgasm, and she found herself kissing Ty back.

He withdrew with a bite to her lower lip, and the vibrations deep inside her kicked up another notch, designed to hurtle her toward an orgasm so intense she found herself to be rather grateful for the cross holding her up.

"That's my girl, come for me now, and I want to hear you scream."

Jeanette didn't need any further encouragement, especially when something hot and wet licked around her clit. The thought of Ty on his knees behind her, send her over that cliff, and she did scream. Long, loud, hard, unable to withstand the dual sensation of the toy inside and Ty's talented tongue against her clit. Up and down her pussy lips, he licked, and nibbled, ran circles around her clit, before he sucked on it hard, bit down, and started all over again.

How many times Ty brought her release this time, she couldn't determine, as one ran into the other, with Ty murmuring encouragement into her pussy. When at long last the vibrations inside of her dimmed to a slow ebb, Jeanette went limp in her restraints. Ty chuckled, the tiny puffs of air tickling on her wet flesh, and another mini contraction rocked her body.

"So fucking responsive and beautiful. I wish you could see yourself, titch. In fact…"

Ty licked a path of heat along her pussy, and Jeanette gasped, as he parted her still smarting ass cheeks, and licked right up to her anus.

No one had ever touched her there, and Jeanette ought to be disgusted, ashamed even, but the opposite was true, especially as the egg's vibrations increased again, as Ty's tongue breached her hole. The sensation of him entering there was strangely exciting, and groaning, Jeanette pushed out her ass, as much as she could. Ty's hold on her butt grew painful as he squeezed the smarting globes, while he continued to tongue fuck her ass.

"Please. I … God, don't stop."

Jeanette grimaced at the needy, breathless quality of her denial, as Ty withdrew his tongue.

His dark laughter washed over her, and in the next instant, the scent of coconut filled her nostrils, seconds before one slick finger entered where his tongue had been moments before.

"Oh believe me, titch, I have no intention of stopping any time soon."

He added another finger, stretching her, and Jeanette had never felt so full. With his other hand he traced a heated path of awareness up her spine, until he could wrap it loosely around her neck. Robbed of her vision as she was, all of her other senses were heightened. She could swear she could feel every one of the hairs on his muscled thighs as he stepped closer, and kissed her again.

The sheer possessiveness of this kiss took her breath away, and she whimpered as he seemingly added another finger, stretching her tiny virgin hole to impossible widths. Yet, there was no pain, just a slight burn which morphed into pleasure when he started to thrust those fingers in and out her ass. The dual sensation of the toy in her cunt and his fingers up her behind, was overwhelming, too much, yet not enough, and she suddenly desperately wanted his cock.

As though he read her mind, Ty withdrew his fingers, and letting go of her neck ripped the blindfold of her eyes.

Temporarily blinded, Jeanette blinked furiously to get her vision to clear, and when she could finally focus, she saw Ty reappearing from the bathroom. Heat rose in her cheeks, seeing him dry his hands on a towel, and winking at her he stepped closer. Her throat went dry when he reached for a condom, and rolled it on his impressive length, and then slathered his sheathed cock liberally with yet more coconut oil.

"Tell me, titch, has anyone ever claimed your luscious ass?"

Jeanette couldn't tear her gaze away from the slow up and downward slide of his fist on his cock, and she shook her head.

"No, Sir."

Ty's dark eyes exploded in a burst of golden flecks at her bestowing that title, and his harsh features softened in a breathtaking smile that she wanted to see more of it.

"Good girl. I'm so glad to hear that. I'm looking forward to being your first then."

He stepped closer still, all lean muscle and sinews, a predator ready to devour her, and Jeanette swallowed hard, when he picked up a remote and flicked a switch. Instantly the toy inside of her went into overdrive, and Jeanette yanked on her restraints, as red hot pleasure surged through her again.

"No, please, I can't … not again, Sir … please."

Jeanette knew she was begging, but she couldn't help it. Everything inside of her screamed for relief. She wanted this torture, pleasure, whatever it was to end, yet she never wanted it to end either.

Ty's body wrapped itself around her again, his kisses everywhere at once it seemed as his hands roamed her body.

"You can and you will, but not until I'm ballocks deep in your ass, my love. Ask me for my cock."

Jeanette shook her head, and the sharp immediate pain to her scalp stopped her. Hands fisted in her hair, Ty stood behind her, forcing her to look at them both in the mirror, and try as she might she couldn't look away from the intense emotions swirling in his dark eyes.

"Ask me, or so help me I'll leave you hanging. I know you want this, so fucking ask me. You're mine, and I'll never let you go, so you might as well just accept it."

His voice broke on the last few words, and it was the intense hunger in his eyes, coupled with that flash of uncertainty that did her in.

Telling that barely still functioning part of her brain to take a hike, she whispered the words on her heart.

"Please, Sir, I want your cock."

Chapter Ten

Ty breathed a sigh of relief, hearing those words from her lips, only that breath came out more as a growl. Jeanette's eyes widened at his response, and he kissed her again. The way she opened to him, went pliant against him, made his chest feel tight with unwanted emotion. He was so fucked and not in a good way. Before he could give those strange emotions a name, he broke the kiss, and smiled at her.

"Good girl."

Taking his cock by the root, he lined it up with her untouched hole, and kissed her shoulder.

"Relax, breathe out as I push in, and yes … just like that. Fuck."

Ty forced himself to go slow, as he breached her hole, and pushed in. Just liked he'd hoped, she opened to him like a flower unfurling in the sun. He grimaced inwardly at the fanciful thought which he'd never live down, if the boys found out, and then he stopped thinking altogether.

A deep throated groan came from his girl, and Ty swore as her muscles clenched around him. The added vibrations from the toy still lodged in her cunt rippled along his dick through the thin membrane separating his cock from her channel. With a groan of his own, Ty pulled out and slowly pushed back in again.

"Oh, God, oh God … I can't … so full … please."

Wrapping one hand around her neck, the other curled around her hip, he started to thrust.

"Yes, you can. Come for me, sweet, because I won't last five seconds. You're so fucking tight."

Jeanette exploded around his dick, the rhythmic clenches around his cock so strong that his orgasm built in record time. His balls drew tight, and with Jeanette quivering in her release, he allowed himself to set the ruthless rhythm he needed. The cross shook with the force of their coupling, and the world went black as he filled the condom with his release while continuing to thrust in and out of her sweet ass.

When his dick stopped twitching, he rested his head on Jeanette's shoulder, and the vision slowly returned to his eyes, coupled with the feeling in his arms and legs. Sweat ran down his shoulder blades, and he struggled to draw breath, as he came down from his high. As for his girl… She stared unseeing into space, her eyes having taken on that glassy faraway look which told him she was floating in the happy place only a good scene could place a subbie in.

Pride warred with affection in his chest, and murmuring his praises to her, he slowly withdrew his softening penis from the tight clasp of her body.

Jeanette moaned, her body still quivering in aftershocks, and having tied off the condom and chucked it on the floor for now, he slowly dialed down the vibration of the egg still inside of her, mindful not to jerk her out of her happy place too abruptly.

The little quivers stopped when he shut the toy off, and Jeanette slumped against the cross. Her eyes fluttered shut, and her head lolled.

"That's my girl. You did so very well. Let's take you off this thing. There you go, my sweet."

Ty wasn't sure if she could even hear him right now, but he kept up his praising of her anyway, all through untying her, and carrying her across to the bed. A whimper escaped her when he fished the toy out her swollen channel, and despite his earlier spectacular release, his cock half hardened again, seeing her sweet cunt so thoroughly used.

Her clit was huge and engorged, and she was so very wet, her pussy hole still quivering in rhythmic clenches which pushed more of her sweet arousal out of her hole.

Giving into the need to taste her again, Ty scooted down the bed, flipped her legs over his shoulder, and lapped up her juices. He would never get enough of her sweet musk, and when she started to lift her hips up and into his face, he looked up to find her watching him.

A small smile played around her full lips, and her eyes had lost some of that glassy look.

"Please, Sir, I can't. It's too much."

Grinning, Ty blew across her pussy, and Jeanette tightened her thighs around his head, as her hips jerked upward.

"Oh, I think you can, baby, and I really want to claim this hole, too." He pushed his thumb into her channel, and her internal muscles immediately clenched around that digit.

Jeanette groaned and screwing her eyes shut, shook her head.

"Not possible, you can't be ... oh." Her eyes flew open in seeming surprise when he got to his knees and slid the tip of his now fully erect dick through her slit, until he could bump her clit. An all over body shiver was his reward, and Ty gritted his teeth against the exquisite pleasure of feeling her naked flesh against his sensitive head.

An image of her covered in his cum sprang to his mind, and it became of utmost importance to him to mark her as such.

"I want to fuck you again, but I don't want there to be anything between us. I'm clean. I get checked out regularly, and I know you've got an implant so..."

He kept up his shallow thrusts along her pussy,

torturing them both in the process, but seeing his girl go cross eyed, her breasts shaking with the force of her breathing was worth it all.

"How do you know that?" She gasped her question, and Ty smiled.

"Alex and James are whizz kids on the computer. I know everything there is to know about you, titch."

"Oh." He marveled at how far she'd come in such a short space of time, because he'd have expected her to argue with him and call him names, but she simply stared up at him.

Bracing himself either side of her head to keep his weight off her, he lowered his head to kiss her, and he inwardly high fived his foresight to have had this conversation when she was all languid from their lovemaking.

The label he had just given their sexual encounter was testament to how much fucking trouble he was in, and deepening the kiss, he put all that unsaid emotion into the kiss he gave her. When she kissed him back after a moment's hesitation with the same desperate need, he flexed his hips, until the tip of his dick breached her hole.

The feel of her cunt muscles gripping his dick, seemingly intent on pulling him inside her, meant he lost his ability to go slow, and wait for her answer.

He bottomed out inside of her in one hard thrust, and Jeanette arched underneath him. Her mouth opened in a silent O as he started to make love to her. And it was love, at least in his mind. They had a lot of ground to cover, still, but this woman was his, come what may. Her legs slid off his shoulder, as he bent down to enable him to rest his forehead on hers, and their gazes locked.

"Tell me this is okay. Tell me you want this. I need to hear you say the words."

Jeanette locked her ankles behind his ass, and slid

her arms around his shoulders, pushing her breasts into his chest in silent affirmation.

"Yes, please, so good. I'm … God … don't stop … yes, there…"

The rest of whatever she was going to say dissolved into gasps and moans as Ty changed the angle of his thrusts. Missionary had never been his favorite position, but with Jeanette writhing underneath him, dropping kisses on every part of him that she could reach, it was fast becoming thus.

The feel of her hot, wet cunt contracting around him as he forced himself in as deep as he could go, her sighs and mewls, and the way she met him thrust for thrust … yeah, that was something else.

Giving into his innate need for control he pinned her arms above her head, while he continued to thrust in and out of her in ever increasing speed. Their gazes locked, and he grinned at what he saw in her expression. Right now she was an open book, vulnerable, exposed, her need and pleasure his for the taking. Ty imagined he probably looked the same, and he had to swallow the words bubbling on his tongue, back down again.

It was far too soon to declare his feelings. Besides this woman had the power to destroy him, to destroy them all, and he had to keep that in mind, no matter what his heart was telling him.

Instead he bent his head and taking one of her hard nipples in his mouth he sucked hard.

Jeanette groaned, and she clamped down on his dick in a stranglehold that made him see stars.

"Fuck, do that again, baby."

He mumbled the words in between switching from one nipple to the other, drinking in the taste of his woman. The harder he sucked the more Jeanette gripped him, and when he felt the ripples of her impending orgasm along his dick, he picked up the speed of his thrusts. Jeanette came around his cock with a gush of liquid to soak them both, and he followed close behind. He climaxed with a shout to rival her scream of completion, and pulling out of her he emptied himself all over her quivering belly, aiming the last spurt at her boobs, before he collapsed on top of her. Ty rolled slightly, mindful to not squash her completely, and pulled her with him until she half lay on him, with her head on his chest.

His limbs felt like lead, and dropping a kiss on her hair, he smiled at her content sigh.

"We should get cleaned up, but I can't move right now, baby."

The slight giggle that shook her shoulders made his grin deepen, especially as it was followed by the soft sounds of her snoring. He wasn't exactly surprised at the fact of her falling asleep. He, too, could do with recharging and pulling the covers over them both with his free hand, he closed his eyes.

****

Jeanette woke up to an annoying buzzing sound, followed by the loss of the nice warm cushion she had been cuddled up to, and the deep rumble of Ty's voice. Reluctantly she opened her eyes, and it dawned on her that she had fallen asleep on Ty. She ought to be ashamed of her actions, but the slight ache in her butt and the delightful soreness between her thighs left no room for shame. Rather it made her clit tingle anew, and she had to force herself to not give into the instincts to lick the scars on Ty's back. Sitting up on the edge of the bed, he was listening intently to the man on the phone, and a shiver of unease crawled up Jeanette's spine when she recognized the voice. It was Huntly, and he didn't sound happy. Neither did Ty, as he replied to him.

"With all due respect, boss, I don't think she's ready for that... Yes, I realize that, but you did give her to me to... No, of course not, sir, but... Very well, I'll make sure she'll be there."

Ty clicked his phone off and threw it toward the bottom of the bed with a sigh, before he got up and ran hand through his dark hair. He started to pace, and froze when he noticed she was awake.

"How much of that did you hear?" he asked.

Jeanette swallowed hard and it was on the tip of her tongue to deny having overheard anything, but the expression on his face stopped her, as he ran his gaze over her exposed chest. Heat rose to her cheeks as she glanced down to see the marks of his possession. His cum had dried on them leaving white marks on her dark skin, and the half-moon bite marks had darkened to form bruises.

The old Jeanette would have been horrified at seeing those all too visible reminders, but this new version of her, the very one who wanted nothing more than to jump the man looking down at her, smiled. She clenched her thighs to relieve the immediate ache between her thighs, made ten times more potent by Ty stepping closer and running his fingers over his marks.

"You look fucking hot covered in my cum, baby. I like seeing my marks on you." He fisted his hand and pulled away with a frown, as though he'd said something he shouldn't have, and Jeanette belatedly answered him.

"What does Huntly want me to do that you think I'm not ready for, Sir?"

Ty's eyes flashed in some deep emotion which made her heart beat faster when she added that title. Amazing how easily it rolled off her tongue now. Jeanette tried really hard to resurrect her anger at Ty, at this whole situation, but she couldn't quite get there. No doubt it would return with a vengeance when she came face to face with Ren, but after the pleasure Sir had wrung from her, she couldn't be angry with him. He had given her a precious gift, after all. She wasn't that frigid cow she had been labeled.

Some of her thought processes must have shown on her face because Ty sat back down and cupped her chin.

"You're thinking mighty hard there, titch. Care to share with me what's going on in that pretty brain of yours? And yes, that was Huntly. He wants you to dance tonight. It seems your disappearance has been noticed, and he doesn't need more police sniffing around. It's bad enough that fucking Wonsan is hanging around, supposedly off duty."

Jeanette couldn't help her wince at the mention of that policeman, and of course Ty noticed. She fidgeted under his silent regard and crossing his arms over his chest Ty waited.

"Is there something you need to tell me, girl?"

The generic "girl" stung far more than it ought to, and it was for that reason alone that Jeannette shook her head.

"Nothing at all. I can dance as long as that's all Huntly expects me to do."

Ty's gaze intensified, and a muscle ticked in his jaw, the only movement in his tense frame.

"Meaning?" he asked.

Feeling far too exposed Jeanette tried to pull the covers up to hide her nakedness.

"No." Ty grasped her wrists and stopped her. "Don't ever cover up in front of your Dom. I like what I see, and I want an answer. What did you mean, as long as you only have to dance?"

Jeanette worried her bottom lip with her teeth,

and immediately stopped when Ty growled his annoyance.

"I don't think I can do anything else. Please don't make me."

Ty's sigh made her insides clench. Her heart did a funny little flip when he smiled at her.

"I would never force you, titch." She couldn't quite help her snort in answer, and Ty flicked her nose.

"Not in that anyway, and neither will Huntly. If you just want to dance, then that's all you'll do. I'll make sure of that, baby. Now, as much as I would love to go for round three, we need to get a move on. Go and clean up."

Jeanette's mouth went dry as Ty picked his jeans up off of the floor and yanked them up his muscled thighs. The fact that he didn't bother with underwear sent another tingle of awareness to her clit.

Ty stopped mid pulling his shirt over his head, and smirked at her open ogling of him.

"You keep looking at me like that, and I'll forget that you're no doubt sore as hell right now, and pin you back to this bed. Better still, fuck you in the shower."

He laughed at her sharp intake of breath and bent to pick up his boots.

"However, we really haven't got the time for that, so you have a shower here, and I'll have one in my room. Meet me in the kitchen when you're dressed. I'll leave the door unlocked."

"You will?" Jeanette's voice rose in her astonishment, and leaning across the bed, Ty dropped a fleeting kiss on her lips.

"Don't make me regret my trust in you, sweetheart."

With one long last searching look at her he took the steps three at a time. The door whooshed shut behind him like it always did, but, sure enough, they were no clunks of bolts being drawn. Adrenaline coursed through her at the thought of freedom.

She could simply run up those stairs and take off. Her muscles locked and she had taken several steps toward that staircase before she caught sight of her herself in the mirror and she started to laugh.

What am I thinking?

She was stark naked, for starters, and no doubt once she made it up those stairs and through the door, she still had to find her way out of here. Jeanette had no idea of the layout of this place, only that it had to be huge. After all, all the Cleaners seemed to live here, and she thought it safe to assume that they would all have their own rooms.

Besides, the mere size of this cellar meant the upstairs had to be humongous. Add to that the small fact that she had no idea where she was exactly, had no money or means of transportation, and she was just as stuck as she had been when chained.

She wasn't going to listen to that little voice in her ear, which insisted that she also didn't want to violate Sir's trust. That would suggest an entirely different motive for her staying put, and she was not about to acknowledge those feelings. Not even to herself, not ever, no sirree.

Having had the shortest shower humanly possible, and dressed in jeans and a simple t-shirt, which she coupled with platform sandals, Jeanette frowned at her messy hair. It would take hours to dry and straighten it, so instead she simply twisted it up as best she could into an unruly half ponytail, and taking a deep breath, ascended toward that ominous looking door.

By the time she got to the top and pulled the handle to find it indeed unlocked, her rapid breathing would have done any marathon winner proud. Her insides churned in fear, or was it hope? Ty had scrambled her brain so effectively that she couldn't put a label on the swirling emotions battering her soul right now, so she stopped trying. Instead she adopted the mantle of feigned confidence, which had served her well up 'til now. It meant she put an extra swagger in her step, and held her head high, as she started to walk down the long hallway.

I will not be intimidated. I will not ... will not...

She valiantly repeated that mantra in her head, as she followed the oriental runner covering the polished floor boards, and tried her best to not gawk at the original artwork on the walls. The solid oak front door loomed large in front of her, and her heart threatened to go into cardiac arrest, when her cursory visual inspection confirmed that it did indeed appear to be unlocked. It would be a matter of moments to turn the handle and see for herself. She hesitated, as male laughter traveled toward her from the back of the house, and presumably the kitchen.

Ren's deep gravelly tones made her stomach churn. She'd hoped to have more time before she had to come face to face with the killer of her sister. Alas, it would appear to not be so.

Fucking typical.

The creak of the stairs to her left made her swing round, and her mouth went dry when she caught sight of the mountain of a man standing on the bottom step. Arms crossed over his massive chest, this guy was watching her with an unwavering intensity that made her fear for her life. This one had to be Josh. She'd heard of the ex-MMA fighter. He sure looked as though he could knock out an opponent with one punch.

A smirk started to appear on Josh's face, as he let his amber gaze travel slowly up and down her body.

Jeanette barely resisted the urge to wrap her arms over her boobs when his gaze lingered there, not least because the t-shirt was a little on the snug side there. It was an age old problem for her. She either spent a fortune on clothes specifically designed to accommodate women who were big up top, or she ended up buying tops three times too big, which dwarfed the rest of her, so that her cleavage wasn't in any man's face. As Susie had bought her clothes, a woman who was clearly very comfortable in her curves, she hadn't thought of that.

If Jeanette had been blessed with the hourglass curves the redhead had been, then maybe she would be, too. Instead she had to put up with bazookas far too big for her slim frame, which always meant folks assumed they were fake. Naturally it also meant that men and women alike always talked to her boobs. All but Ty, and she realized with a start, Ren, Huntly, and Susie, too.

Even this guy, once he seemed satisfied with what he'd seen, kept his gaze focused on her face.

"You scrub up well for Myrtle's sister."

The mention of her sister brought Jeanette's chin up higher, and amusement danced in this man's eyes at her reaction.

"Ty let you come out to play then? I sure hope you weren't thinking of shaking your tight little tushy out of that open door, subbie."

Jeanette fought and lost to the blush stealing into her cheeks, and to hide her discomfort, she inched her nose even higher and gave him what she hoped was her best haughty look.

"My name is Jeanette, not subbie," she said.

Josh threw his head back and laughed, an action which meant Ty stuck his head through the open kitchen door. He frowned at the other man, and held out his hand toward Jeanette.

"There you are, titch. Come on in. We've just brewed a fresh pot of coffee."

"Are there cookies to go with that coffee?" Josh's deep rumble from her side held such a comically hopeful note that Jeanette had to smile as she glanced toward him. He looked far less menacing now that he grinned, and rubbed his rock hard abs.

Ty laughed and winked at Jeanette.

"Trust you, Josh. This one only ever thinks with his stomach, titch, as you'll discover."

"Oh, not just that." Josh made a lewd hand signal before he rubbed the rather impressive bulge hiding in his jeans, and Jeanette took several steps back as Josh stalked toward her. Hands either side of her face, he crowded her against the wall, when that structure stopped her retreat, and Jeanette threw Ty a nervous glance when this Josh leaned down and sniffed the air right next to her ear.

"Hmm, she smells good enough to eat." He pulled back at Jeanette's sharp intake of breath and shook off Ty's hand which had landed on his shoulder.

"Chill your beans, Ty. We all know she's off limits." Giving her another one of those slow appraisals which made Jeanette feel as though she was standing naked in front of him, he eventually grinned. "So, as I can't partake of her services, tell me she can at least cook, like Susie."

Ty gave him a shove, and the big guy stepped away from her. Jeanette had never been more willing to take someone's hand than when Ty held out his, and yanked her to his side.

"Answer the oaf, Jeanette," Ty said. "Though I have to say, the longer we're debating this, the slimmer the chances of there being any cookies left for you. Susie made a fresh batch, and I know Ren must have had half of them already."

"Fuck that."

Josh looked utterly outraged, and Jeanette couldn't suppress an involuntary giggle, when the huge guy stuck his bottom lip out in a pout that wouldn't have looked amiss on a schoolboy.

"See, what we have to put up with, girl. First Ren won't share, now Ty won't, and they're keeping the food goodies away from me, too. It's not fair. Please tell me you make cookies."

Jeanette shook her head, and another giggle escaped her, when Josh sighed in rather overdramatic fashion, and put his hands over his heart.

"Oh, you wound me. So, if you don't cook, what can you do, apart from dance that is?" Clearly judging her surprised expression accurately, he nodded at Ty behind her.

"Ace filled me in on the performance she gave in her audition. He said it was spunk fodder for ages."

Ty growled his seeming annoyance behind her, and pulled her closer to him, while splaying his large hand possessively over her midriff. The tips of his fingers brushed the underside of her breasts, and Jeanette gasped. She was far too aware of him as it was. Great sex appeared to turn you into a raving nymphomaniac. Then again the feel of his cock hardening against her ass might also have something to do with her thoughts immediately turning to sex. She gave a little wiggle, and Ty groaned and pulled her closer, still. It made her feel much better about her wayward thoughts, as did the way Josh winked at her. It took some of the sting out of what he was saying.

"You can tell Ace from me to find some other material to rub off to."

Josh laughed and started to walk toward to the

kitchen.

"Tell him yourself, Ty. I'm not doing your dirty work for you."

"Neither should you." Ren's deep voice put a dampener on Jeanette's mood. Standing in the entrance to the doorway, he blocked the way in, and he looked far from happy.

"You haven't answered the question, girl. What are you going to bring to the house, other than fucking trouble, and a few convenient holes for Ty to use? And I gotta tell you, dancing is not going to cut it. We can get that at the club."

Chapter Eleven

Jeanette tensed in his arms, and Ty groaned under his breath. Despite his earlier talk with Ren, the man seemed determined to disrespect Jeanette. Ty really didn't want to start a fight with his best mate, but they were fast heading that way.

"Don't be such an ass, Ren," he said, instead of acting on the impulse to rearrange the man's face with his fists.

"I'll stop being an ass, when you start thinking with your head instead of your dick, Ty. You can't trust her."

Something sounding like a growl erupted from the woman in Ty's arms, and before he could say anything, she'd shaken off his hold on her, and advanced on a bemused looking Ren. Ty shook his head at Josh, who looked ready to grab her as she stormed past him in the narrow hallway. She stopped inches apart from Ren, and taking a full swing slapped him hard around the face with so much force she left a red handprint behind. Susie gasped behind Ren, and the head of the Cleaners stopped the next slap aimed at his face with ease. Grasping her wrists, he twisted Jeanette around until she faced Ty and yanked her arms up in a way designed to hurt. Sure enough tears sprang into her eyes, but she fought against the hold anyway.

"One slap is all you get, girl. Tell your woman to behave, Ty, or she'll live to regret it." Ren gave Jeanette a shove which sent her flying past an uncomfortable looking Josh, and into Ty. Before she could spin back round to have another go at Ren, Ty repeated the move Ren had used on her.

"Stop it, titch, I don't want to hurt you."

His grumbled words at last got through to her,

and she stopped struggling. If looks could kill, however, Ren would be six feet under for sure, because she continued to glare at him.

"Let me go, Sir."

Ren quirked an eyebrow at hearing Jeanette address Ty so, and Josh whistled through his teeth, whereas Ty was hard pushed not to high five the air in triumph. As that would have been highly inappropriate he hid his smile in his girl's shoulder, and added for her ears only.

"Good girl." Pulling back slightly he raised his voice. "Only if you promise to behave yourself, titch. Assaulting any of the inhabitants of this house is not permitted."

"I wouldn't, just him. And I slapped him. Hardly made a dent in his thick hide. If you want to see assault, however, I shall gladly comply with your request ... *Sir.*"

Jeanette's sassy reply made Josh laugh, and even Ren's dark eyes twinkled in amusement.

"I should fucking kill him for what he did to my sister."

Ren's amusement dissipated instantly, and Jeanette pushed back into Ty's body as though she was seeking his protection. While he inwardly rejoiced at her instinctive reaction, his gut twisted seeing the quiet fury on his friend's face. Ren stopped inches away from Jeanette, and while she yanked her head up to look at him, Ty didn't miss the tiny tremors shaking her frame.

"Let go of her, Ty, and let's see if she actually has the guts to try that."

"Sir, please." Susie's plea made Ren tense further, and the redhead flinched at his sharp reply.

"Stay out of this, Susie."

Josh grumbled something under his breath, crossed his arms over his massive chest, and glared at a spot at the opposite wall. Out of all of them Josh had the biggest soft spot for Susie, and it always irked him tenfold when Ren upset her.

"No, I won't stay out of it, Ren." Susie's trembling words must have caught her dearly, and Ren swung 'round to glare her instead. Ty had a hard time processing hearing Susie address Ren by anything other than "Sir", himself. Even Jeanette gasped softly, clearly recognizing the enormity of this moment. "Myrtle was her sister, and regardless of what we all thought of her, she is entitled to be upset over her death. Just let her say her piece and then we can all move on. I'm sure she wouldn't really want to kill you, right, Jeanette?"

Arms crossed under her chest, Susie glared at the trembling woman in Ty's arms, and he released his hold on her when she slumped against him and shook her head.

"No, I should, but lord help me, I couldn't do that. Not now." Her whispered words tore a strip of Ty's heart, because there was a wealth of unshed tears behind them. Raw grief, which he recognized only too well, and the desperate need to make sense of it all.

Ren sighed, ran a hand through his silver hair, and facing Jeanette again, grasped her chin to study her expression.

Something like fleeting remorse crossed his ragged features, and he flicked a glance up at Ty and nodded.

"She had to die, girl, and I'm not sorry I killed her, but I *am* sorry she was your sister." Jeanette and Susie both gasped at those murmured words.

"I can only imagine how much it must hurt to lose a sibling." Ren paused, and a quiet look of understanding passed between him and Ty. Ren had no siblings, but he'd been there for Ty, when Ty's brother had been blown to smithereens, had witnessed Ty falling apart, and he was clearly drawing on those times right now to offer the olive branch to Jeanette.

"Were you close to your sister?" he asked.

He stepped back whilst speaking, and Susie scrambled into his outstretched arms with a small squeal. Ren pulled her close and kissed the top of her head, his harsh features and tense stature relaxing with every second he held his girl in his arms.

"Not, really, but … if I had been then … damn it." All the remaining fight went out of Jeanette, and when Ty grasped her shoulders and gently turned her to face him, he wasn't at all surprised to see the tears clinging to her eyelashes.

"You couldn't have stopped her, even then, baby," Ty said.

Jeanette shook her head.

"Listen to Ty, girl," Ren said. "He's right. Myrtle was a law onto herself. She enjoyed the dancing and the whoring she did." Jeanette flinched at those words, and Ty glared at his friend over her head. A small smile played around Ren's lips at Ty's reaction, and he flipped him the finger.

"It's the truth, Ty, and you know it. She was never a victim in this. That bi—your sister," Ren corrected himself at the last minute with a wry grin at Ty, "knew exactly what she was doing, and far more importantly she knew the consequences for her actions, yet she *chose* to betray the trust Huntly had placed in her anyway. I wouldn't want to even hazard a guess as to what drove her. Greed, I suspect, and a complete and utter disregard for the feelings of others, let alone the danger she placed anyone else at the club under by her actions. By all means mourn the sister you remember, the sister who inspired such loyalty in you that you came to the club, determined to seek your revenge, as misguided as those actions were. Don't mourn the bitch we threw in the canal, however. She deserved everything she got and more, and any guilt you might feel about not being there for her, dismiss that right now. It's not worth your life, and believe me, were it not for Ty here, you wouldn't be standing there right now, so I suggest you'll be nice to him and *let this go.* I have no wish to have more blood on my hands. We've got enough to do with the fucking turf war to expend energy on fighting among ourselves, and as much as I don't like the idea, Ty's claimed you, which makes you one of us. So, obey the rules, and we'll all get along just fine."

Susie lifted her head to look across at Ty and Jeanette, and she smiled when she saw Jeanette nod. It was the slightest of movements, but a veritable weight lifted off Ty's shoulders anyway, and Ren relaxed further.

"We need to hear the words, titch." Ty grimaced at the hoarse quality of his voice, and Josh smirked at him. Yeah, talk about wearing your fucking feelings on your sleeve. Had it not been for Ren and Susie, Ty knew he would have been the butt of jokes in the house for months. Probably still would be, until the next one of the Cleaners fell hard, and Ty couldn't shake the feeling that they all would sooner or later. Nothing quite like having a happy couple in your midst to make a man reevaluate his life, after all, not that Jeanette and he could be classed as such, but he hoped in time they would be. She sure as fuck couldn't leave their protection, so one way or the other she was stuck with him.

"I'll try, that's all I can promise."

Jeanette's whispered words carried in the stillness of the hallway, and not caring about their audience, Ty fisted his hand in the loose ponytail at her neck, tipped her head up and kissed her. The fact that she immediately opened to him on a soft whimper, and pressed herself closer into his solid frame, every soft curve a perfect counterfoil against him meant he took the kiss much deeper than he'd first intended. When they eventually broke apart, it was to catcalls and whistles from the Synn brothers.

"Get a room, for fuck's sake. You'll make us bring up our breakfasts."

Alex and James wore identical smirks on their faces, and ignoring them Ty pulled Jeanette past them and into the kitchen.

She hesitated at the entrance seeing Ren sitting at the table with Susie by his feet, resting her head on his thigh, but at Ty's gentle nudge she adopted a similar position by Ty's feet when he sat down. Wordlessly Josh slid two coffee cups across the table, and when Ty handed Jeanette one, she accepted it with trembling fingers. After a moment of hesitation she inhaled deeply, closed her eyes, and then proceeded to sip the fragrant brew slowly. Ty froze halfway to drinking his own cup, and his dick punched forward with a speed that made him glad he was sitting down. Fuck him, if Jeanette didn't make the simple act of drinking coffee look as though she was making love to the cup. She seemed utterly unaware of the effect she had on the assembled males in the room. Alex and James readjusted themselves with a groan, Josh swore under his breath, and even Ren seemed transfixed by the sight of Jeanette's full lips wrapped around the rim of the cup.

A slight blush spread across Jeanette's features, when she opened her eyes to find everyone staring at them, and then Ace's mocking voice broke the moment.

"Well, isn't this fucking cozy? Haven't you bunch of assholes got jobs to get on with? Huntly wants your woman at the club, Ty, and the rest of you, I've got a tip-off that shipment's going down this afternoon. We can't go in en masse but I need a few of you guys."

Jeanette blinked, Susie paled, and Ren fisted the air.

"Finally, Ty has babysitting duties." He smirked in Ty's direction, as he said that. "I've got a meeting with Huntly, after I dropped Susie off at work, but then I'm all yours."

Josh and the twins added their agreement, and they all filed out of the kitchen to discuss strategies out of earshot of Jeanette and Susie, who never liked to hear the particulars.

Having lost the use of her Sir's thighs, Susie stood and took another batch of biscuits out of the oven. The aroma that filled the kitchen made Ty's stomach rumble loudly, and laughing the redhead plated the few remaining ones of the earlier batch she'd made and placed them on the table in front of Ty, before she sat down on the chair Ren had just vacated.

"There, that's all that's left, I'm afraid. Give it five to let those ones cool down, and you can demolish them." She hitched her thumb over her shoulder, and addressing Jeanette patted the seat of the stool next to her.

"Come sit at the table to eat. That's all right with you, Ty, yes?"

Ty didn't miss the unspoken challenge in Susie's voice, and he smiled. Little Susie was submissive through and through, but she had spirit in spades, and it seemed she had decided to take Jeanette under her wings. Sure enough her next words confirmed that. "We got off on the wrong foot you and I, but if you're staying here, I'd like us to be friends. I sure could do with another woman in the house to keep these domly types in check, I tell you."

Ty laughed, just as his phone started to vibrate in his trouser pocket. Pulling it out he frowned at the display, and stood.

"I've got to take this. Go and eat something, titch."

****

The tone of his voice gave Jeanette pause as Ty shot to his feet and left the kitchen. Not being able to lean on his legs also left her feeling strangely bereft, which made no sense at all, as she struggled to her feet and looked after him with a frown.

"Here sit, and let's talk." Susie's calm voice meant Jeanette did just that. She shook her head at the plate Susie nudged toward her.

"No, thank you, I'm not really one for biscuits. I'll have some more coffee though. No, don't get up. I'll get it myself." She tried to stop the other woman, but Susie shook her head, and did it anyway.

"It's no bother, you sit there. You've a lot to take in, after all."

Susie getting up, and refilling her cup, gave Jeanette a few precious minutes to gather her thoughts. Ty's deep rumble carried up the hallway. She couldn't hear what he was saying, but he didn't sound happy, and her heart squeezed painfully in her chest at that thought.

She took the fresh brew Susie placed in front of her, as Ty's voice grew more distant.

"Who do you think is on the phone? He doesn't sound happy, does he?"

The minute the words were out of her mouth Jeanette frowned. What did it matter if he was happy or not?

"It's confusing isn't it?" The quiet understanding in Susie's voice further rattled Jeanette, and instead of answering her, she shrugged and took another sip of coffee.

A not entirely comfortable silence fell between them, and eventually Jeanette had to say something.

"I don't understand any of it. I should hate him, yet … fuck."

Susie's giggle seemed utterly inappropriate under the circumstances, but it also put Jeanette at ease.

"I know, yet you can't help but love him, can you?"

Jeanette's immediate denial hovered on her lips, but the knowing look in Susie's eyes stopped her.

"I can tell you're not ready to admit that to yourself, and that's okay. There's no need to say it, when your feelings are there for all to see."

"I'm not sure I know what you mean."

Even to her own ears that protest sounded hollow, and sure enough, Susie simply smiled.

"You've come a long way in the last week or so, Jeanette. You wouldn't have accepted Sir's apology, which, by the way, I'm still amazed he made, at all a week ago. Probably would have kneed him in the balls I reckon, or at least tried."

A grudging smile formed on Jeanette's lips at that mental image.

"I still might," she said, but she knew deep down that she wouldn't. Not least because she dreaded to think how sore her ass would be if she pulled a stunt like that, but because it would hurt too much to see the disappointment in Ty's eyes. "Dammit, I should hate them all."

"But you don't." The quietly utterly statement held such conviction that Jeanette let it sit in the room. There was no point in arguing the truth.

"They killed my sister. They're all criminals, for fuck's sake."

Susie stretched across the table to put her hand over Jeanette's. The simple comfort made her want to cry again.

"They are, but they're also good guys in their own right."

Jeanette snorted in answer, and Susie squeezed her hand and leaned back in her chair.

"They are, and believe me I know how much of a mind-fuck that is to admit, especially to yourself, and especially with what happened to your sister, but Sir is right. The sister you knew and the one we met, are not the same. Not by a long shot. No offense but Myrtle was a royal bitch." Jeanette flinched hearing those words, but she didn't contradict Susie either. What was the point? She was right, after all.

"That raid they're planning tonight…"

Susie's voice broke, and when Jeanette looked up, it was her turn to reach out to the other woman, because she looked utterly terrified.

"They'll be all right, I'm sure," she said. "They seem to know what they're doing after all."

Susie offered her a wobbly smile.

"They do, but taking on the Priestlys like that is dangerous, not least because the police always seem to turn a blind eye to their schemes. I mean, I know Huntly has some of the police in his pockets, but clearly they do, too, and it turns my stomach. Their girls … well, they're not there because they want to be, and some of them are so damn young. The Priestlys are scum, that's all."

Susie's words gave Jeanette further pause for thought, and they also made her feel slightly better about her growing feelings toward Ty.

"The boys never discuss their work in front of me, because they know I don't like to think about them out there, getting in harm's way, but I know what they're up to anyway. Tonight's thing has been in the planning for months. It's a major dent in the Priestly operation if they can pull it off."

Jeanette gave Susie's arm another squeeze.

"Surely Ty should be there, too, then?" she asked and Susie shrugged.

"He should, but Huntly needs me at the club, and those fucking injuries mean I'm not at my best, so Ren won't let me attend." Ty's voice held a quiet fury which raised the fine hair on Jeanette's neck, but it was the worried undertone that got to her more. Sure enough when she turned her head to look at him, a deep frown marred his features, and he didn't quite look at her.

"Have you finished, because I really need to swing by somewhere on the way to the club?"

Jeanette shot to her feet, and nodded.

"Sure, but why… I mean, yes, Sir."

Ty's smile in answer didn't reach his eyes, and nodding at Susie, he held out his hand and when Jeanette took it, he pulled her along and out of the house.

It seemed strange to be in the outside, and Jeanette blinked in the sunlight that hit her in the face the minute she stepped out through the front door. She blinked again, in sheer surprise this time, when Ty pulled her along to a huge looking motorbike, and handed her a helmet.

"Glad you're wearing trousers, because there's no time to change. The boys will need the cars, so this will have to be our transport. Here put this on, too." He took a leather jacket off the seat, and draped it around her shoulders. "It will be a bit big on you, but it'll offer you some protection, should anything happen."

Jeanette swallowed hard at the immediate gruesome images that sprang to mind, mainly of them being tangled around a tree or something.

Ty laughed as he helped her into the jacket, when she struggled, and having zipped her into it he placed the helmet on her and secured the chin strap.

Flipping her visor up, he flicked her nose with his index finger.

"Ever ridden pillion before, titch?" he asked.

"No, Sir."

"Well, then, you're in for a ride. And don't worry, I do know what I'm doing, and you'll be perfectly safe. Just hold onto me and don't fight the movements, okay? The back of a motor bike is not a place to be sassy."

"Okay."

"Good girl, hop on then."

Ty put on his own helmet, and got on. Once she'd managed to climb on behind him, the engine purred to life underneath them, and Jeanette gasped at the vibrations travelling up through her core. Ty rolled the bike off its stand, and she scooted closer to him with a shriek. His big shoulders shook as though he was laughing at her, and Jeanette frowned.

"It's not funny." She had to shout to make herself heard over the roar of the engine. "Where are we going to anyway?"

Ty tensed under her hands.

"To see my mum."

Chapter Twelve

Ty felt rather then heard her gasp of surprise, and to stop any further conversation, he flipped his visor shut and revved the engine hard before he cruised off the driveway. Opening the throttle he tanked it down the road, and despite the knot of worry churning in his gut, he grinned at the death grip his girl had on him. He was pretty sure you couldn't get a hair's width between them. Every inch of her delectable body was molded around him, and under any other circumstances, his dick would be making a bid for freedom right about now, but that particular body part had gone into hiding.

If he lost his mum now ... no, that didn't bear thinking about. Mama was tough as nails, and she'd had these funny turns before and been perfectly fine after them, or as fine as a frail old woman with a chronic heart condition could be. He took it as a good sign that she had refused to go to the hospital. The nurse he'd spoken to had sounded positively harassed and at the end of her tether, which either meant his mother was running rings around her, or she was sicker than the nurse had let on.

Mum would not want to worry him, but the staff was under strict instructions to inform him of any change in her condition, and as Ty hadn't managed to visit her in close to a month now, he wouldn't rest until he'd reassured himself of her state of health with his own eyes.

Taking Jeanette to see her so soon had not been in his plans, but that couldn't be helped. Like it or not, until she had proven her loyalty, one of them—and preferably him—had to watch over her.

It made missing out on tonight's raid slightly easier to bear. Ty smiled grimly at Jeanette's terrified shriek as he leaned right over into a corner. He didn't miss the fact that she did as she'd been told, which was just as well, because any sudden moves from her at the speed he was taking these bends would have ended up with a wobble of the bike he might not have been able to recover from.

Banishing all maudlin thoughts from his head, Ty gave himself over to the sheer joy of riding the Harley. When he had to slow down to weave in and out of traffic, he smiled at the glimpse of their reflection he caught in shop windows. If he had to hazard to guess, his little titch had her eyes screwed shut and was probably praying.

To reassure her a little he switched on the intercom between their helmets.

"How are you holding up back there, girl?" he asked. Her death grip loosened as she startled in seeming surprise, and her sharp intake of breath rang in his ears.

"You're trying to kill me, right?"

She thumped his thigh when he laughed at that, only to grab tight again when he moved away from the traffic lights.

"There are easier ways of doing that than taking you on a ride, darling. Relax and enjoy it."

He grinned at her lack of an intelligible reply, when he opened up the throttle again to take the A-road which would take them to the leafy suburb his mother's nursing home was located in. She relaxed enough to talk to him when she realized he didn't need to take any corners on the almost straight road.

"So, your mother?" she asked. "Why are you taking me to see her? I mean, won't she wonder who I am, and such like. What do you want me to do? Pretend to be your girlfriend or something?"

"Or something."

Another sharp intake of breath and a rather prolonged silence was his reward for that response. In truth he had no idea what he was going to say to his mum. It all depended on what he would find when he got there, after all. If Mum was with it, and he sure as fuck hoped she was, she would look through any lies, so he'd have to stick as close to the truth as he could.

"Let's just play it by ear, titch. She's in a nursing home, and she's not well." Another one of those sharp intakes of breath, which said a thousand things without the use of words.

"And before you ask, no, she does not know what I do for a living. She thinks I work in security, and I'm just a club bouncer. I would appreciate it if you didn't disabuse her of that notion."

Silence greeted his earpiece, and he could almost hear the wheels turning in her head. Nothing further was said until he pulled up in the car park of the former country house which now housed the exclusive nursing home. Ty waited for Jeanette to scramble off the bike, then pulled it up on its stand and killing the engine got off himself. By the time he'd taken off his helmet, Jeanette had managed to get hers off, and having plonked it on top of the pillion seat attempted to rescue her hair. He rather adored the messy locks she was currently sporting, but judging by the muttering she did under her breath as she tried to finger comb the ebony mass Jeanette was less enamored of her hair.

"Leave it, titch, you look beautiful."

Jeanette pulled a face, and she looked all poised to argue with him, until he quirked an eyebrow, and fixed her with a look daring her to disagree with him. Placing his helmet next to hers on the seat, he held out his hand, and after a moment's hesitation she took it. A gasp escaped her when he pulled her into his body.

"Come on, let's go."

The gravel crunched under his boots, as he

rounded the corner to the entrance of the building, at which point he finally became aware of the reluctance at the end of his hand.

"Wait, Sir, please. I'm not sure … maybe you should go in by yourself."

Turning on the bottom step of the wide stone entrance, he regarded Jeanette through hooded lids. The urgency to see his mother burned a hole in his guts, but seeing his girl worry her bottom lip with her teeth, as she followed the slow progress a nurse made up the ramp with an elderly man in a wheel chair, bothered him almost as much.

"I can't leave you here," he said.

"Why not? I don't even know where we are exactly. It's not as though I could make a run for it, now is it? Besides where would I run to? You Cleaners would only track me down, and I really don't want to end up as the next lot of fish food."

Her voice broke on the last few words, and Ty gentled his hold on her hand. A sigh escaped her when he ran his thumb over the back of her hand, and grasping her nape pulled her close enough to him to rest his forehead on hers.

"That's not going to happen, girl. I told you already you're mine now, and no one is going to touch you, but me."

Another one of those rapid inhales, and when he pulled back and tugged on her hand again, she followed without any further resistance.

His gut churned anew as he approached the front desk, and the receptionist gave him a distant, slightly apologetic smile, as she continued her phone conversation.

She must be new, because he didn't recognize her, and subsequently he remained rooted to the spot, rather than charging up to his mother's rooms. Besides she might well be in the hospital wing, if she was bad, and that thought darkened his mood further.

He hadn't realized he'd fisted his free hand by his side, until Jeanette stepped around him, grasped that hand, and smiling up at him briefly, turned to ring the bell on the desk repeatedly.

The receptionist glared at her, and Jeanette reached over and with a smile hit the disconnect button on the phone.

"Hey, you can't do—"

"I think you find I just did. Especially as I'm sure you don't get paid to make personal phone calls, especially when you have anxious clients waiting. This man…" She glanced back at Ty, who was watching the proceedings with a certain amount of amusement. Jeanette had beaten him to it. While he didn't want to create a scene, he had been on the verge of throttling the raven-haired receptionist, when it dawned on him that she was on a personal call.

"He's received a phone call saying his mother is not well, so, unless you want me to scream blue murder and take this to whoever manages this expensive dump, you give him some attention, and tell him what he needs to know."

Jeanette pulled a much needed breath into her lungs, and Ty intervened before she could carry on ripping the now mortified looking receptionist a new one.

"Breathe, titch," he murmured and pulled her back behind him. "I've got this."

Jeanette shot one last venom filled look at the hapless woman behind the desk. Arms crossed under her impressive rack, Jeanette stepped to the side.

"I'm sorry, sir, I didn't realize, I—"

"Never mind that." Ty interrupted the

meaningless apology with a flick of his hand, and the girl, Chelsea, according to her name tag, paled. "Theresa Mason, how is she and where is she right now?"

He took it as a good sign that Chelsea blinked and started tapping on her keyboard. Had there been any further emergency that morning, his mother's name would surely have rung a bell with her. After all, private calls notwithstanding, she had to be good at her job, otherwise the home wouldn't have employed her. Ty chose this place for its high standards, after all.

After several seconds of tapping, which seemed to drag on forever, she finally looked up and smiled.

"Ah, yes, I see. Mrs. Mason was seen by our in-house doctor early this morning, after complaining of chest pains. She was pronounced well, but then took a turn for the worse." Chelsea shot him a glance from under her fake lashes.

"This must have been when you were called. Her carer logged a phone call to the next of kin. Mrs. Mason refused further treatment, but it says here, she brightened up considerably once she heard her son was on his way. Sounds as though she just wanted to see you. Happens all the time. I see it's been a while since you last visited, after all."

Again she smiled at him, and Jeanette made a rather disgusted sound at the back of her throat. She was positively glaring at Chelsea.

"So you're a doctor now, as well as a useless receptionist?"

Chelsea blinked, her mouth doing silent goldfish impressions until she recovered.

"I'm not. I mean, I wasn't suggesting that … heavens, I shall just find out where she is right now."

"I would appreciate that, Chelsea." Ty gave the flustered woman his best *melt any female's panties in an instant* smile, and sure enough a slight blush spread over the young girl's cheekbones.

Jeanette positively bristled next to him. It was almost as though she was jealous, which should have been a ridiculous notion, because that would mean that she had developed actual feelings for him, yet the way she continued to stare down the other woman, made him wonder.

Placing his hand on her nape he pulled her closer to him. It broke the death stare she was giving Chelsea, and he shook his head at Jeanette. A mutinous flare of something crossed her features, before she dropped her gaze to his collarbone and left it there.

"Ah, here we are. I believe she's in her room. Let me check with her carer."

Chelsea picked up her phone again, and after a quick conversation she addressed Ty.

"Mrs. Mason is currently in the garden. She requested some fresh air. If you want me to—"

"No need, I know where she'll be." Ty interrupted the woman, and turning on his heel strode off, after nodding at Jeanette to follow him.

****

Jeanette stared at Ty's departing back, and mindful of the curious looks she got from the other people milling about in the foyer, she hotfooted it after him.

What else could she do, especially after the foolish way she had acted in front of that Chelsea person?

Jeanette still wasn't entirely sure what had made her act so out of turn, but seeing Ty all tense and worried left standing there, while that blasted woman planned her next night out, and then the shameless flirting the hussy had exhibited, not to mention the careless way she had dismissed Ty's mother's symptoms… Yeah, she had seen red. Okay, maybe to call it flirting was an exaggeration, but that blasted woman had definitely liked what she'd seen in Ty, and he was hers, dammit. And when he'd smiled at the damn woman…

Jeanette almost tripped on the stairs going down into the garden, as that thought slammed into her brain.

When had she started thinking of Ty as hers? He'd said she was his, but then he no doubt meant that in the possessive term only. She was his to punish, after all, and her butt still smarted a little bit, after the lashings with the belt he'd given her. The bike ride had aggravated the few leftover bruises. Bruises she had traced in the mirror after her shower with a small smile.

Yep, I've lost the plot, pure and simple.

As much as she would like to claim temporary insanity however, she couldn't deny the tightness in her chest and the lump of emotion which clogged up her throat, when Ty's rapid steps slowed to a halt, as he approached the pond. There under the shade of a willow tree sat an incredibly frail old lady. The clothes hung off her frame as though she had lost a fair amount of weight recently, and the mobile drip located next to the bench spoke volumes. Clearly Ty's mother was far from well, a thought which must have occurred to Ty, too, because he scrubbed his palm over his face, blinked away suspicious looking moisture in his eyes—an act which made her already tender heart soften a little more toward him—and taking a deep breath in, visibly collected himself before he made his presence known.

"Mummy, will you stop scaring everyone?"

Ty's mother startled, dropped the crossword she had been engaged in, and her lined face broke into a wide smile, when she spotted her son. Jeanette hung back, as Mrs. Mason held out a hand, fingers thickened and curled by arthritis, and her heart missed a few beats, when Ty got to his haunches in front of his mother, and kissed the inside of her hand, before his mother placed it on his face.

"Well, it got you here, son, didn't it?"

Ty threw his head back and laughed, and Mrs. Mason smiled again. Her blue eyes, still surprisingly clear and intelligent, considering her advanced age and frail health, twinkled in amusement, and she shrugged when Ty berated her gently.

"Don't do that, Mummy. That phone call scared the bejesus out of me. They made it sound as though … well, never mind. I'm just glad you're okay." He glanced up at the drip, and taking both his mother's hands in his sat down next to her on the bench. "What's that for?" he asked.

"Oh, apparently I'm not drinking enough, and I've got an infection in my waterworks, so the doctor put me on extra fluids. Waste of time, I tell you. All that does is make me wanna pee every five seconds, and who's got time for that nonsense? Anyway, he wouldn't let me go and come sit on your father's bench, unless I agreed to this, so…" She frowned at the line going into the back of her hand, and Ty sighed.

"You've been told about this before, Mummy, really."

Jeanette's heart gave another suspicious little bump in her chest, but, seriously, hearing him call his mother *mummy*, especially in that affectionate tone of voice … well it seemed a livewire straight to her libido.

Belatedly she noticed the plaque on the back of the bench.

In loving memory of Albert Mason, much loved husband and daddy. May you always sit in the sun.

Another emotional punch to her fragile emotional

state, because it was pretty clear that Ty's family were close, unlike hers.

She couldn't hear the rest of the conversation between mother and son, as they both dropped their voices. Mrs. Mason seemed to have noticed Ty's bruising, because she ran her fingers over his face and was clearly telling him off.

Ty threw a glance at Jeanette over his mother's head, and her heart beat faster when he disentangled himself from his mother's caress and stood.

"I brought someone to meet you. Mummy, this is Jeanette. She's a…" He hesitated briefly as he held out his hand to her, and stepping closer Jeanette finished his sentence for him.

"I'm a friend of your son's. Nice to meet you, Mrs. Mason."

Ty frowned at her, but he didn't contradict her, and Mrs. Mason intelligent blue eyes drew together in a frown. For several heartbeats she simply looked between Jeanette and her son, and then finally patted the seat next to her.

"Sit, sit, don't make an old woman crane her neck. A friend you say? Really, is that what you call it nowadays?"

"*Mother.*"

Jeanette sat down with an inelegant thump, and Mrs. Mason laughed, and waved Ty away.

"No need to 'mother' me. You don't ever bring a girl home, so excuse me for being curious. You sit down, too. You're spoiling the view."

Ty frowned, but dutifully sat down on the opposite side. Jeanette couldn't quite decipher the dark look he aimed at her, and then her attention was taken up by his mother, as she grasped her hands.

"He doesn't?" Jeanette inwardly winced at her

inane question, all too aware of the intensity of Ty's gaze burning into her.

Instead of replying his mother grasped Jeanette's chin in a seeming effort to study her. Jeanette barely resisted the urge to fidget under that silent examination. Whatever the other woman had read in Jeanette's expression seemed to satisfy her, however, because she nodded, smiled, and then released her hold on her.

"No, he doesn't, my dear. *Friend* or otherwise."

"Mother, *please*. You're embarrassing her." Ty's voice held a note of exasperation, and his mother shooed him away like you might an annoying fly.

"Hopscotch. Besides, that blush is rather becoming on her skin tone. Tell me, you're mixed race, right?" At Jeanette's nod, she smiled and flicked a glance toward an uncomfortable looking Ty. "Thought so, who was what, if you don't mind me asking?" she said.

"Mummy, I really don't think, that's—"

"Hush now, boy. You can't expect me not to ask these questions, when you bring a girl to see me." Mrs. Mason cut off Ty's protest with a flick of her hand, and it was rather amusing to see him snap his mouth shut.

"I have an interest in genetics you see, and besides it will help me to picture my future grandbabies."

Jeanette blinked in surprise, and Ty shot off the bench with a growl.

"Mother, really, whatever makes you think that…"

Ty stopped talking when his mum fixed him with a look only a mother could give to her child, and it was rather fascinating to see the dark stain spread across his cheekbones.

"Besides, you don't mind answering my nosy questions, do you, Jeanette?"

Jeanette opened her mouth to say, yes, she did

mind, actually, but the desperate hope shining back at her out of the depths of this fragile woman's eyes stopped that denial.

"No, of course I don't, but I have to say, I have no intention of having babies anytime soon, with your son or anyone for that matter."

Mrs. Mason's gaze intensified, and Jeanette got the distinct impression that this woman was seeing far more than she let on.

"Is that so? Are you or are you not having sex with my son?" Ty's mother asked. Another one of those delicious growls came from Ty, and Jeanette could see him start pacing in her peripheral vision. In any other circumstances she would have found his discomfort rather amusing, but she seemed to have left her sense of humor back on the Harley. Her throat closed up, and she simply nodded.

"Well, then, it is reasonable to assume that such activities will eventually lead to babies. No contraception is one hundred percent effective after all, is it?"

Mrs. Mason's gaze never once wavered from Jeanette's face, and not knowing what to do she threw a glance at Ty. If she had hoped for any help from him, however, she was sorely disappointed, because he simply threw his hands up in the air, and shook his head while glaring at the back of his mother's head.

When the silence stretched to uncomfortable lengths, Jeanette managed to mumble her reply.

"I guess not, no, Mrs. Mason."

"Call me Theresa, my dear. Mrs. Mason is far too formal under the circumstances. So, who was black, your father or your mother?"

Jeanette blinked again, and answered without thinking.

"My sperm donor."

Theresa blinked, and Ty went as still as a statue.

"My mother was white, and before you ask, I never knew my father. I have very vague recollections of a large, black man, who made my mother cry, before he disappeared never to be seen again. Good riddance if you ask me."

Theresa grasped her hands, stilling the frantic movement of her fingers, and the silent compassion in her blue eyes made Jeanette's walls crumble.

"I'm so sorry, my dear. That must have been hard to witness."

Jeanette tried for a nonchalant shrug, and failed miserably.

"It wasn't that bad. My sister had it worse." Ty drew in a sharp breath at her mention of Myrtle, and she daren't look at Ty, as she continued.

"She was never even sure who her father was. I'm pretty sure mum didn't know either. She was too far gone on booze and drugs to care much about either of us, but that was okay. We had each other." Jeanette smiled remembering those times, when Myr followed her around, and Jeanette could do no wrong in her eyes. "I was five years older, so it fell to me to look after her. It was us against the rest of the world, you see."

Theresa squeezed her hand in silent understanding.

"You sound as though she's not…"

Jeanette sniffed loudly and nodded.

"Yes, she was mu… I mean she passed away recently."

Ty stepped around to place his hands on her shoulders, whether to reassure her or to warn her to be careful what she said, Jeanette couldn't quite determine. As his spicy cologne and the very essence of virile male surrounded her, she did lean back into his strength, however, drawing comfort from his presence.

An action which clearly wasn't lost on his mother, because she released Jeanette's hands and smiled.

"I'm so sorry. We lost Ty's brother far too early, too. It's never easy when that happens, regardless of the circumstances, and I can tell they weren't the norm. Is that when you met my son?" Theresa asked.

Ty saved Jeanette from having to answer that far too dangerous question by responding.

"Jeanette dances at the club I work security for. We met at her audition."

Theresa blinked twice, and Jeanette couldn't bring herself to look at the older woman, sure to read disgust in her eyes now.

"I see. What sort of dancing if you don't mind me asking?"

Jeanette wanted the ground to swallow her whole, and again Ty answered for her.

"The usual sort that happens at a club, Mum. She's very talented, a dance teacher in fact, and she volunteers at a center that teaches underprivileged kids."

There was a clear challenge in Ty's voice as though he dared his mother to disagree with him. Some sort of silent communication seemed to be going on between mother and son, not that Jeanette paid too much attention to them. She was still trying to process the fact that Ty had clearly run a background check on her, and that he almost sounded … what? … proud of her? That couldn't be right, however, could it?

She was saved from coming up with an answer to that question bouncing round in her head by Ty's mother however.

"I see, well that's very admirable. One last question, if you'll indulge an old lady, please." She grasped Jeanette's chin again and smiled.

"It's clear to me by the dagger looks my son is throwing me that he cares very much for you." She held up her free hand to seemingly interrupt Ty, whose hold on her shoulders grew painful for a second before he relaxed his viselike grip. His sharp exhale brought with it the hint of coffee and mint, and stirred the strands of hair determined to fall into her eyes.

"So, let me ask you this? Do you love my son?"

Chapter Thirteen

Ty stopped breathing for the long interminable seconds it took before Jeanette answered his mother. He never should have brought her here, but the only other option would have been to confine her back in the cellar, and he hadn't wanted to do that either. They were finally making progress after all, and leaving her locked up would have set them back again.

Jesus, though, Mummy is in form today.

"I ... I don't know. We haven't known each other long enough ... and it's complicated."

Jeanette's halting reply made warmth spread through his chest, and he was hard pushed not to grin like a fucking fool. He couldn't help himself from sliding his hands up her shoulders, until his thumbs caressed the sensitive skin under her ears. Sure enough her heart beat jumped under his fingertips, and from his vantage point, he could see her t-shirt strain over her boobs as her breathing sped up.

His mother flicked him an amused glance, and then smiled at his girl.

"It doesn't have to be complicated. I knew from the minute I laid eyes on Ty's father that I was in trouble. I fought it, of course. We can't make it too easy for these men, after all." She stopped and fingered the delicate day collar around her neck, which Ty knew hadn't left its place since his father had placed it on her. Growing up he hadn't known what that meant, but he'd known its significance since he'd been a teenager. Back then he'd been horrified at the mere thought of his parents having sex, let alone of the kinky sort, but as a grown man he'd appreciated the fact that his mum and dad had had the sort of relationship he could only hope would one day be his.

He felt rather than saw Jeanette's surprise, when it no doubt dawned on her what that was, and his mother tucked the collar back away under her clothing.

"Anyway, I think I'll go and have a lie down now. It was nice to meet you, Jeanette. Ty call Anton over here, he'll take me back to rooms. No, he will." His mother forestalled his protest. She hated him seeing her in a wheelchair, he knew that, and she wasn't strong enough to walk more than a few steps nowadays, so one would be needed to take her back to her room.

"Give me a kiss, son, and find him for me. He was lurking in the shrubbery earlier."

Sure enough Anton appeared as though he'd been anticipating his mother's move, and maybe he had. The middle-aged carer seemed devoted to Theresa, after all, and approached now with a wide smile.

"I'm here, so you can stop giving your son grief now, Theresa."

He smiled at Jeanette, who had scrambled to her feet, and looked at anyone but Ty, it seemed. She startled when he grasped her hand and bent down to kiss his mother's paper thin cheeks.

"Don't take so long to come see me next time," Theresa said, and traced his left over bruising again. "And be careful out there. I couldn't bear to lose you, too."

"I will, Mummy, I promise," Ty said.

Jeanette stepped forward when Theresa held her hand out.

"Look after my son, my dear. He's got a tender heart under all that bluster, just like his father did. If you let him, he'll never make you regret being with him."

Jeanette didn't say anything to that, and Ty rolled his eyes.

"Stop meddling, Mama."

"It's a mother's job to meddle, son, now be off with you."

Taking his cue, Ty kissed his mother one last time, and pulled Jeanette along behind him. He didn't stop until he was out of sight behind the shrubbery and then turned to watch the painfully slow process that was transferring his mother from bench to wheelchair.

"Fuck."

Jeanette tugged on his hand to get his attention, and when he glanced her way it was the quiet compassion in her expressive chocolate eyes that did him in.

"We should go, Sir. She wouldn't want you to see her like this."

Ty knew she was right, but he couldn't *not* watch either, until Jeanette rose on her tiptoes and kissed him.

It was a mere brush of her lips against his, but he groaned anyway, because it brought with it the scent of his woman. Caramel, spice, with a hint of coconut oil and the unique sweet musk that was his girl, and he wasted no time to take the kiss deeper, while moving them further into the dense foliage and out of sight. He crowded her against the tree, and the breath left her lungs on a soft moan, which he caught in his ever more passionate kiss, as he ground his rock hard dick into her cunt. Catching onto the idea, Jeanette brought one of her legs up around his hip, and she whimpered, when he dry humped against her in a pretty good fucking imitation of what he wanted to do for real.

Tearing his mouth from hers, he glanced down at her flushed complexion, and seeing the same need reflected back at him, he growled his next words.

"I want you, girl."

The most delightful blush spread across his girl's features, as he reached between them and fumbled with his zipper.

"Now, here, Sir?" she asked, the slight tremor in her voice such a fucking turn-on, he groaned as his hand freed his dick.

"Right now, girl. This would be a fuck load easier if you wore a skirt, but we'll just have to work with what we've got. Pull your jeans and panties, down, spread your legs and face that tree, *now*."

Jeanette jumped, and her gaze snared on his heavy erection, as it bobbed to his abdomen when he succeeded in yanking his own jeans off his ass.

Instead of obeying his order, the sassy little minx sank to her knees and before he could stop her, wrapped her hands around the bottom of his shaft. Ty saw stars when she closed her mouth around his sensitive head and swirled her tongue around and under his corona. A moan escaped his girl when he grasped her hair to keep her right where she was. The vibrations of that moan traveled down his dick and settled in his balls with a speed that left him lightheaded. Bracing one hand on the tree, he fisted her hair harder, causing her to moan again.

Forcing himself to look around, and satisfied they were not about to be arrested for lewd conduct, he growled his demand.

"Fuck, yeah, you work my dick, titch. Make it good now, and don't you dare spill a drop."

Seeing and feeling her nod, her gaze locked with his, while her plump lips stretched around his dick robbed him of the last of his restraint. When she slid one of her hands down to his balls and started to fondle them, Ty swore again.

"That's my girl. Fuck, yeah, take me deeper, swallow, that's it, so fucking good."

All conscious thought left him, when she started to deep-throat him in earnest, and his balls drew tight in record time. Ty took over, fucking her mouth with every forward jerk of his hips, loving the feel of her throat muscles tightening around his dick, as she swallowed and gagged around his length. The barely functioning rational side of his brain told him to take it easy, that they were in public, and making far too much noise, but the exquisite pleasure her talented mouth and tongue wrung from him in that moment paid no heed to any caution.

Ty hurtled toward his release with the velocity of a high speed train, and when he forced his eyes open not wanting to miss the moment he pumped her sweet mouth full of his spunk, the sight of his saliva slickened cock disappearing into her mouth proved too much.

Pushing in as far as he could, he emptied himself into the soft, wet haven of her mouth with a muffled curse. He wanted to growl his release into the air, as tears streamed down Jeanette's face with the effort required to keep on milking him. Nostrils flaring she swallowed convulsively, trying her best to take all he gave her, and seeing the dribble of cum escape her mouth and trickle down her neck was the hottest fucking sight ever, made ten times more erotic by the sound of people walking past. When his dick at long last stopped twitching Ty pulled out of her mouth and grasping her by the shoulders, yanked her up to her feet. Crowding her back against the tree, he kissed her, tasting himself in with the sweet scent that was his titch. She gasped into his kiss, when he got her jeans open with one hand, and slid his hands down her quivering abdomen and into her panties, until he encountered her slick folds.

"Always so fucking wet for me. Time to reward my girl for a job well done." He growled the words into her neck, while he licked away his cum off her sweat dampened skin, and finger-fucked her with ruthless precision. He caught her needy mewls in his mouth, while pumping two fingers in and out her quivering channel, and rubbing his thumb across her clit.

Jeanette tensed and shook, her thighs trembling around his hand, as she came with a gush of her arousal coating his fingers. Ty clamped his free hand over her mouth to stop her from making too much noise as she convulsed under his fingers, eyes wide and staring right into his soul. Something shifted inside Ty at the utter trust he saw in her gaze at this moment, and his dick surged back to life.

"That's my girl." He whispered the words, in between delivering kisses along her jaw. "You're so fucking beautiful when you come for me."

Before Jeanette had even stopped shaking in aftershocks, he spun her around, pulled her jeans past her hips and down to her ankles, and yanking her ass back spread her wide for him.

"Hold onto that tree, my love, and bent over. I need to fuck you properly."

With a strangled groan Jeanette complied, and Ty damn well near swallowed his tongue seeing her submit so freely and without inhibition.

There was something incredibly dirty, primal, and downright hot seeing her pert ass stuck out at him. Faint bruises from his belt marred the otherwise perfect skin. He squeezed the marks, and a deep throated groan escaped his girl.

"Oh yeah, this ass is mine. Tell me you're mine, girl, to do with as I please, anytime, anywhere."

He ran a hand through her glistening slit, her labia still delightfully swollen, and Jeanette gasped, when he reached around and shoved his digits slick with her arousal into her mouth.

"Taste how wet you are for your Sir. Such a perfect little slut for me, aren't you?"

Jeanette tensed and shook her head, and withdrawing his fingers Ty grasped her hair to pull her head around.

Tears shimmered in her eyes, and Ty felt a right heel when she whispered her denial.

"Please don't call me that, Sir."

"Why not?" he asked, and she swallowed hard.

"I don't like it. Please, Sir."

"Good girl, I won't then."

"Thank you, Sir." Her tremulous smile made him feel ten feet tall, and grasping the root of his dick he lined it up with her hole and pushed inside. Jeanette's eyes fluttered shut and her mouth opened in a silent scream, while her internal muscles clamped down on his dick like a warm, wet fist.

"Fuck yeah, you keep doing that, and it will all be over in seconds." One hand buried in her hair, the other grasping her hip, Ty pulled out until only his thick head remained inside her sweet cunt, and then thrust back in all the way. Jeanette moaned, his balls hit her clit, and she pushed back against him. Together they found a fast, furious rhythm, the wet sounds of their rough coupling barely masked by the noise of an airplane flying low in his approach to Heathrow Airport, whose flight path the nursing home was on.

When he reached around to flick her clit, Jeanette exploded around him with a muffled shriek as she bit into her arm, and Ty followed her right over that cliff. Pushing in as far as he could, he emptied himself deep inside her body, and as Jeanette's legs gave way, he grasped her around the waist to stop her fall. Together they collapsed onto to the mossy, slightly damp grassy area that made up the ground of their impromptu sex den. Pulling out of her caused an avalanche of their combined fluids to splash onto the grass. He sat his naked ass down, and pulled his still shaking girl down onto his lap. She winced as her no doubt sore pussy made contact with his hairy thighs, and pulling her head on his shoulder, Ty rubbed soothing circles along her back.

By the time both their breathing had returned to somewhat normal patterns, his backside was going numb and he didn't even want to contemplate what exactly was poking his asshole.

His lips quirked at the ridiculous sight they must make, both of them with their jeans round their ankles, all sweaty and spent from their strenuous escapades, and when he nudged her chin up to see her expression, she, too, smiled.

"Feeling better now, Sir?" she asked, and Ty kissed her nose.

"Much, thank you, my sweet girl, but we make a ridiculous sight, and we need to get out of here and cleaned up."

Heat suffused his girl's cheeks, and she dropped her gaze to his collarbone.

"Though it was fucking hot. The only way we could have improved on that would have been if I'd had my ropes. Hmm, just think, you out in the open, spread wide for my pleasure, tied between trees, and completely at my mercy."

He chuckled at Jeanette's sharp intake of breath and the feel of her wet pussy rippling along his naked thigh.

"Oh, my naughty girl likes that idea, I see. We'll have to do that then, though perhaps not in the gardens of my mother's nursing home, huh?"

A lighthearted giggle shook Jeanette's frame, and she buried her face in his neck.

"God, do you think anyone heard us? And even if they didn't they'll all know what we've been up to. I must look such a mess."

"Hush, now girl. You're beautiful and look thoroughly fucked."

Jeanette flinched, and he shook his head at her reaction.

"That's a very good thing in my book, and fuck what anyone else thinks. Besides, I pay this place enough hard cash to turn a blind eye. They do a good enough job of looking after my mum, but they have zero business turning their nose up at anything I do."

He paused when he noticed the quiet intensity in which Jeanette was studying him.

"How long has she got?" she asked, and Ty swallowed hard against the sudden sharp pain slicing at his insides.

"I don't know. No one knows." He scrubbed a hand across his face, and closed his eyes to stop the tears lurking there. He wasn't a fucking pussy, damn it.

The feel of Jeanette tugging his hand off his face made him scowl at her, but it didn't seem to faze her.

"Stop pretending to be the big bad," she said. "Even serial killers love their mothers, especially when they have a mum like yours."

"Is that what I am in your eyes? A serial killer?"

His voice sounded far too fucking hoarse even to his own ears, but fuck him, if her answer to that question didn't mean far too much to him.

"Are you?" Her whispered reply left him reeling, and it also forced him to take a good, long look at his life.

"Serial killers are psychopaths. I'm not. Have I killed? Damn straight, baby, and I'll continue to do so when it's necessary. There's a lot of bad shit happening out there, and if I can make a small difference by whatever means, legal or illegal, then you can bet your cute ass that's what I'll do. Do I sometimes get a kick out snapping some asshole's neck?"

She gasped at that question, and Ty swallowed down the rapidly rising bile at her horrified expression to his words and continued.

"The fuck I do, yes. There's great satisfaction in seeing the lights go out in some cunt's eyes, and before you ask, yes, sometimes I go hard. Guess that makes me a monster, after all, but you've asked me a question, and I'm not going to lie about it. Do I need violence to get off? Nope, but it sure gets me in the mood."

He let his words sink in, and when Jeanette didn't take off down the path screaming her head off he relaxed a little.

"I *am* the big bad, titch, don't ever think I'm not. We all are, but we don't go 'round killing indiscriminately, despite what you might have been told about us, and despite the treatment you've received at our hands so far. If we were, we'd have killed you the minute we found out who you were."

Jeanette flinched but she also slowly nodded, and the weight crushing his chest slowly lifted.

"I realize that … Sir."

She offered him a tremulous smile, and giving into the need to taste her again, he kissed her. Jeanette fisted her hands in his shirt, and kissed him back. It took tremendous effort to break the kiss, and even more to will his burgeoning erection away.

"We should get going. Huntly wants you to sign a contract, and I dare say there are things you need to do to prepare for dancing tonight."

He smiled grimly when she slowly nodded, his blood reaching boiling point already at the thought of other men lusting after what was his.

"That's all I'll have to do, though, right? Dance?"

Ty framed her face in his hands, nodded, and kissed her again, putting all his unsaid emotions into the kiss, and this time when they drew apart he stood up, taking her with him.

Wordlessly they righted their clothing, and after Ty had checked they were unobserved, they exited from their hidey-hole.

Ty ignored the curious glances aimed their way, and once they reached the cool interior of the hall, he gently extricated his hand out of the death grip his girl had on him, and steered her toward the toilets.

"Go freshen up a bit. I'll meet you back out here."

Head down, Jeanette took off toward the ladies' as though the hounds of hell were after her, and chuckling to himself, Ty took the door marked *Gents*.

When he reemerged five minutes later, he wasn't surprised to see Jeanette hadn't come out yet. He leaned back against the wall to wait, only to be approached by Anton.

"Glad you're still here, Mr. Mason," the other man said, and Ty frowned at Anton's odd tone of voice.

"Is my mother okay? Has something happened?" He stared up at the wide staircase leading to the residents' rooms and breathed a sigh of relief when Anton shook his head.

"No, Theresa is fine. Well, as fine as a lady of her age with a fatal heart condition is ever going to get."

Ty swore under his breath, and Anton put a hand on his arm.

"Look, son," he paused when Ty shook his hand off and glared at him.

"I'm not your son, Anton."

Far from looking suitably remorseful the older man grinned.

"Once you get to my age, you're all youngsters. Figure of speech, only, I don't mean no disrespect, and I know I'm overstepping the mark here, but don't leave it so long until you come to visit her next time, especially not looking like that."

He gestured to Ty's face, and Ty's scowl grew in proportion to the need to rearrange this man's face with his fists.

As they were in public, however, and a wide-eyed Jeanette approached them now from the ladies', he tempered his words, and voice, and slowly relaxed his fists.

Even so, some of his thought processes must have shown on his face, because Anton's smile slipped, and he took a step back.

"Don't you think I fucking know that, man? Why do you think I stayed away all this time? I didn't want her to see me like this."

Jeanette stepped closer and slipped her hand in his in a silent gesture of support, which worked wonders at deflating some of his anger.

"She'd rather see you battered and bruised, and know you're alive, son. Your mother is a shrewd woman. She knows what you do."

Chapter Fourteen

Ty's arm jerked in his surprise, and Jeanette squeezed his hand to help. Why it mattered to her she couldn't even begin to fathom, but hearing his mother knew of his real job had clearly come as a shock to Ty.

"I'm sure I don't know what you mean."

Ty's voice could have cut glass with its clipped cadence, and to hide her body's immediate response to *that* tone of voice, Jeanette snuggled closer into his side. It had the added advantage of hiding her disheveled appearance somewhat, as there were far too many people milling about. She'd been utterly horrified to see her reflection, because she looked like she felt. Dragged through a hedge backwards, with a stupid grin on her face, her eyes far too bright and shiny. In other words, like a woman who'd just been laid, and damn good at that.

Choosing to ignore the conflicting emotions bombarding her insides, she'd dashed inside a cubicle, and cleaned up as best she could. Her sopping wet knickers were ruined beyond repair, so she chucked them in the bin. Going commando under her jeans felt oddly freeing, and certainly beat the feel of damp undies.

She should have known that the surprises weren't over yet. Her whole life seemed to have been turned into one giant rollercoaster ride from the minute she clapped eyes on the man, who now ran a hand over his face in a telltale gesture she was fast coming to love.

Her heart turned over and missed a few beats at the mention of the L-word, just like it had done when Ty's mother had pinned her in place with her far too knowing gaze and had asked if Jeanette loved her son.

What she felt for Ty was just lust, that's all. It had to be, because any other alternative didn't bear thinking about.

He's a goddamn killer, remember that.

So what if there was much more to him than that? So what if his voice shook as he addressed Anton?

"She can't know. She would have said something to me."

Despite herself, Jeanette pressed closer still, and there was something almost desperate in the way Ty put his arms around her and pulled her in front of him. It meant she couldn't hide behind him anymore, but somehow, that didn't matter. Not when the arms holding her tightened and he nuzzled briefly into her neck and inhaled.

She heard him swear softly for her ears only, as Anton resumed talking. Jeanette stopped listening, far too aware of Ty tensing around her, and when the two men at long last parted company, she wasn't entirely surprised at Ty simply pulling her along and back to the motor bike.

He looked deep in thought as he helped her back into the jacket and helmet.

"Do you want to talk about it?" she finally asked as he shoved his own headgear on.

"No, there's no point. She must be so fucking disappointed in me."

Jeanette's bruised heart broke a little more for him, and she shook her head.

"I don't think anything you could ever do would disappoint her. Your mother loves you. You're lucky."

Ty's gaze intensified as he focused on her, and he surprised her again when he smiled. This moment, right here, he didn't look like the hard-nosed killer he was. Instead a myriad of emotions chased each other across the darkened landscape of his eyes. Like fireworks in a night's sky they exploded in his dark gaze in flecks of amber which held her spellbound. He looked as though he cared, truly cared, and that thought really shouldn't make her feel giddy with happiness. It did, however, and Jeanette found herself smiling back at him, like a besotted, lovesick fool.

"I know I am, titch." He paused, flicked his visor down, and the resulting click in her ear told her he'd also switched the intercom on.

"I'm sorry you didn't have that growing up, and for what it's worth, I think you've grown into a remarkable young woman that any mother ought to be damn fucking proud of."

The words settled deep inside Jeanette's hurt soul. Neither one of them said anything, as Ty started the engine and cruised out of the car park. Jeanette simply hung on tight, and once they reached the open road, she had to concede there was something about being on the back of a motorbike, handled by a clearly experienced rider. She's been too terrified to let herself enjoy the ride over, but as she relaxed into the knowledge that Ty had her, she took note of other things. The feel of the wind rushing by, the steady vibrations which added delicious pressure to her core, the hard muscles she was touching under her fingertips. With a sigh, Jeanette snuggled in, and screeched in delight this time, when Ty expertly took a corner, and straightened them up again with ease.

His amused laughter rang in her ear.

"That's my girl. Starting to enjoy this now?"

"Maybe."

Ty reached back to pat her thigh with his gloved hand, and she bit back a grin.

"Minx."

By the time they finally pulled up outside the club, and Ty had secured the bike out back it was late afternoon, and the inside of the club was a hive of activity.

Susie was busy behind the bar, and Ty handed Jeanette over to a curvaceous blonde.

"Meet Kim. She'll show you around backstage, and get you your outfit to dance in. I've got to see Huntly."

"Ah, okay."

Ty dropped a quick kiss on her lips, slapped her ass, and disappeared, leaving a Ty-shaped hole in her heart.

Jeanette hadn't been aware of staring after him until Kim snapped her fingers in front of her face.

"Earth to the newbie. I know Ty has a rather cute ass and all that, but focus here, will you?"

Susie laughed and regarded her through narrowed eyes, while she continued to polish the glass in her hand.

"Did something happen while you were out riding with him, Jeanette?" Susie asked. "You kinda seem different."

"Riding, huh? Bet she rode him hard or vice versa." Kim laughed, and Jeanette fought the blush stealing into her cheeks.

"Nothing happened okay, well, other than meeting his mother."

Susie almost dropped the glass in her seeming astonishment, and Kim whistled through her teeth.

"Well, I never. Ty dotes on his mum, according to Josh, so, he must really like you, huh?"

Susie shrugged at those words, and Jeanette thought it wisest to simply stay quiet on that subject.

"Oh come on, it's obvious. I bet you all my tips tonight that Ty'll hover around you like a mother hen when you're dancing. Heaven help any punter trying to cop a feel." Kim laughed as though she'd just made the biggest joke over, and Jeanette swallowed hard to rid herself of the rising panic in her gut.

"That's not gonna happen, is it?" she asked, hating the shakiness of her voice, and Kim visibly sobered.

"Not unless you're okay with that. The boss runs a tight ship here, and makes sure we're all safe. Talking of the devil, I think he wants you."

Kim took Jeanette by the shoulders and turned her in time to see Huntly stroll up. Dressed, as ever, in an impeccably tailored business suit, the club owner's expression gave nothing away, as he slowly looked her up and down, and then smiled.

It didn't reach his eyes, however, and he seemed preoccupied when he addressed her.

"Once Kim has shown you around, swing by my office and sign your contract, will you, girl?"

"Which one?" Jeanette asked, and Huntly stopped mid-adjusting his cufflinks and this time gave her his full attention.

"The one you asked for. Mason phoned me to say you changed your mind and want to dance only. Is that not correct?"

"No, yes … I mean…" Aware that she was babbling, Jeanette slammed her mouth shut, and not knowing what to do with her hands shoved them in the back pockets of her jeans. The action stuck her boobs out, and the already stretched material of her tee thinned out further. Huntly's gaze briefly dropped to the girls, and then returned to her face. A slight smirk played around his lips this time, and for some reason that made Jeanette even more nervous.

"Hmm, Ren tells me you're not usually lost for words, so out with it, girl. Do you want to dance in my club or not?"

The mention of her sister's killer made her gut churn, but the usual flash of simmering hate didn't come this time. With a burst of sudden insight Jeanette realized that she couldn't hate the man for what he'd done. As everyone had been at great pains to point out from the beginning, the sister she mourned was a very different person from the one these guys had known and dealt with. Forcing her mind back to the present, she pushed her shoulders back more and shook her head.

Kim gasped, and Susie swore under her breath as Huntly's gaze turned to sharp steel. She was reminded of the old saying to not provoke the sleeping tiger, and hurried on to explain.

"I mean I would rather not have anything at all to do with the club and everything that goes on in here, but as you won't just let me walk away, yes, dancing is all that I want to do. I'm not a whore."

Huntly's gaze softened just a tad as he continued to study her, and he eventually laughed.

"No, you're not, are you? Besides, Ty would probably take a swing at me if I put you to work like that, and I rather like my face the way it is." Huntly winked at her, an action so at odds with his stern persona that Jeanette could only stare and blink. She was also uncomfortably aware that she wasn't immune to the man. There was something dangerous, yet oddly intriguing about Owen Huntly, and any woman would be hard pushed to resist him, should he turn on the charm.

"I don't know about that." Jeanette murmured her reply and dropped her gaze to the man's tie.

"No, hmm, is that why Ty is standing right there watching you like a hawk then, even though he's got work to do?"

Huntly grasped her chin while he spoke, and sure enough Ty stood by one of the doors leading out back, arms crossed over his massive chest, and looking as though he wanted to kill Huntly.

Jeanette offered him a tremulous smile, and Ty's tense features relaxed a little, when Huntly let go off her.

"I value my Cleaners, and I like to keep them happy. Ty has very much claimed you as his own, which means you're off limits to anyone, including me." He grinned when Jeanette startled and looked up at him. "More's the pity." Again with that wink, which left Jeanette to simply stare up at him.

"So, now that we cleared that up, sign the contract, and dance your luscious ass off tonight. You're one of us now, and we'll keep you safe from everyone."

It was on the tip of her tongue to ask who would keep her safe from the lot of them, but Kim's shake of the head stopped any further argument.

"Are we clear here, or do I need to demonstrate further?" Huntly asked, and Jeanette shook her head.

"Crystal. I'm safe as long as I do what's expected of me." Huntly gave her one last look and turned to leave. Jeanette didn't know what possessed her, but she blurted the words out without thinking. "Otherwise I'll end up like my sister, right?"

Huntly stopped mid walking away, and you could have heard a pin drop in the club, as everyone seemed to look at her. At least Ty wasn't staring at her anymore. He must have left to do whatever it was Huntly needed him to do, because that doorway was empty, and Jeanette breathed a sigh of relief. Somehow she got the impression her ass would be red raw for this outburst anyhow, but she wouldn't have put it past Ty to march over here, bend her over the bar and deliver that punishment right now for speaking to his boss like that.

As it was Huntly looked ready to deliver such treatment himself, when he turned round and stalked back toward her. Jeanette took several steps back until the edge of the bar stopped her and she focused on

Huntly's Adam's apple, as he put one arm either side of her, effectively caging her in against the bar.

"Ty's girl or not, watch your mouth about her. What happened to your sister will not be repeated, ever. Not least because I know better than to trust another piece of wet cunt."

Jeanette gasped at the cruel words, but Huntly wasn't done yet.

"Don't ever bring that bitch up in front of me again, are we clear?"

"Yes, sir. I'm sorry, I didn't mean that the way it came out, it's just … she *was* my sister, and I guess, I have a hard time letting it go, that's all."

Huntly continued to stare at her without an ounce of compassion on his features, and she hurried on to make herself clearer.

"I will, though, sir, please, I promise."

"Good, and for the record. If you betray the Cleaners and thus me, I'll rip you apart myself, girl." He smiled grimly at her horrified gasp. "Ty says you can be trusted. Don't let him down."

With that he pushed away from the bar, and Jeanette drew much needed air into her lungs.

"God, Jeanette." Susie shook her head at her, and Kim looked all but ready to sock her one.

"Jesus, girl, have you got a death wish talking to him like that? You must be a damn good dancer for him to even let you up on stage after that. Enough of this now, come on and show me what you've got."

Kim turned on her heel, and knowing better than to argue, Jeanette followed the other woman.

Dancing was something she was very good at after all.

****

Ty scowled at the woman gyrating around the

pole as though she had danced like that forever. Jeanette wasn't dancing, she was *one* with the fucking thing, and Ty bet his hard-on that every man in the place sported a boner to rival King Kong's watching his girl dance.

And she damn fucking well was his. His talk with Huntly had made sure of that. The club owner had smiled, shaken his head, and tapped his long index finger on his nose.

"You'll vouch for this girl? Especially considering who her sister was?"

"Jeanette is nothing like Myrtle, and she is fiercely loyal. Even though she knows what her sister got up to she still cannot let go, and defends her whenever she gets a chance."

"That must make life difficult at the house…"

Huntly hadn't needed to state the obvious.

"Ren and she are good. They won't ever be best buds, but they won't kill each other either."

Huntly had smirked at that.

"I'd like to see anyone, let alone a female try, unless she's Susie, of course, and that girl has proven her loyalty without a doubt. Can you say the same for your woman?"

Ty had forced himself to hold Huntly's gaze.

"Yes, at least I hope so."

Huntly had sighed.

"For all our sake I hope you're right. We still have to address where she got her intel from. It wasn't the Priestly fuckers, so, my guess is on Wonsan. If he turns up tonight, and I bet he will, watch him with her. Do *not* intervene."

Huntly had held up his hand to stave off Ty's immediate protest.

"She looks like she can handle a bit of rough treatment, but I want her to have the chance to hang herself … or not."

Huntly had waved him away, and Ty had been left to ponder the question of his girl's loyalty, not least when he'd heard of the near altercation she'd had with Huntly.

Kim had given him a blow by blow account, which had made him seek out his insolent subbie in the locker room, bent her over his knee and spank her ass until it had glowed a nice shade of red. The sex that had followed had been fucking hot, and the caveman in him had grinned at the thought of sending his woman on stage clearly marked by his hands, and with her pussy still wet from his cum.

It would serve as a nice little reminder of who she belonged to, when she was turning all those fuckers on. Sure enough to start with her dancing while fluid had been somewhat guarded, but as she relaxed, seemingly reassured that no one could touch her, after Ty and the other bouncer assigned to watch the dancers tonight, had facilitated   the exit of several jerks who thought they could touch the dancers, her moves had been spectacular.

Ty had taken particular delight in breaking the nose of the asshole who'd made a grab for Jeanette's ass when she'd hung upside down off the pole.

While she'd jumped and paled at the blood which had hit the stage, requiring a quick clean-up and a break from dancing for her, she had also mouthed a silent *thank you* at him.

Ty flexed his bruised knuckles and grinned. A grin which froze when he spotted Wonsan wander into the club. Ren and Josh trailed after him, and as relieved as he was seeing the sharp nod from Ren to signal tonight's operation had gone down well, the sight of Wonsan made his blood boil.

Especially as he made a beeline straight for Jeanette, who was waiting by the side of the stage to take over from Kim. When Wonsan came up right behind her and spoke to her, Ty moved to intervene, but Ren's hand on his shoulder stopped him. Josh, in the meantime, got right in his way, and he couldn't look past the mountain of a man.

"Move your fucking ass, man, I can't see her."

Josh smirked and crossed his arms over his chest.

"That's the point, Ty. Ren has visual. Besides, I thought you trusted her." The mocking tone made Ty want to take a swing at the bigger guy, but that's what Josh wanted him to do. Operation, "keep Ty from spoiling the trap which had been set for Jeanette", was very much a go, it seemed.

"Fuck this, what is she doing, Ren? Please tell me she is ignoring him."

"No can do, Ty, she's talking to him."

"Son of a fucking gun, let me see."

He shrugged Ren off, and Josh reluctantly moved out of his way. What he saw made his gut churn. Perversely it also held him in place, because he knew her body language well enough by now to know that his titch was far from happy. While she was smiling at Wonsan it was rather forced, and the way she subtly leaned away from him, told him all he needed to know.

"So, they're talking. She's not inviting him backstage."

No sooner had he said that, Jeanette turned sharply and made her way toward the back, with Wonsan right on her heels. One of the new guys stepped forward to stop the slimy detective from following her backstage, and Ty swore again, when she leaned in, batted her eyelashes at him, and the fucking idiot let Wonsan through.

Strictly speaking the boy wasn't doing anything wrong. The girls were allowed men of their choosing backstage, but…

"Fuck it all. This can't be what it looks like."

Josh got in his way again when he made to go after them, and Ren slapped him on the shoulder.

"Give them a minute."

Ty turned on his best mate, and the pity in Ren's eyes felt like a punch to the stomach.

"This isn't what it looks like."

"I'm sure you're right, but let's see. Wonsan tries anything, Alex and James are out back watching the monitors. They'll get to her faster than us. We'll sort this."

****

Oh God, oh, God, oh God … where's Ty? I just have to hold on until he comes to find me.

Taking a deep breath in Jeanette turned in the narrow corridor to face the sweating detective. He reeked of body odor and booze, and something else. Taking another quick sniff, Jeanette swallowed the rising bile. Cannabis for sure.

She'd recognize that stench anywhere. It had permeated everything in her childhood after all. It was a wonder Wonsan had been allowed in the club at all. According to Kim, Huntly had a strict no drugs allowed on club premises rule while the place was open to the public. All sounded rather ironic to her, considering the crime lord had his fingers in many pies in the city, and drugs was definitively one of them, but it seemed he didn't shit in his own back yard.

Then again, he was on the police radar now more than ever, so she guessed he had to be careful not be caught with his hands in the cookie jar.

"Okay, you've got me in private. What is so urgent that you need to talk to me?" Jeanette forced herself to smile at the detective, and to not let her disgust show when he stepped right into her personal space.

"Oh come on, girl, you stop the pretense now. We're on our own. I've come for answers. What have you got for me?"

More bile rose in Jeanette's throat as she stared at him. He looked so damn smug and expectant. Even a few days ago, she probably would have given him the answers he sought in a heartbeat, but she couldn't, wouldn't betray Ty like that.

She put her hands up to stop him from advancing further, and Wonsan frowned.

"I have nothing to say to you."

Wonsan sucked in air through his teeth and shook his head.

"So, they got to you, too, huh? Well, in that case you can pay me back in other ways."

He laughed at her gasp of horror. "Come on, whore, you're working here now, so be nice to me. I'm here as a paying customer after all." She flinched when he ran his index finger along her jaw, and then lower, to trace the tiny straps holding up her dance costume. "A man could drown in those babies, I reckon."

Jeanette slapped his finger away and took a step back, only to have him follow her. The light of the surveillance camera mounted high in the corner of the hallway, mocked her with its blinking intensity.

Kim had said she was perfectly safe, so why then wasn't anyone bursting the damn door down. Someone had to be watching?

"I'm not a whore, damn you. I simply dance, and I don't appreciate you talking to me like this."

She twisted her head sideways when Wonsan bent his head to kiss her, and giving him a shove managed to twist out of his way. For a half drunk guy he moved surprisingly fast, however, because he twisted his hand in her hair and slammed her back against the wall with enough force to make plaster rain down on them.

Temporarily winded, Jeanette had no defense as he ground his hard dick into her ass.

"Play hard to get all you want, but you can't fool me. Besides, I want the information you came here to get for me."

"I don't know what the hell you're talking about. Let me go."

Wonsan yanked her hair hard, and Jeanette cried out in pain.

"Don't play dumb with me, girl. You know what I want. Same as you, sweetheart." He licked along her jaw, and Jeanette screamed.

"No, get the hell off me. Help."

Finally, the door at the other end of the hallway burst open, and the Synn brothers burst through it like avenging angels. With one quick move they'd brought Wonsan to his knees, at the same time as the other door flew open, and a murderous looking Ty appeared. Jeanette didn't even think about her actions. She threw herself into his arms and buried close. It felt so damn good to be back in her Sir's arms, to breathe in his clean, spicy scent, and to feel safe.

"It's okay, I've got you, titch."

"Get that fucker out of here, boys." Ren's deep voice penetrated her consciousness and she swallowed nervously when Ty pushed her away, and Ren grasped her chin. She was dimly aware of Alex and James carting a protesting Wonsan away, before her attention was taken up by the guarded intensity in Ren's eyes.

"Did he hurt you?"

"N-no…. not really."

"If he had, police or not, I'd rip his fucking balls off." Ty's growled words at her back sent a shiver down her spine. Not of disgust, as she might have thought, but relief that Ty had her. Sure enough, he reached out to draw her back into his solid frame, and she closed her eyes, when he nuzzled into her neck erasing the feel of Wonsan's tongue.

"I reckon I'd let you, Ty. What information was he referring to, girl?"

"Ren, really, she hasn't—"

"It's okay, Sir, let me answer that."

Ren's eyebrows shot up when she interrupted Ty, and his sigh ghosted across her neck. Josh chuckled, and Huntly's cool voice made her shiver.

"Yes, I'd be most interested in hearing that answer, too."

Huntly leaned against the wall, flicking an imaginary speck of dust off of his suit, to all intents and purposes without a care in the world, but the tick in his jaw gave him away.

"Detective Wonsan approached me after Myr died. We'd met briefly at the police station, when they'd brought me in to question me about her. I didn't know anything of course. He had these pictures."

She shuddered recalling the horrific images, and leaned more on Ty, when he squeezed her hip in silent support.

"His partner didn't seem to like his approach, and then the next day I got a visit at my flat. He had more pictures, not just of Myr, but other people you're supposed to have … well anyway. He said he needed my help, 'cause he'd run out of options, and I…"

"That wanker fucking used you, baby."

Ty's annoyed growl vibrated through her, and Jeanette dropped her gaze and nodded.

"I realize that now, but at the time I simply wanted revenge for my sister. I let her down, see. If I had been a better sister, come looking for her sooner, then, maybe I could have—"

"If is a useless word, which doesn't change a thing, baby. Believe me, I know." Ty's quiet voice at her back made her blink away tears. "Your sister was a grown woman who made her own choices. Nothing you could have done. Let it go, now."

Ren let go of her chin at last, nodded at whatever he saw in her eyes, and addressed Huntly.

"Now, can I kill that fucking detective?"

Much to Jeanette's surprise Huntly shook his head.

"I told you, he's got a young son and a wife."

Ty snorted his disgust, and Huntly smiled grimly.

"I know what you're thinking. He can't be much of a husband and father if he hangs around clubs in his spare time, right? That being as it may, until we know what his game is, he's more valuable to us alive. The rate he's been spending money here and elsewhere, he's gonna need cash soon. Hopefully, he'll come to me. If not … well, then he's all yours, boys. Jeanette, you look done in. No more dancing for you tonight. Ty can take you home. You should all scoot. Where's Ace?"

Belatedly Jeanette realized there was no sign of the tall guy.

"Hospital," Josh said, and Jeanette gasped.

"He's not hurt, well, minor scrapes only, which he can take care of himself, but the girls tonight were…" Josh glanced at her clearly unsure of how much he should say.

At Huntly's nod he continued.

"Too fucking young. None of them were over twenty, and the couple he took to his contact in the hospital looked about fourteen, if that, and utterly traumatized. They need proper care and their parents traced, so he's taking care of that."

"Oh my God." Even though Jeanette whispered the words they sounded far too loud in the heavy stillness which had descended upon the hallway.

"Right," Huntly finally said. "Good work tonight, guys."

As quickly as the hallway had filled with people, it emptied again, leaving just Ty and her.

"You heard the boss, titch, let's get you home." Ty gently turned her until she was facing him, and she swallowed hard when he cradled her head in his large hands.

"I'm sorry," he said.

"For what?"

"For putting you through tonight, but we had to be sure."

"This was a set-up?" How she managed to get the words past the huge lump in her throat she would never know. Ty clenched his jaw, and when he simply nodded, she wanted to hit him. How dare he put her through this?

The anger she needed just wouldn't come however, not when he looked at her as though she was the most precious thing to him. His hands slipped lower until he could massage the base of her skull, right where Wonsan had tried to rip her hair out so cruelly, and Jeanette closed her eyes. That gentle pressure felt way too good on her sore scalp, and when she moaned Ty stopped.

Heat flared in his dark eyes when her eyes fluttered open and their gazes connected.

"Say the word, and I'll hunt him down, orders be fucked. I hate that he got to hurt you, even just a little bit. No one will ever touch you again, I promise. You're mine now, if you want to be, that is." He paused, his face contorted as though it cost him dearly to say those words, and she had to push him a little more, just to be sure what her heart was telling her right now was the truth. Ty was hard to read at the best of times, after all, and this could all simply be chalked up to her being overwrought.

"And if I don't want to be?" she asked.

Ty closed his eyes briefly, his hold on her tightening for one precious second, before he dropped his hands and stepped away from her. It took every ounce of self-control she had to not close the distance between them. Goosebumps broke out across her exposed skin, and the cold hand of dread squeezed her inside and made breathing difficult. She could almost see the wall going up around Ty, as he schooled his face into an expressionless mask.

"You're free to go wherever you want to be. There's accommodation here, if you'd rather not come back to the house, with me."

Ty's strained words belied the careful way he tried to hide his feelings, and Jeanette's heart beat faster.

His voice held that deep, delicious growl, which never failed to get her wet. She licked her lips to get some saliva into her dry mouth and the way Ty's gaze dropped to her mouth instantly, as though he wanted to devour her, made her moan.

"I have a better idea, Sir," she said.

"You do?" Ty's face cracked into that sinful grin she loved, when she nodded, and flung her arms around his neck.

"Yes, Sir, take me home, and show me what it means to be yours."

Ty pulled back to study her, and that slow grin morphed into a full on smile. It lit up his dark features, and made him look far more approachable

"Are you sure, titch?" Even as he said that, he pulled her closer into his frame, dropping kisses along her jaw, and neck, his stubble creating delicious friction and making her feel gloriously alive. "'Cause I gotta tell you, once I got you in my bed, I'll tie you up and won't ever let you go. Even if you beg me. I'm not that fucking noble that I can keep my hands off you, or let anyone else touch you again, ever."

He pulled back to study her face, and the depth of emotion that shone from his dark eyes soothed the last of her misgivings. Fuck everything else. Fuck notions of right and wrong, this, right here in her Sir's arms was where she wanted to be. He might be the big bad, but he was *her* big bad, and together they would make it work. Besides, the world was a damn scary place, and who better to keep her safe than the Cleaners?

"I think it sounds wonderful, Sir."

"Thank fuck for that."

Ty picked her up, pinned her to the wall, and proceeded to kiss her senseless.

When he finally let her come up for air, the world was spinning and Jeanette knew that her life as she'd known it was well and truly over. A new adventure was waiting for her, with the man she had fallen head over heels in love with, when she hadn't been looking.

Ty flicked her nose and grinned.

"You know my mother will be even more impossible now."

Ty pulled a face and Jeanette giggled.

"I like your impossible mother, but why would she be?" she asked.

"Because, my little unruly subbie, she told me years ago, that the day she asked a girl I brought home, whether she loved me..." He shook his head and laughed. "That would be the girl for me."

The End

THE CLEANERS

www.dorisoconnor.com

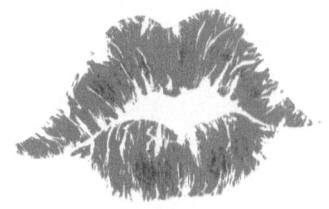

EVERNIGHT PUBLISHING ®

www.evernightpublishing.com